This is a work of fiction. Any si
events, methods, technologies, ... or people,
living or dead, is entirely coincidental. References to
office holders or other people in the National Criminal
Intelligence Service, the Secret Intelligence Service, the
Police or any other body, organisation or company are
also fictional and are not intended to relate to any
actual person who may have been in the post or
position mentioned at any time.

Copyright © by Jo Calman 2021
All rights reserved

www.jo-calman.com

ISBN 979-8-4974-2265-8

An Undeclared Contest

by Jo Calman

The ultimate in disposing one's troop
is to be without ascertainable shape.
Then the most penetrating spies cannot pry in
nor can the wise lay plans against you

Sun Tzu, *The Art of War*

Chapter 1 - Montreal, Summer 2003

After careful consideration she had selected three subjects for the demonstration. In her own mind she had no doubt at all that the scheme would work, but she recognised that all the others, the many names on her list, would need to see evidence of what she could and would do. Then they would comply or face similar consequences to those she had heaped on her unfortunate subjects. She read the short-list one last time as she sipped her warm green tea.

Her apartment was silent, calm, just as she liked it. At this early hour the streets outside were still quiet before the tourists arrived and the cafés opened; before the loft studios and workshops came to creative life. As far as the neighbours were concerned she was just another artist - a photographer - working on her own. She was cordially polite but did not exude any signals inviting closer contact or friendship. She stood and stretched her tight limbs, stiff after so many hours at her screens. Walking over to the open double doors she went out to the balcony and looked down on the sleepy river. A steamer ploughed its way westward towards Toronto and the Great Lakes. She decided to have a shower, and afterwards she would go back to her screens and start it all.

******

In Ouchy, on the north shore of Lake Geneva, life was good. A sunny Monday morning heralded another busy and fruitful week. Jean-Luc Weisser took his breakfast on his shaded terrace with a view over the lake. He looked across towards Evian on the French side and watched the elegant white passenger boats plying their trade up, down and across *Lac Léman* - Lake Geneva. Jean-Luc checked his Blackberry for emails and quickly scanned the morning headlines on his laptop seeking out gossip and celebrity stories. All was well.

In an hour he would take the fast train to Geneva airport and head off to New York and his latest commission, the extensive remodelling of a mansion on Long Island for a member of Hollywood royalty, which would pay extremely well. Jean-Luc's architectural and design practice was flourishing, and now that he'd secured access to the homes of the rich and famous he was the go-to guru for style and sophisticated but still comfortable elegance. That he held his clients and paymasters in complete contempt was his little secret. The entry-phone suddenly buzzed impatiently.

Jean-Luc listened to the voice speaking at the street door below. The police needed to talk to him, urgently. He invited them up to his penthouse and waited by the door. As always in Switzerland, the police were polite. The detectives, there were three of them - two men and one quite attractive if slightly over made-up woman - each shook hands with him and declined coffee. How could he help?

"Jean-Luc Weisser?" the attractive woman detective asked. "Is this your name?"

"It is, Inspector."

"And this is your usual address? You don't have any other home addresses in Switzerland?"

He nodded.

"Do you have business premises in the Place du Chateau in Lausanne?"

"What's this about, Inspector?" Jean-Luc remained calm and was still smiling as he spoke to the woman.

"Do you have any computers in this apartment?" She hadn't answered his question.

"Of course I do," he said. "Look, I'm sorry but I'm leaving in a few minutes for New York and I need to hurry. I'll ask you again, what is this about and how can I help you?"

"What credit or charge cards do you have?" she asked.

"That is none of your business, Inspector!" he replied, a bit too loudly, rattled by the intrusive financial nature of the questions. The male officers remained silent, letting the woman lead.

"Jean-Luc Weisser," she stated, "I am Inspector Bovet of the Canton of Vaud police vice and child-protection brigade. I have a warrant for your arrest issued by examining magistrate Schultz. I also have a warrant granted by Maître Schultz to seize and examine any computers or other electronic recording devices in your possession, and to search your apartment and any business premises you have within his jurisdiction."

"Arrest me? Search? For what? I've done nothing wrong!"

"The case concerns your purchase and distribution of extreme child pornography over the internet - material of the most serious and abhorrent kind," Inspector Bovet stated coolly.

Jean-Luc was stunned. He staggered slightly and leant heavily on a table.

"I know nothing of this! I have never purchased any pornography of any sort. I'm leaving for New York.

Can you sort this out with my lawyer? There has been a terrible mistake - you must want another person with a similar name."

"We are taking you into custody, Monsieur Weisser," Inspector Bovet stated. "You won't be going to New York; you can call your lawyer when we get to headquarters. Maître Schultz will see you there and he will take your statement, but he has already signed the order committing you to prison on remand pending the conclusion of our enquiries. The evidence against you is very compelling, and it is straightforward. I have a police van downstairs with uniformed officers to take you. My colleagues and I will search your apartment and your office while you are being processed."

Inspector Bovet used her mobile phone and a few seconds later two officers in the grey uniforms of the Canton of Vaud police appeared at the door. Without a word one of them swiftly fastened handcuffs on Jean-Luc's wrists and they both led him away. He was in shock. He had absolutely no knowledge of any child pornography; he had never seen any and had never wanted to.

That evening, a tearful Jean-Luc Weisser, architect and designer to the stars, cried himself into a listless exhausted sleep in a cell in police headquarters, an ugly concrete complex just off the motorway skirting Lausanne. The examining magistrate had shown him copies of dreadful images he claimed to have found on his computer, together with credit card statements for one of his cards showing numerous purchases from a website - purchases which the magistrate stated were of the dreadful images and many worse - made by Jean-Luc in the previous few months. The magistrate wasn't very interested in Jean-Luc's denials and protests of innocence. In the morning he would be formally charged and committed to the remand wing of the prison complex at Orbe to await trial. The magistrate had explained that the evidence had been gathered as part of an international investigation into a global paedophile network, coordinated by Europol and the FBI. On the evidence available, including the extreme nature of the disgusting pictures, the magistrate stated that Jean-Luc should expect a significant custodial sentence.

Jean-Luc took no comfort from his one short meeting with his own lawyer, who said he reluctantly agreed with the prosecutor about the strength of the evidence and the probable outcome. His lawyer suggested he plead guilty and put forward arguments of mitigation on the grounds of, for example, extreme work-related stress.

The custody officer had removed Jean-Luc's belt and shoes. He still had his trousers, shirt and undershirt. In the cell there was a steel toilet fixed to the wall, a metal bed with a thin mattress, and a single small rigid plastic chair. He lay awake at 2 in the morning, unable to sleep any further. Jean-Luc removed his shirt and undershirt. The undershirt he tied to a leg of the plastic chair to form a loose loop which he put over his head. Using the chair as a lever he wound the loop tight and kept winding. When he could barely breathe he forced the chair under the bed to stop it moving and writhed and twisted on the floor, tightening the loop around his neck still further.

The custody officer found him at 4am on a routine check. Jean-Luc Weisser was cold to the touch, and he was dead.

******

The morning after they found Jean-Luc Weisser's dead body in the police cell in Switzerland, the usual calm of Amelia Armstrong's chambers in a quiet square in central London was broken by insistent phone calls from national newspapers and TV channels. By 11am there was a small army of shouty reporters camped outside the offices of one of the UKs, if not the world's, most renowned and successful (depending on your point of view) divorce lawyers. Amelia's secretary was in tears; Amelia herself was uncharacteristically flustered. She sent for her partner, Christopher Llewellyn.

"What do they say they've got, Amelia?" he asked her.

"They say they've got hold of statements made by our client in the Wilmslow case, the statements in which she specifies and describes the abuse she's suffered. They say they're going to publish the details in the Sundays, complete with vehement rebuttals from the husband. I'm trying to get hold of the client but she's on a yacht somewhere; she is going to blow her top!"

"How the hell did the press get the statements, for God's sake?"

"How should I know? Not from me, obviously!" Amelia shouted. "I made notes as I spoke to her, as I always do with clients, and afterwards the notes were typed up and filed on the system, again as usual. I had the client sign a printed copy of each for the evidence bundle, again as bloody usual. One of the editors, who I know slightly and who owes me a favour, emailed me a copy of the stuff he's got. It's only fucking genuine, Chris! Every bloody detail of what he did to her and what he made her do. It's lurid, to say the least! The tabloids are going to lap it up."

"What can we do, Amelia? Do they want money or something?"

"It's the national press, not some third-rate blackmailer! We're done for, Chris! Our reputation for confidentiality and protecting our clients' privacy will be ruined. Knowing her, the client will undoubtedly sue us and once all the dirt is out in the open her reputation will be shot to bits too. She can forget the settlement we'd just about agreed with the husband. She'll sue us for that as well!"

"So, what can we do? Can we ask the papers not to publish this?"

Amelia gave him a withering look.

"Brilliant, Chris, I never thought of that. Of course we can't, and even if we did there's no way they'd all agree. Apparently it's leaked out onto the internet already so it's too late for any meaningful injunction."

The tearful secretary knocked on Amelia's door.

"Sorry to interrupt, but I thought you should know. Three clients have just given us notice that they're getting their legal advice from somewhere else. The clerk is saying that his phone has stopped ringing too, no enquiries from solicitors or anyone. And I've just had that hysterical client on the phone, the one in the Mediterranean. A reporter found her and called the yacht on a satellite phone and told her what they're going to print about her. I can't bring myself to repeat exactly what she said, but in essence we're fired and can expect to hear from her new lawyers soon. Sorry, Amelia."

******

In a spacious airy office high above the sweaty streets of Houston the General Counsel of one of the world's major oil companies was having a difficult conversation with a serious young attorney from the Department of Justice.

"I hear what you're saying, sir," the DoJ lawyer said, "and we will continue to investigate. However, there is no escaping the fact that we have received a large number of documents which appear to corroborate the allegation that your company has been paying significant sums of cash to the family of the president of the country concerned. I know you're familiar with the Foreign Corrupt Practices Act, so I don't need to explain the corporate implications to you."

"Don't give me all that, Jonathan," the General Counsel snapped, "I was a lead-attorney at DoJ when you were still in diapers! This evidence is cooked up! It's all baloney!"

"I can get a subpoena, sir, or you can do what I ask. Have your IT people search all your systems and electronic records. We need to see all transactions and payments relating to that business unit for the relevant period. I've given you the dates and the amounts specified in the allegations. If it *is* baloney and you can prove it, all well and good, but if you have anything relevant at all in your records I need to see it. You know I have to warn you about tampering with evidence or removing it, it's the law. I also have to warn you that the nature of the allegations makes it probable that there will be a criminal investigation against named individuals in the company as well as an FCPA case brought against the corporation. You might want to instruct criminal lawyers to represent your executives and the individual managers in the country concerned."

"You're going too far, Jonathan. The Chairman is a good friend of the Attorney General, and the President come to that. You aren't really suggesting that the corporation is knowingly and willingly paying bribes to operate in that country? That the Chairman himself knows about it, and that executives and senior managers are colluding? This is a major corporation, Jonathan, not some two-bit wildcat outfit. If you say you have evidence, show it to me!"

"If you insist, sir. Can we resume in an hour? I need to have an associate with me when we go through the evidence. It's the rules."

Three hours later the General Counsel called an urgent meeting with the Chairman and the Chief Financial Officer. The Department of Justice did indeed have what appeared to be *prima facie* evidence, seemingly passed to them by a whistleblowing insider, which proved almost categorically that the corporation had paid millions of US dollars to the son and daughter of the president of a West African country where the corporation had extensive and highly profitable operations. The three of them discussed it for hours long into the evening and pored over the printouts which the DoJ had left with them, together with formal notification of imminent proceedings under the Foreign

Corrupt Practices Act. Also, the FBI were calling and wanted to see the General Counsel urgently.

"No, sir," the General Counsel said to the Chairman, "I don't think a holding statement will do it. I suggest we try to do a deal with DoJ on the FCPA allegations, it is still possible, but the criminal case with the FBI is a different matter. This could be another Enron. We'll need to conduct a full forensic examination of our records, and we have to hope this is a clever scam. If not, well……"

"Are you saying you think our people actually did this? And they managed to keep payments of several million dollars off the books? That some very senior people were conspiring to do it? Is that what you're saying to me, Counsellor? Our people would never do that!" The Chairman was getting angry.

"But it is looking very much like they did," the General Counsel said, calmly. "By the way, and this may not be the best time to say it, but I quit. Effective immediately. Sorry, but I can't handle this for you."

With that, the General Counsel stood and left the room.

The CFO, who had until then been silent, looked at her Blackberry.

"It's getting out. Our stock is in freefall," was all she said.

Chapter 2

Commander Julia Kelso, known to those closest to her as Jake, was taking a few minutes out alone in her office at New Scotland Yard. She usually thrived on pressure, but today was not going so well. The morning had been taken up by the monthly meeting of senior officers in the specialist crime-fighting squads and departments to hear updates on the most difficult, complex or high-profile investigations that were ongoing. Julia was there with the others, and she'd presented a few cases which her own teams were working on. Her contribution had been largely constructive, highlighting the use of novel technologies and analytical methods to break into organised crime groups. Input from some of the others, though, left her feeling uneasy.

The homicide chief had been using his investigation review team to look at several high-profile cases over the last year or so, too recent for the usual cold-case rake over, but he had his reasons. He had found some very circumstantial forensic leads that might *just* be able to link forensically the murders of three gangsters and the serious wounding of a fourth the previous spring with some other killings. Granted, none of the gangster murders had been committed in the Metropolitan Police District, but the others had. Four separate shootings had occurred in London in a short space of time, in addition to the attempted murder of Commander Kelso herself. There were indications that the DNA evidence that had initially led to a conclusion that Ukrainian mercenaries had been responsible may not have been wholly correct. Nothing conclusive, but very small traces of other, as yet unidentified, DNA had been found at the scenes of both sets of killings. The DNA traces were too minute and too corrupted to allow evidential sequencing, but the head of homicide was worried about the possibility of an unknown serial killer, possibly a professional, being on the loose. The two people, currently serving long sentences for crimes associated with the killings, the Murstons - a father (formerly a Member of Parliament) and son team of corrupt and corrupting financiers who had attempted to manipulate the cocaine market with adulterated narcotics - killing dozens of users in the process - were still squealing loudly that they had been entrapped by a person named Thomas Donohue. Donohue had never been found but had been declared killed in Liberia.

The head of one of the organised crime teams had been trying to tie up loose ends relating to the human-trafficking networks that Julia Kelso had been so closely involved in disrupting. Everything was pretty much done and dusted, but one of the suspects convicted of running the networks had given several statements implicating an unlocated person by the name of Paulo Silva, of whom no one had ever heard. Enquiries to identify and locate him through Europol and the Portuguese police had produced nothing to date. The only other loose end was the kingpin (or should it be queen pin?) of the whole business, the elusive Dido Sykes who had run the entire conspiracy. Like the missing Paulo Silva, no trace could be found of Sykes anywhere in the world. It was as if neither of them had ever really existed.

Julia Kelso knew otherwise, certainly about Paulo Silva, but she said nothing. She could also hazard a guess about the mysterious DNA traces, but again was saying nothing. She had quietly hoped that these cases would have been overtaken by other events and that energies would be directed elsewhere for a good while, but her colleagues were keen to clear the decks before the war in Iraq, which had started a couple of months previously, began to have its inevitable repercussions in London.

Back in her office Julia sat alone for a few minutes, thinking carefully. Her peace was disturbed by her faithful assistant Raj who knocked loudly.

"She's on the phone again, boss," he said.

"Who is?" Julia asked.

"That lawyer, Amelia Armstrong, QC."

"The divorce Rottweiler? What does she want?"

"She wants to talk to you, personally. Says it's urgent, but nothing to do with any divorces."

"That's a relief, not that I can think of a reason why I'd be involved in any divorcing. Put her through."

A few seconds later Julia's phone warbled.

"Commander Kelso," she answered.

"Commander, this is Amelia Armstrong. I need to see you urgently. I have a highly confidential ongoing matter, and I think I've been the victim of a serious crime."

"I'm sorry to hear that, Ms Armstrong, but the usual procedure is to report crime to a police station to get the ball rolling. Why have you come straight to me?"

"As I said, it is a very confidential matter. You clearly know who I am and what my specialism is, and presumably you are aware of the type of clientele I have. You have a very good reputation, unlike many of your colleagues with whom I've had the dubious pleasure of dealing over the years, no offence intended of course."

"If you say so, Ms Armstrong. I'm extremely busy, but I could find half an hour tomorrow morning if you can get to me at the Yard." Julia was expecting a rebuff or a protest.

"That is so kind, Commander Kelso, I'm very grateful." She sounded genuinely relieved.

"10.30 then. I'll send someone to get you from the front desk."

"Thank you, Ms Kelso. I look forward to meeting you."

Julia hung up.

"Raj," she called, "is there anything in the news about that woman, Amelia Armstrong?"

"I haven't seen anything, boss. There's often something about her in the Sundays, the massive settlements she gets for her clients going through divorces and stuff."

"Could you ask Press Bureau if they've got anything about her in the pipeline, just in case? She's coming to see me tomorrow morning."

"Have you put it in the diary?"

"Not yet. Sorry Raj, she's coming at 10.30."

"I'll do it then, shall I?"

"Don't sulk, Raj, or I'll have to fire you," Julia said this with a smile.

Julia's phone warbled again, an internal call.

"Commander Kelso," she said.

"Commissioner's compliments, ma'am. Can you spare a few minutes in his conference room?" despite the polite tone it wasn't a request.

Julia took a moment, then decided to change into her uniform. She took the lift to the eighth floor and walked to the Commissioner's extensive corner suite of offices and meeting rooms. She was shown into the main conference room by a staff officer, who took a seat at the end of the table and prepared to take notes. There were four others at the table, apart from Julia and the staff officer. All were men, and none were in uniform. The Commissioner looked tired. His tie was loose, his jacket creased and open.

"Thank you for coming, Julia," he started, "you know Commander Idris from Specialist Operations, and of course DAC Connaught. This gentleman is from the American Embassy," the Commissioner indicated a nondescript individual with neat, short grey hair, a button-down shirt and a strangely fitting sports jacket.

"Harvey Olson, ma'am. I'm the Legat at the embassy."

Julia nodded at him. A Legat, or Legal Attaché, is the most senior FBI representative at a US diplomatic mission.

"Mr Olson has some information that I'd like you to hear, and possibly comment on, Julia. I'm sorry to say it is of a personal nature, so from now on this meeting is not to be minuted." He nodded at the staff officer, who took the hint and left the room.

"Thank you, sir," Olson said. "Back in the spring we had information that a US citizen, a special forces veteran, was running what was basically an assassination agency from a mountain shack in Colorado. The shack was remote and difficult to approach, so it took the Bureau several days to work out the best way to deal with the problem. Eventually it came down to an assault by a SWAT team dropped from helicopters. It wasn't quiet, and the suspect did not survive. We believe he took his own life, but there was a lot of gunfire and we can't be certain. He tried to set fire to the shack and was quite successful. Almost everything was destroyed, including several computers and phones. Our forensic teams have been working on these without much success.

"We did recover some papers, though, which is why I'm here."

Olson slid a thin folder towards Julia. She noticed that the others around the table already had one. She didn't open it.

"The papers we found relate to a surveillance operation by a private investigator here in the UK. We've been speaking to Commander Idris about it. The target of the surveillance operation was you, Commander Kelso. You might want to take a look now."

As Julia opened the folder, she saw the others round the table do the same. The top sheet of paper had notes of a route out of London, with dates and times and distances. The second two sheets were copies of grainy photographs, blown up to A4 size. In the first one Julia Kelso could be seen, naked and from the waist up, with a man standing behind her wrapping his bare arms around her. His face was concealed by her neck, which he seemed to be kissing. She was smiling, her eyes closed. To one side of the couple was a tall young woman in an unfastened dressing gown holding what seemed to be a tray with cups and plates on it. Julia felt her face getting hot and blood was pounding in her ears. The second photograph was a zoom of the first, this time showing Julia's face and breasts in close up, and the top of the man's head. Both photographs were in colour, but the light level was low and the hair colouring was not clear. Julia closed the folder but said nothing.

She looked up, regaining her composure and containing her anger. Under her glare the men closed their folders and looked at each other awkwardly.

"Can you tell us anything about these, Julia?" the Commissioner asked.

"What do you want to know?" she said.

"Is it you in the photographs?"

"You can all see it is. I take it these photographs will go no further than this room."

"Of course, Julia, but we need to know about them. What were the circumstances? The implication is that the assassin in America had you in his sights and he had hired someone to follow you."

"If I can add, Commissioner," Commander Idris chimed up, "we've identified and spoken to the photographer. He's a private investigator, a former police officer but not with the Met, who believed he had been hired for a divorce job, routine stuff. He had no idea that his material and reports were being sent to an assassin. He told us that he followed the subject, that is Commander Kelso, to Devon. The subject drove a car, a blue BMW convertible, with a single female passenger. They parked at a house on the bank of the River Dart, which he could not watch at close quarters. He found an observation point across the river, and early the next morning he was able to take a few pictures of the occupants of a first-floor room of the house opposite with a telephoto lens. These two pictures are the only ones which survived, and he hasn't kept copies. He states he was unable to find out anything about the house and who was in it, but he believes it to have been an out-of-season holiday rental. So far, we haven't made any further efforts to identify the occupants or the circumstances. We thought it best to speak to you first, Julia."

There was a pause, a long pause. The Commissioner looked at her expectantly.

"Alright, if you must know I'll tell you," Julia began, "but this is very personal. I went with my partner, my female partner, for a weekend away. I drove us to Devon, we stayed near Dartmouth in a borrowed house that belongs to someone else, I don't know who. It's immaterial. My girlfriend, partner, is the other woman in the first photograph," she paused. "The man is someone we met by arrangement. We do this from time to time, although it's really none of anyone's business. The man, whose name was Steve as I recall, had arranged the use of the house and we'd agreed to meet him there. We had a nice weekend and my partner and I left on Sunday afternoon. That's all there is to it."

"So, you can't identify the man?" the Commissioner asked.

"No. He's just someone we met through a network we know of."

"What sort of network?"

"What sort do you think, sir?" Julia said, archly.

"And your girlfriend is?"

"She's Demelza Dunn, she works at NCIS. She's living with me at the moment. Will that be all?"

"If I may say, Commander Kelso," Olson said, "you don't seem too concerned that a hired killer put you under surveillance, or at all interested in the reasons for it."

"Being hated by criminals is an occupational hazard, Mr Olson. I cut my teeth on organised crime in Glasgow, you may have heard of it. If the neds and gangsters weren't wanting you dead it meant you weren't hurting them, not doing your job. My only concern here is about how I was too preoccupied with tying up a major investigation to notice that I was being followed. That won't happen again. And since you're saying that the hired killer is dead, I think that's an end to it."

"It would be, Commander Kelso, if we didn't have reason to think that a contract has been taken out on you, and possibly your 'girlfriend' too, and that there is a strong possibility that someone has taken a down-payment. Our studies of assassins and hit-men suggest that once a down-payment has been made the contract remains in force until it is executed, literally."

"I agree with Mr Olson, Julia," Idris said, "so I think that both you and Ms Dunn should have armed protection until this matter is completely resolved."

"Last time I had armed protection from your department someone was able to get close enough to take a shot at me. If it's all the same to you, I'll book out a weapon and look after myself and Ms Dunn. I'll discuss it with her later and if she thinks she wants or needs protection from your department I'll let you know. Now, unless there's anything else?"

She stood up and glared at each of the men in turn, daring any of them to look in the direction of her breasts. No one said anything.

Chapter 3

Julia opened the door of the flat she was currently sharing with Mel Dunn. It was a temporary measure because, despite her performance in front of the Commissioner, Julia was very well aware that both her life and that of Mel Dunn could be in great danger. Her family friend at MI6, Hugh Cavendish, had offered her the use of one of his service's apartments; they kept a few to house sensitive visitors and the odd MI6 field officer who had to return home at short notice.

"Mel?" Julia called.

There was no answer. The flat was empty. Julia felt soiled and weary, and the thought of going out for a run was not appealing. Instead, she undressed and took a cool shower. Mel came back while Julia was sitting on the sofa in a lightweight dressing gown watching the evening news with a glass of white wine.

"'Lo," Mel called, "it's warm out, isn't it?"

Mel had been running and her polo shirt was wet with sweat, her long hair damp and plastered to her head. She went straight to the bathroom, hardly glancing at Julia. Julia heard the shower running. A few minutes later Mel emerged, wrapped in towels. She helped herself to a glass of wine and slumped in a chair. For a few seconds there was silence between them.

"Had a good day?" Julia asked.

"Average," Mel replied, "you?"

"Fucking awful, Mel. We need to talk."

"Sounds ominous. What about?"

Julia explained briefly about the case review meeting and the uncomfortable interview with the Commissioner and the others.

"They had these pictures, Mel. Pictures of me and Alf - but you couldn't see his face - with you in the background at that house in Devon. There was a private investigator watching us, hired by that crazy assassin we heard about. Four men, including the bloody Commissioner and my own boss, staring at pictures of my tits while Alf was chewing my neck! I was furious. The only thing I could come up with on the spot was to say you're my girlfriend and that we had a weekend away, picking up a guy for some extra fun. It was weak, but all I could manage. They said we need protection, you and me."

"You said I was your girlfriend?" Mel asked.

"Yes. Do you mind?"

"No, but you do know I'm not though, don't you Jake? I'm not your girlfriend. I'm a friend, a close friend, but I'm not 'your' anything, I'm not anyone's anything, you do know that?"

"If you say so, Mel."

"And you said Alf was just some random bloke we'd picked up? Who happened to have you wrapped in a loved-up bear-hug the morning after? Not particularly plausible, is it?"

"I never said it was, but I had to come up with something. I couldn't say who he really is, the supposedly dead Detective Chief Inspector Alan Ferdinand, who is also the late Thomas Donohue and the mysterious Paulo Silva, could I?"

"I suppose not. Do you think this is still something to do with that mad cow Dido Sykes? Is she still after you, I mean us?"

"I'd rather hoped she got herself distracted with some other nasty scheme. I'm not entirely convinced that she's still on the warpath, but with her you can never tell. If she's taken out a contract it could have died with that guy in Colorado or wherever it was, if not we'll find out soon enough."

"You mentioned protection. You mean like bodyguards and things?"

"They offered. I said I'd prefer to take my chances. If you want protection, it can be arranged - but it means having someone with you all the time, wherever you go, whatever you do, and whoever you do it with."

"Well fuck that, Jake! I'll take my chances too. Anyway, you've got three weeks to get this sorted out."

"Why three weeks?"

"Because I'm going on holiday, and when I get back I'm moving out, Dido Sykes or no Dido Sykes. I need my own place and space, no offence, and not that I'm not grateful to you and Hugh Cavendish for this bolt-hole."

"Oh! I was kind of getting used to us being together."

"I know, and that's one reason I'm off. I'm never going to be half a couple, you know that, or even a third of a trio with you and Alf."

"Where are you going?"

"On holiday or to live?"

"Both, either."

"No idea where I'm going to live, at least not yet. Holiday-wise I'm going to Crete. I'm taking two diving courses back-to-back, and then I'm going to do some underwater archaeology. I told you a while ago I was interested in it. You can get to advanced open-water standard in two weeks apparently. They've got a few decent historical dive sites and they're always after trained diving archaeologists to volunteer for a week or so. I've been thinking about it for ages."

"When did you decide to do this?"

"Just now, before I went out for my run. I booked it online, flights, hotel, everything. To be frank, I've been feeling a bit cooped up at work. NCIS has gone a bit flat for me, and the last year or so with you and Alf have knocked some of my stuffing out. I might be looking for some big changes. I'll see how I feel when I've got some sand between my toes and a bit of sun on my back. Talking of which, could you give it a rub later? It's a bit stiff."

"Only if you rub mine too. I'm feeling very stressed and tense."

"Sounds like you need a bit of Alf. Why don't you go and see him and get him to 'rub your back'?"

"I'm not sure I want to wait that long, and you're here now. Plus, I've no idea where he is. I know he's left Portugal; I'll try to find him while you're gone. When are you going to Crete?"

"First thing tomorrow morning. NCIS owe me some leave."

"Oh, I see. Best I get my back rub in now then," said Jake.

Later, the two friends lay together in bed, stiffness and tensions gone.

"Don't get me wrong, Jake," Mel said, "it's not that I don't want to be around you anymore or anything, I just need to be on my own a bit more. I'll still like doing this with you, just not every night."

"Stop explaining, I get it. I do know you quite well. Now, what's the best way for me to keep in touch with Alf?"

"Just use two mobiles, ones that aren't used for anything else. You need to get one, a brand-new pay-as-you-go. He needs the same, wherever he is. Keep them turned off with the batteries out but have set times to call each other, don't send text messages. Then only make short calls and never, ever use them to call anyone else, especially someone you've called from your work phone. That's how I'd do it."

"I'll try to get hold of him on the email and get it fixed when we meet up. I do want to see him."

"Good idea. Now I'm going to get some sleep. I need to pack first thing and get a cab to Gatwick by 6."

Chapter 4

Julia woke up after Mel had gone. She'd left early, trying not to disturb Jake as she slept. Julia was briefly unsettled by the stillness of the flat, aware only of her own presence. It would take some getting used to, she supposed. Mel's announcement of her intended departure had prompted her to think about her own accommodation needs - she didn't feel she could impose on Hugh Cavendish much longer. She'd start looking soon, maybe next week. Or maybe she would try to track down Alf and go to see him instead, wherever he was.

She decided to walk to work, using a complicated set of back-doubles to make sure no one was following her. Raj was already at his desk when she arrived, a rare occurrence and one that pleased him greatly. Try as she might, Julia could not shake her flat feeling, her sense of vague and uneasy disappointment. It couldn't just be the thought of Mel Dunn moving out, could it? She hoped not.

At 10.30 Raj knocked.

"Ms Armstrong to see you, boss," he announced.

Amelia Armstrong was probably a couple of years older than Julia, and quite a bit taller. She wore skilfully applied make-up and an imposing business suit, complete with black high heels. Her hand was warm and dry, her handshake extremely firm.

"Julia Kelso," Jake said, "coffee?"

"Amelia Armstrong. No thank you, just water please."

They sat at Julia's conference table.

"How can I help you, Ms Armstrong?"

"Amelia, please. May I call you Julia?"

Jake nodded.

"I have a major problem, Julia," Armstrong began, "one that I suspect has criminal origins. Let me explain; as you may know, I have a very successful legal practice with my business partner, Christopher Llewellyn. We've become known as divorce specialists, but that's not how we started out. Many of our clients are household names, so we are constantly aware of the risk of information leakage, not only to the media but also to lawyers representing our opposing parties. Until a few days ago we'd never had a problem."

Armstrong paused. Julia said nothing.

"Anyway," Amelia continued, "last Tuesday we started to get inundated with calls from journalists and TV and radio stations. They said they had copies of statements made by one of our current, now former, clients concerning the abuse she said she'd suffered at the hands of her husband, and about the degrading nature of things he'd forced her to do with him and others. Needless to say, the husband is rebutting everything and says he can prove it. Our client is both mortified and infuriated, and this morning we received notice that she is implementing legal action against us for gross negligence. She says she will be seeking a very large sum in compensation for what should have been a sizeable divorce settlement, plus a further even larger sum in exemplary damages for the harm done to her reputation. Our insurance won't come anywhere near covering it, but I digress. In short, our practice is all but ruined."

"I'm sorry to hear that, Amelia," Julia said, "but I don't see how I can help."

"I'm coming to that," Amelia almost snapped. "The statements in the hands of the press are unfortunately real, exact copies of genuine documents. They can only have been stolen from us. In cases as sensitive as our client's we keep very tight control of private information and documents. Only myself and my secretary will have seen the statements - nobody else in chambers. I take notes during interviews with the client, my secretary then types the notes up in statement or affidavit form for agreement and signature at the next meeting. The documents are kept under password protection on our IT system, within which we have strict access controls for all files. I am the system administrator who grants permissions. No one apart from myself and my secretary have had access to these documents. So, you'll be thinking one of us must have leaked them or mislaid them somehow."

Julia looked at her but still said nothing.

"Well, we didn't. I'm certain of it. My secretary has been with us from the very beginning. She has an equity interest in the practice and is facing a very significant personal loss if the business collapses. She is loyal and utterly professional. As for me, I would have absolutely nothing to gain and everything to lose if I did anything to jeopardise my practice. Neither of us is responsible for the disclosure. Which means someone else must be. I'd like you to find out who, and why."

"If by that you mean the police, we will do what we can as and when we've established that it's likely a crime has been committed. If, as you're suggesting, material was removed from your computer system by an unauthorised third party, existing legislation is quite limited in scope unless there's evidence that it's part of another crime. I take it you haven't received any communication from anyone, no demands for money or action, anything of that nature?"

"No, nothing at all. If it was simple blackmail I wouldn't need to come to see you. I need your help because you have a reputation for integrity and intelligence and, may I say, lateral thinking. I've been following your career, Ms Kelso. Julia."

"Do you know of anyone who would want to damage or destroy your practice? I can guess the answer, but I need to ask."

"Most of our clients are the wives, Julia, and we usually obtain significant settlements for them. We keep a very large file, a paper one, containing all the threats we receive from annoyed ex-husbands. We refer the very worst to the police, but for most of them we just respond to with a stiff legal note which usually does the trick. This case was nowhere near settlement. The husband is convinced he's going to win, or at least get off with a minor financial inconvenience - nothing to warrant this sort of thing. If I were to hazard a guess, outlandish as it may seem, I would say that we have been set up as an example. Maybe to encourage others to comply with blackmail demands. Can you help?"

"Before I answer, why do you think this particular case has been disclosed? Is there anything special about it?"

"The people are well-known, of course, and the intimate details are distasteful to say the least, but not really. Many of our clients are just as well-known and often have very dirty secrets too. I suppose that disclosure of this case could be particularly damaging, not just to my practice but to the lives and businesses of the parties concerned. Why do you ask?"

"If this case has been specifically selected rather than chosen at random it means that whoever did the disclosing has probably had access to the other cases on your system as well. If the cause of the leak is outside your practice you should probably assume that all your information has been compromised and may be in hostile hands already. We'll need to conduct a full forensic examination of your IT system. We have some limited in-house capacity, so depending on how complex your system is we may need to buy in some expert help. It will mean your practice will be out of action for a while."

"It's already out of action, Julia, probably permanently. What then?"

"If we find that there *has* been some outside interference, we'll try to find out by whom, and why. If we find the person responsible, and they're within our jurisdiction, we can consider a prosecution. Usually, though, if we're talking about a sophisticated computer hacking operation, the culprit will be in another country. If it's not the US or the European Union we're often stymied. I'm sorry I'm not being overly optimistic, but it pays not to set expectations too high at the outset. My recommendation is that you as a business run a private IT investigation once we've done our criminal one, and that will give you the option of pursuing a civil case against any identified perpetrator in a wider range of jurisdictions than a criminal case could reach. Our computer crime team will do the criminal side, and make sure that anything your civil investigation finds is of the appropriate evidential standard. How does that sound?"

"It sounds appropriate, Julia. I'm not sure what I was expecting - not a silver bullet I can assure you, but maybe a little hope. Is there much of this sort of thing going on?"

"I'm not sure what you mean by 'this sort of thing', but international computer crime is surging everywhere. Law-enforcement and governments are running just to try to keep up with the criminals, many of whom are technically far more astute than the police, politicians or even lawyers. We've seen a few examples of trans-national computer-based blackmail, mostly using something called 'ransomware', where the criminals lock users out of their IT systems until a ransom payment is made. The payments are usually quite small, and often the locks can easily be overcome by legitimate computer experts. But the potential is certainly there for sophisticated criminal hackers to take it further. I'll speak to the computer crime people and one of them will call you later. Meanwhile I'm going to take a personal interest in this."

"Thank you, Julia. I can't ask for more. It's been good to meet you."

"You too, Amelia. Let's keep in touch."

After Amelia left, Julia reflected on the meeting. Despite appearances, the powerful lawyer was all but broken; her world shattered, her authority and expertise washed away in an instant. Julia hadn't been expecting to like her but she found she did, and she felt sorry for her too. She picked up the phone and called the computer crime team.

Chapter 5

She watched the sun come up on the river, bringing colours back to life. Montreal was starting to warm up for the day ahead. She had already watched the European news and checked her feed online, and she had mixed feelings. She hadn't wanted the Swiss architect to give up so easily; there was good potential to exploit the information she'd planted on him. That he had killed himself so quickly was annoying, not sporting, but nothing could be done about it now.

The oil company hadn't given up and was fighting hard, but she would take it down when it suited her, and she knew she had the means to do so. She had already made a large sum of money shorting stock in the company, not that it was money she wanted or needed. It was power, power and control.

As for the parasitic lawyers in London, she was going to enjoy herself with them. The outed client with her extraordinarily depraved habits had become very vocal and had declared her intention of suing her former lawyers. Several people had come forward to state that far from being an exploited victim, the lady client was in fact the instigator and driver of the many sordid orgies she claimed to have been forced into. The tabloid headlines were lurid and salacious. *'Gang-Bang? Yes Thank You, Says Ma'am!'* was typical. She'd chosen the case carefully, having gone through the entire library of past and current files, and she knew she had enough material to keep things going for a long, long time. As long as it took in fact, as far as Amelia Armstrong was concerned. She'd already planned the next steps and lined up a new set of subjects.

She made herself some tea and started to eat her breakfast. A bowl of nuts and chilled luscious berries, a slice of sourdough toast with honey, freshly squeezed fruit juice. A long way from the cold, bitter stewed tea and stale cereal soaked in sour milk that her mother used to make her eat all those years ago in Hull. As she ate, her thoughts turned to Julia Kelso. She had amended the contract, having made sure she could get hold of the contractor after the lunatic in Colorado tried to shoot it out with the FBI. The contractor who'd taken on the task of dealing with Kelso, the Dunn woman and that bastard Silva or whatever his name really was, was Dutch. He lived on a houseboat near Haarlem, not far from Schiphol airport, with his wife and baby daughter. The wife worked with him and was as proficient as he was with a blade, a pistol, toxic substances or a petrol-bomb. They doted on their little one but had no qualms at all about taking the lives of other people's sons and daughters - as long as the price was right.

She had contacted them through secretive and circuitous channels involving the dark web and various email complexities that made tracing or monitoring their communications very difficult, if not almost impossible. She had told them to continue to deal with Dunn who, she had learned, would be spending three weeks in Crete. That gave them plenty of time to put the necessary arrangements in place to fulfil the first part of the contract. They were also to continue to attempt to identify and locate Paulo Silva, which she was also trying to do, and put together a plan to deal with him. If luck was on their side, Silva might even show his face in Crete as well. As for that bitch Kelso, she told them to wait. She wanted to draw it out with her; she wanted to hurt her first, then own her, use her and finally break her. When she was done the Dutch couple could have her if they wanted. OK, they'd said.

After breakfast she went out for a brisk walk in the early morning sunshine. She didn't like to run, and now that she had no need to practice her skills with whips and tight leather, even though she was still in superb shape she was slowly losing condition. Some exercise was needed, she'd decided, and she had bought some equipment that now stood in a distant corner of her loft apartment-cum-studio. She would get round to using it one day, but this morning she would walk, then come back, have a sauna and do some yoga for a while before having a long shower. Then she would be ready to start her day's work.

Her day's work involved sending some emails; she had already composed them. All would be sent using the system she had devised so that any attempts to trace them back to her would meet a solid impenetrable wall. The system had taken some time and considerable effort to set up using a variety of email providers, account aliases, re-direction of mail through servers she controlled, and a series of hijacked Virtual Private Networks with encrypted pipes back to other servers she could access at will. It all meant that replies to her messages would sit somewhere remote, unopened until she decided to read them, and only she would know where they were. It was a good system - not infallible, but too hard for the cops and governments to deal with.

The first set of messages went to named executives of major corporations around the globe, to their own personal emails, not the ones that were opened, read and dealt with by staff and assistants. Each contained an extract of one or two documents pointing to major violations of the strict US anti-corruption laws, violations which had been either sanctioned or condoned by a corporate officer. The documents were all genuine, obtained while she mined the companies' hacked information systems. The context for the documents was less clear, and in most cases wholly innocent. But in isolation they all looked bad enough to cause significant damage to the reputations and stock prices of the companies concerned, and to prompt very public investigations by law-enforcement or worse, financial journalists. She didn't demand anything. She just suggested that they took seriously any future communication they received containing a given codeword.

The next set of emails went to partners in a couple of dozen leading law firms, some in the UK and Europe, others in offshore territories in Latin America or the Caribbean. What they all had in common was their lists of very wealthy and / or well-known clients. Each email had two documents attached, taken surreptitiously from the firms' own electronic systems. One document related to a client and his or her financial or personal circumstances. Had she had any sort of shame or conscience she might have been embarrassed by some of the content. The second document gave an example of action taken by the firm in question or advice given to enable a client to evade justice, taxation or liability. Each example was worded in such a way as to infer acceptance by the firm that what they were doing was illegal, or at best immoral.

As with the corporate emails, no direct demands were included, just the advice to respond rapidly to any future communication received with a given codeword included.

The final set of emails went to a handful of soldiers in the armies of sycophants who serviced the egos of superstars. Each recipient was shown documents implicating them in the supply of drugs, illicit art works and objects, vile pornography, dubious personal services or human sexual playthings, regardless of gender or age, to ease the pampered but nevertheless tortured lives of their masters or mistresses. Like the other sets of emails no demands were made, just the strong advice to respond immediately to future communications. In addition, this set of recipients was told in no uncertain terms that if any of them contacted the police or any other agency things would not go at all well for them or their paymasters.

As she sent the last email she felt satisfied. She wouldn't check for responses until tomorrow at the earliest; she would set the timing for this phase of the project. It was late afternoon, still warm in the summer sun. She stood and stretched, took a cool drink from the fridge and went to the balcony. In the streets below the tourists and artists mingled, the old docks were busy. She put on shorts, a tee shirt and some sandals and wandered through the crowds towards the Place des Arts, the spectacular hub of Montreal's colourful cultural life. She had nothing in mind, but there was always something entertaining or amusing going on. She would find somewhere to sit and watch, to be with other people but at a distance, on her own.

Chapter 6

Julia had eventually contacted Alf. He changed the draft of their unsent email, saying simply *'got a phone'*.

'whoopee' she changed the draft.

'2314567761086' appeared next time she opened the mail.

'?'

'think of my little pony'

'FFS!'

'work it out'

Julia wrote the long number down. It was too long, but it must be the new phone number in some sort of code. She had told Alf once that as a girl she'd had a pony, her first ever, and she loved it even after it had thrown her one morning. The pony had been called Spangle. After half an hour messing about with the number and any numerical association with her pony, she found that dividing the number by the number of letters in Spangle's name gave a 12-digit number beginning with 33. It was a French mobile phone number.

'got it. need to see you'

It was two days before the text of the message changed again.

'go dover calais as a foot passenger. call from your new mobile when you get off the ferry. tell me what date first no sooner than 2 days' time.'

Two days later Julia told her assistant Raj that she was taking a long weekend off; she'd cleared it with DAC Connaught. She would not be contactable but would let Raj know when she was back in circulation, three or four days at the most.

She took a train from Victoria to Dover Priory the next morning. It seemed to take forever, and by the time the train got to the tatty, run-down station she was starting to feel depressed. The shuttle bus to the ferry terminal did little to raise her spirits, but once she had bought her ticket and gone through the very cursory passport control she started to feel excited about seeing him again. She found a seat in a quiet part of the boat and watched the water as the ferry steamed purposefully onward. Although she'd been over it in her head more times than she cared to remember, she couldn't come up with any rational explanation for the intimate situation she was currently in with Mel Dunn and the ostensibly late Alan Ferdinand. She was an ambitious, capable woman who held a very senior leadership position in the nation's largest police service. She had been in control of her life, her emotions and her destiny until she'd got tangled up with the two of them. Was it really only 18 months ago?

She was now 38 years old, unmarried - much to her mother's disappointment - deeply involved in both a sexual and intense relationship with a headstrong and slightly strange woman who loved sex but was incapable of making love, and another with a man who had once been her subordinate until his untimely staged death at Beachy Head. The late Alan Ferdinand, known as Alf, had become her secret weapon in a personal crusade against the corruption of justice. He was also her lover, not just a friend and sex partner like Mel. He was very capable of making love to her, and she was looking forward to him doing it again. The fact that he was also sexually entwined with Mel Dunn, on pretty much the same terms that she herself was, was neither here nor there and they didn't discuss it anymore, well not so much.

Mel Dunn had stirred in her a very different Julia Kelso to the one she had always known. The Julia Kelso that Jake had been all her life, until that first night with Mel at Dolphin Square, had woken up the next morning as a sexually aware and sexually interested being, open to new ideas and new experiences. She had probably had more sex, certainly better sex, with Mel and Alf than she had had with anyone else, ever. Not that there had ever been that much.

Julia turned her thoughts to other things as the ferry ploughed on. Mel was safely tucked away in Crete. Alf was clearly now in France, but she had no idea what he was up to. She was concerned about the contract that Dido Sykes had taken out on her and her two friends, and she was struggling to find a way to deal with it and with her. She didn't know where Sykes was, or what name she was using. She had no idea who had accepted the contract and was presumably working out how to kill the three of them.

She could look after herself, at least that's what she liked to believe, and she was fairly confident that Alf could handle anyone foolish enough to come after him. Mel was the vulnerable one, the brilliant intellectual analyst who was uncomfortable with confrontation and violence, unlike her two friends. Mel was fiercely independent and she guarded her privacy. Although Jake and Alf knew about her other special friends, 'the group' as she called them, neither of them had ever met them and they knew they never would. Mel maintained her separate life, away from work and away from Jake and Alf, a life in which she was part of a small group of close friends who also had a deep sexual connection. Mel said she needed the group when she got fed up with trying to teach Jake and Alf how to be good at sex. Sometimes, she said, she needed to be the pupil again, to learn from her group and try new things out with experienced people who trusted each other implicitly. The group needed her too, obviously. Who wouldn't?

Claxons were sounding; the ferry was docking. Julia joined the queue of foot passengers waiting to disembark. Standing in the next queue for the shuttle bus to town she used her new pay-as-you-go mobile to call the number she had worked out for Alf. She hoped she'd got it right. It rang.

"You're here!" he said. "Don't speak. Get on the shuttle bus to the train station in Calais, then get the train to Boulogne Ville. There's one every fifteen or twenty minutes. Call again when you're on the train." He hung up.

She did as she was told. Thirty minutes later she called him again.

"When you get to Boulogne Ville leave the train. Walk slowly towards the Old Town, that's up the hill toward the basilica, you can't miss it. Wherever you want, find a café you like the look of and sit at a table. If I don't show up within 30 minutes, walk back to the station and get a train back to Calais and go home." He hung up again. She frowned at her phone.

In Boulogne she again did as she'd been told, not that it sat easily with her. She wandered through the streets, looking in shop windows. Once or twice she thought she may have caught a glimpse of him, but she couldn't be sure. Just inside the Old Town she found a quiet bistro with shaded tables on a small terrace looking onto a square. She spoke quietly to the waiter and sat at the table he directed her to. The waiter brought her a *café crème* and a glass of water. Julia was wearing a pale cream linen suit and flat shoes. She had a shoulder bag containing clean underwear and a fresh shirt, a few toiletries and a book she was reading. That was all. She wished she had a hat or sunglasses and was glad when the sun disappeared briefly behind a cloud. Then he was there. He just appeared out of nowhere and was suddenly sitting opposite her at the small table. She was about to speak.

"It's OK, you're clear," he said, "no one's following you. You're looking great, Jake. How are you?" Alf reached across the table and took her hand.

She looked at him. He was a bit greyer than when she'd last seen him, and maybe he'd put on a couple of pounds, but not too many. He was inconspicuously dressed in jeans and a crumpled linen jacket. His smile was brighter than the sun.

"You're looking good too," she said. "I've missed you, Alf." She squeezed his hand.

"Shall we eat, or do you want to go somewhere quiet to talk?" Alf asked.

"We'll go somewhere quiet for talking and anything else you want, but I need some food first. I'm starving! The stuff on the ferry looked awful."

They ordered omelettes, salad and glasses of white Bordeaux. Fifty minutes later Alf led her to a small hotel in the lower town and took her to a room on the second floor. It was comfortable and spacious but not luxurious. They hadn't kissed or held each other, not yet. She evaded his arms when he moved towards her.

"Shower. Me first, then you," she said, stepping out of her cream linen trousers and unbuttoning her shirt.

When Alf came out of the shower, Jake was lying in bed with a sheet just concealing her breasts. She threw it back, presenting her perfectly formed body to him in its stark white glory. He dropped his towel and got in beside her. Their reunion was passionate and prolonged. It was almost evening when they both lay back, breathing heavily and satisfied.

"Well, Ferdinand, that was quite something," Jake said eventually, "Mel would be proud of you! I'm glad we ate first."

"With you I never want it to stop," he said. "You do know I love you, don't you?"

"I'd guessed. I love you too, Ferdinand, but it does make life complicated."

She nestled into his chest.

"Do you want to talk now?" he asked.

"How long do we have?"

"As long as you want. I've got the room for three days."

"Do they do room service?"

"I wouldn't have thought so; this is France, after all. Why?"

"I've only brought one clean pair of knickers, and if I don't get fed, I get scratchy. I'm not sure going commando in fine linen trousers is a good idea."

"As I said, this is France, and I'm sure no one would mind, but if it bothers you I can be your hunter-gatherer and you can stay in bed."

"I'm liking that idea. Can you hunter-gather us some alcohol?"

"Already done, ma'am. I'll just need to pop downstairs for some ice."

"Don't be long. I think you're just starting to wear off and I need some more of you. Better get two ice buckets."

"I've missed you, Kelso," Alf said, forcing himself out of bed.

The following morning they had breakfast in the room. Alf had gone down to the salon and come back with a tray laden with coffee and croissants. They'd opened the narrow doors onto the small balcony, but wary of potential prying eyes they sat out of sight in the room.

"They're still digging for Thomas Donohue, Alf, and Paulo Silva. I was in a meeting at the Yard the other day. They're trying to develop some DNA leads they've unearthed. When you 'died' I put in the usual routine request to have your elimination fingerprints and DNA destroyed. I'm really hoping that it was done quickly and properly."

"They won't find anything else on Donohue. They've found his passport already, and by now they'll know that the referee on the application form does not exist. Donohue is gone. As for Silva, well he never existed anyway. His passport was a good fake, an expensive one though. That's why they won't have found any official trace of him. But you're right; if they tie Alan Ferdinand to any of the cases, we will have a problem."

"Not we, Alf, me," Jake said.

"You can't blame yourself, Jake, you had no idea I was going to fake my own death and go after the Carltons. You had no idea I'd be using other identities."

"Not for the Carltons, but I did know for the others. I was part of it too, remember?"

"Let's not worry about that for now. How's Mel?"

"She's in an odd mood, quite withdrawn sometimes. I told you she's moving out, didn't I? When she comes back from playing at being Jacques Cousteau. I'll miss her, but I do get her point. She needs space to be herself. I've got used to her being around, which she says is part of her problem. I think she liked it better as it was before, friends with benefits."

"Is that how you like it too?"

"I do, but I blur things sometimes. I enjoy being with her, but I have to keep telling myself we're not 'together'. We're still close and I hope it stays that way. Why don't you try to see her when she's back? She'd like that, I think she misses you. Let's change the subject. Where are you living now?"

"I've bought a place here in France, in the west, near Poitiers. It's quiet, I've enough space and people leave me alone."

"You've bought a place?"

"I need some roots somewhere, Jake. It was starting to do my head in being permanently impermanent. It's still anonymous, bought through a shell company, and on paper I look like a tenant paying rent. I'm currently Belgian, by the way, Dutch speaking. I'm working on a passport, but with a Belgian identity card I can travel freely in the EU. By the way, I've got you one too."

"Got me what?"

"A Belgian ID card, and a driving licence."

"Why?"

"Sometimes it pays to be able to be someone else."

"Where did you get them, and yours for that matter?"

"There are a few bars in Antwerp near the docks where you can buy most things. Luckily the photographs on Belgian identity cards are always rubbish. You're much prettier in real life than in your photo."

"Tell me about your place."

"It's quite large, an oldish country farmhouse. Not a chateau or anything, but comfortable and big enough, and strangely for France it's got really good plumbing. It's got a couple of barns and some outbuildings that a previous owner used as *gîtes*. There's a smallish bit of woodland, a nice garden, and a pool of course. The nearest village is a twenty-minute walk, and the neighbouring properties are a good way off. I've not met my neighbours yet. I've picked up enough bad French for the locals to believe I'm Belgian and not want to talk to me. You should come and see it."

"It sounds amazing. Book me in for my holidays."

"What about these death threats, Jake? The contract that Dido Sykes took out?"

"Later, Alf. Let's not spoil the moment. I'm going to have a shower and go back to bed for a nap. You can make yourself useful and go to the pharmacy down the street and get us something cool and lubricating - I'm out of practice. And don't forget to put the 'do not derange' sign on the door when you go out."

"You've changed, Kelso. I blame it on that Mel Dunn."

"I do too. I hope you remember to thank her when you see her next. Off you go."

Chapter 7

The diving courses had been fun. Mel was now a qualified Advanced Open Water scuba diver. Ten consecutive days with the same pair of instructors and a variety of fellow students had flown by. As usual, when their dive boat returned to port in Elounda they all went across the road for cold beer in the local bar the dive school always used. Bottles of chilled Mythos served in glasses straight from the freezer, accompanied by bowls of olives. Most of the others left after one beer, but Mel stayed on for a second with a fellow student and both instructors. One of the instructors was the dive school owner, a Cretan former fisherman named Fotis who smiled a lot but said little. The fellow student was a shy lad from the west of England whose name Mel couldn't remember. The fourth person, the second instructor, was a bubbly French girl called Stella, petite and pneumatic.

"Stella is not my proper name, Demelz'," she said at the end of day two, "it is Florence. They call me Stella because I am from Artois, in the north of France. There is a beer called Stella Artois - I think it is an English joke, no?"

Stella always called Mel Demelz'.

They chatted on in the bar for a while.

"Tomorrow I'm going with Fotis to an archaeological dive site, just south of here, to try it out," Mel was saying.

The shy lad nodded enthusiastically.

"You will adore it, Demelz'. Crete is wonderful for historic sites. For archaeologic dives you need perfect buoyancy control, which you have. Most historic dive sites are quite shallow, less than 15 metres, so you can conserve your air, but keep a close eye on your timing. It is very easy to stay down too long."

Fotis smiled. The lad nodded. Mel decided it was time to go. She had enjoyed the evenings of solitude, her simple room in the small dockside hotel, her meals at the taverna she had adopted where they were content to let her sit with a glass of wine and a book long after she had finished eating. She was content.

As Mel was leaving the bar Stella came up behind her and tugged her arm gently.

"Demelz', can I talk with you? Will you come to eat something with me, I invite you? I might not see you again."

Mel looked down at Stella, whose large brown eyes seemed to be pleading. Mel knew what was happening and what Stella wanted; she looked as if she could be quite needy. Mel just wasn't in the mood for any of that, but she liked Stella and her company over a plate of *souvlaki* and a glass of wine would be welcome. She would let her down gently when the time came.

"OK, Stella, that would be nice. But I can't stay long; I'm tired and I need to be up early tomorrow."

"Thank you Demelz'. Attend, I will get my bag." Stella hurried back into the bar, Mel stood on the pavement outside, enjoying the evening sunshine as the air started to cool. Stella emerged and they stepped off the kerb to cross the wide street to the waterside.

"*Merde!*" Stella tripped on her flipflop. She stumbled but didn't fall.

Mel slowed and started to turn towards Stella, but she'd recovered and was trotting to catch up. Mel hadn't noticed the red Suzuki jeep emblazoned with a local car-hire company logo. Its engine idling, it was parked on the kerbside behind her and to her right. As they walked towards the dockside the little jeep's engine was gunned and it hurtled towards them. Mel looked to her right. The jeep was being driven by a man wearing a conspicuous yellow track suit, a baseball cap and dark glasses, and it was heading straight for her and Stella. She grabbed Stella's hand and started to run for safety. Mel was fit and fast but hanging on to Stella slowed her down. They weren't going to make it.

Stella was to Mel's right when the jeep struck, and she took the full force of the impact. Both women were thrown high into the air by the accelerating jeep, which kept going and sped off out of town. They landed close together in a broken heap on the hot tarmac. Stella lay quite still, blood trickling from her ears and nose. Mel stirred, wracked with burning pains all down her right side. She felt cold, very cold; her head hurt. The coldness crept on and grabbed at her heart, she gasped for breath as everything went dark and silent.

Chapter 8

Julia arrived back in London on Sunday afternoon. Sitting alone in the empty borrowed apartment she felt sad and downbeat, despite the physical and emotional lift she'd had from a few days with Ferdinand. She had a leisurely bath and went to bed early, and as she dozed her mind was filled with images of alternating ecstasy, first with Mel Dunn and then with Alan Ferdinand, currently known as Piet Kuyper.

She was in her office before 7 on Monday morning, reviewing everything that had come in during her few days away. There was a message from the computer crime people asking her to call them when she could. She had been half expecting some kind of message from Mel, a jokey postcard or something, but there was nothing. She'd be back at the end of the week and Jake would prepare a special welcome-home for her, probably involving gin.

Julia called the computer crime people at 9.

"Inspector Chakrabarti," a female voice said.

"Commander Kelso, I have a message to call you," Julia said.

"Oh, thanks for getting back to me. I have some news about the Armstrong case you referred to us. Can I come and see you to talk you through it?"

"Please do. Are you free right now? I've got a ten o'clock but I'm clear until then. I'm in Room 540, Victoria block."

"I'll be five minutes, ma'am."

Inspector Chakrabarti arrived exactly five minutes later. Julia met her in the outer office, Raj having been delayed on the train, as was usual for a Monday. She stood and shook hands.

"Inspector Chakrabarti, I'm Julia Kelso."

"Tanisha, ma'am. Pleased to meet you."

Tanisha Chakrabarti was in her late twenties, a little shorter than Julia, and with a slightly fuller figure. Her hair was a lustrous black, swept back off her face and tied in a ponytail. She wasn't in police clothing, choosing instead the unofficial uniform of people of her sort of age. She wore blue chinos, dark blue trainers and a shapeless open-necked polo shirt.

"Tanisha, then. I'm Julia. What do you have for me?"

"Well, I went over to Amelia Armstrong's rooms, her chambers she calls them. She showed me her IT system, if you can call it that. It's pretty basic, primitive even. People don't really get the internet yet, or how to set up a secure IT system that's connected to it. It's not just a question of plugging in a computer and setting a password, there's a lot more to it than that. Anyhow, it didn't take me long to check out her access logs. She thought that they were something she had to fill in herself when I mentioned them, and I had to explain that the machine does all that. It logs everything that's done on it unless someone who knows what they're doing goes in and wipes the records clean. And that's what's happened to hers. I checked the access logs for every file on her system, not that that's very many, just a few thousand, and every single one has been wiped, but not at the same time. Someone has been spending ages carefully going through every file on her system, and when they've done with each one, they wipe the access log record."

"That doesn't sound good, Tanisha," Julia said.

"It isn't. It tells me that someone who knows what they're doing, and that excludes Amelia Armstrong and her dozy but loyal secretary - neither of whom would have a clue where to start - now knows every secret the firm has, its own and its clients. They've accessed all the business records too, accounts, billing and payment details, and of course all the case files, current and past. The closed case files have scanned copies of all the other side's papers too, so including all the statements and disclosures made during the court proceedings, which as you know are mostly about juicy and expensive divorces. I would guess that copies have been made of everything, but there's no way I can confirm that. I've asked Amelia for all her Internet Service Provider records of data usage and time spent on-line. That might tell me a bit more, but nothing that's going to surprise me much.

"There's something else. Every device on the internet has a unique identifier, a number, called the Internet Protocol or IP address. Whenever one device 'talks' to another a record is made of the contact and where it came from."

"You're not going to tell me that's been wiped too, are you?"

"No, worse than that. I can see all the IP addresses that seem to correlate with the times when the hacker was probably rummaging in Amelia's dirty laundry. The incoming IP addresses are all different, I mean all of them. Some are genuine and still exist, others are no longer in use, one or two never existed at all. Every IP address has a geographical component, so you can see where in the world a given device is. Our hacker's addresses are all over the place, from Iceland to Argentina and anywhere in between. It means that the hacker can spoof his or her internet presence at will, using hijacked machines and cut-outs and all sorts. It's sophisticated, Julia."

"Just so I get this right," Julia said, "you're saying it seems pretty certain that someone somewhere who looks like they know what they're doing has been into Amelia Armstrong's IT system over a considerable period. Are you sure they've been able to access everything? Amelia told me that every file was password protected."

"Every file has been opened, otherwise the access logs couldn't have been changed. Amelia gave me the passwords she uses. They're laughable. Anyone who can read up on her would be able to make a guess with a good chance of being right. The timescale is quite long, though. The first file access logs were wiped around six weeks ago, the most recent just two weeks ago, so it was going on for a month. The password thing is quite interesting, despite what I said. Everyone thinks that computer hackers are just a bit nerdy, and some of them are, but people who hack for a proper reason, criminal or otherwise, are also students of people. They're as good at psychology as they are at mathematics, that's why they find it easy to break passwords."

"Where did you learn all this, Tanisha?"

"At uni. I actually did computer science as my first degree, but alongside it I did an OU psychology degree, to save time. I'm thinking about a PhD next, but we'll see."

"So, how come you're in the police?"

"I could ask you the same, couldn't I? You've got a first from Oxford and you're in the police."

"Fair point, but how come?"

"I'm interested in clever criminals. No one's really twigged yet, but internet crime is going to be the biggest law-enforcement challenge of the century. The internet is going to explode, figuratively speaking, it's going to intrude into every aspect of people's lives. Now that it's started there's nothing that can stop it, and it can't be controlled. It's beyond governments. Sure, countries can try to block internet access over the public phone system, but within a decade or so we're all going to be so dependent on it for everything that there'll be riots in the streets if anyone tries to turn it off. The law can't keep up with the technical advances. The only chance we have is to have a lot of people on our side who are as good as the hackers, the criminal ones I mean."

"What do you mean by that?" Julia asked.

"Well, there are good hackers and bad hackers. We need to have the good ones on our side. In the new techie terminology they're known as 'white-hats'. The bad guys are the 'black-hats'. Not very PC, I know."

"And you're a 'white-hat hacker', I'm assuming."

"You're a senior officer and I've only just met you, so I'm going to take the fifth. Like I said, the law can't keep up and white-hat hacking isn't technically legal, not yet."

Julia smiled; she was warming to this sparky and smart young woman.

"So, what can we do for Amelia Armstrong, if anything?"

"Not much. If it was just an everyday blackmailing hacker, I'd have a fair chance of getting a steer on who it is, or at least where. This one has a different feel to it, it's someone who really knows what they want to do, and it's not simple blackmail or a ransomware scam. I've seen lots of those; the usual perpetrators have a style, almost a signature. This one has extreme confidence, enough to dip in and out at will, wiping away their fingerprints after every visit. It's like a burglar stealing the Crown Jewels from the Tower of London a bit at a time - strolling in to take one or two pieces whenever he wants. It's bold, Julia. What I'm not getting at the moment is the why. There was no gain for the hacker in just releasing material to the papers. It was just inflicting damage and pain. My psychology degree is kicking in, and I'm going to suggest that the Armstrong hack is not an end in itself; it's part of something else."

"Like what?"

"Like activism; like a much bigger blackmail; like seizing power. That might seem extreme, but you shouldn't underestimate what can be achieved through the internet, Julia."

"OK, I get it. Now, what do we tell Amelia Armstrong?"

"Whatever she does, all she'll be doing is bolting a horse to her stable door, or whatever the saying is. Her stuff's gone, period. Her clients are going to go nuts and her opponents are going to be very happy, I expect, unless the information she had on them gets let out by the hacker too. If she's still in business in a couple of weeks, she'll be needing a new IT system. We can point her towards a reputable system designer and installation manager, but as you know we can't recommend anyone."

"What about the culprit, the hacker? You're using the singular?"

"Almost certainly a loner, Julia, a chess player rather than a rugby team, if you'll excuse the analogy."

"OK, thanks Tanisha. I'm going to want to take up more of your time to educate myself on this, hacking and computer crime, I mean. How's your workload?"

"Mad. We haven't got enough good people, Julia, and you can't just go out and hire one off the street. I'm not bragging, but it probably takes as long to train a good forensic IT investigator as it does to train a doctor. And once you do there are dozens of consultancy firms out there wanting to snap them up for three times what the Met Police or the government will pay them. I get six offers a week."

"Why don't you take them?"

"I'd only spend the money on inappropriate men and fast cars. Seriously, I'd rather do the right thing than the most lucrative one."

"Which is why you and I are in the police, isn't it? Tanisha, I've enjoyed meeting you, and we'll continue this over lunch or something, and soon. OK?"

"It would be a pleasure. I've done a report on what I've found. Do you want me to take it to Amelia Armstrong? If I do, I'm sure she'll shout at me."

"If you could, Tanisha. If she does shout at you I'll deal with her. I can shout back."

Julia stood and shook hands again with Tanisha Chakrabarti. Quite a girl, she thought.

A few minutes after Tanisha had gone Julia's assistant Raj poked his head round the door.

"Got a Mrs Dunn on the line, boss, she says it's personal and urgent."

"Mrs Dunn?" Julia's heart froze as she realised who Mrs Dunn must be. "Put her through, Raj."

Chapter 9

In Montreal she finished reading the report from the Dutch couple. They had used the information she had given them to trace the Dunn girl in Crete. They had completed their work, destroyed the evidence by setting fire to the stolen car and had driven their own legitimately rented hire car back to their hotel in Malia to continue their holiday in the sun. They were satisfied, so was she.

She started to read Julia Kelso's overnight emails - God, her life was boring! Dull reports on this and that, complaints from subordinates about resources, endless meetings. But there was never anything personal that she could get her teeth into. Nothing about family, lovers, friends, home, money - nothing useful. She hadn't even found a personal email account yet, nor a personal mobile that might have text messages stored on it. She was starting to think that Kelso might actually be quite savvy; on the other hand, it might be she just didn't have many friends. If the Dutch couple's report was correct, she now had one fewer than she did last week.

The lawyer woman seemed to have gone into meltdown. Her emails were flying everywhere and were getting ever more hysterical. It seems she'd been given a report by the police stating that all her practice information had been stolen in a sophisticated hacking attack, and that it wasn't possible to say who had done it. Of course it wasn't possible, she thought. The lawyer's hysteria was attracting media attention. Time, she thought, to take the next step.

She had prepared another series of emails, fifty in all, to former clients of the fizzing lawyer or to their ex-husbands. Each one referred the recipient to media coverage of the ongoing collapse of Armstrong and Llewellyn, divorce lawyers to the rich and famous, and stated that specific information concerning the recipient's personal affairs would be released to the British and European media within five days unless substantial donations were made to specified charities. She listed five (four of which were genuine and one of which was not) and specified the amount to be donated to each. The total demanded in each email ranged from £50,000 to £1 million. The addressees could easily afford what she was demanding. The fictitious charity was her own, one she'd set up earlier to handle these payments. It was in an accommodating and poorly regulated country, one which had a lax and available banking system. She didn't need the money; she just didn't like working for nothing.

She spent an hour or so sending the emails and sat back to wait. She would have to head back to Europe soon if she was going to deal with Kelso the way she wanted to, but that would have to wait until she'd turned up the heat under the other subjects she'd selected for her experiment. And she also had to get a handle on the man known as Paulo Silva. She was expecting some progress on that front soon. Silva's death or downfall was part of her plan to bring Kelso to heel. She owed it to Drew Strathdon, who was presumably rotting in a British jail. She had no emotional or sentimental attachment to Strathdon. He'd been good to her, and she had quite liked him, even respected him for a while, but he had been well-rewarded at the time and now he was no longer of any use to her. She would avenge him, though, because she could and because she wanted to. And Kelso deserved it.

******

In Charente in western France, Piet Kuyper was painting the side of one of his barns. A previous owner had given it a coat of an incongruous bright green which Kuyper couldn't stand a minute longer. The morning sun was warm on his back and he was sweating slightly. He didn't hear his phone ringing. When he'd finished applying the first coat he saw that the green still showed through the pastel grey-blue he'd applied and he resigned himself to giving it a second one tomorrow. He went into the house for a cold drink, and he picked up his new phone. There were four missed calls, all from the same UK number: Jake's number that she used just for him. He called her back.

"Get to Crete," she said when she picked up, "Mel's been hurt, badly hurt. We need to go to her."

"What happened?"

"I don't know yet. I had a call from her mum earlier. The hospital in Heraklion called her and told her to get there immediately, but she can't because she has to look after her husband who's very sick. Mel had spoken to her about me, and she's asked me to go. I'm booked on a flight leaving soon. I'm at Gatwick now."

"OK. I'll get there as soon as I can. Keep your phone on when you land."

He opened his computer and searched flights to Heraklion. He found one leaving Nantes, a couple of hours' drive away, at 5 that afternoon, arriving at Heraklion at 9. He phoned the airline. They only had business class seats available so he booked one and packed an overnight bag. He extracted his current car, this one an aging Peugeot 504 saloon, from one of the barns and set off after a quick sandwich. He was at the airport terminal before 3, paid cash for his ticket and cleared check-in with no problem using his Belgian ID card as a travel document.

Waiting in the lounge he helped himself to a cold beer and tried to stop imagining what could have happened to Mel Dunn. He hoped she was alright, or at least alive. The wait seemed to go on forever, but eventually the flight was called and he boarded. He declined the meal but accepted a couple of tiny bottles of whisky from the steward. The plane landed on time and he walked through the Schengen lane into the evening warmth. He called Julia.

"I'm here. Where are you?"

"I'm at the hospital, it's bad - she's in intensive care. I don't think it was an accident; I think someone's tried to kill her, deliberately. The girl she was with has died, and Mel's only hanging on because she's so fit. Get to the hospital, the University Hospital - it's south-west of the airport and you'll need a taxi. I'll see you by the Intensive Care Unit. Please hurry!"

He was there in twenty minutes. For the first time he saw fearful tears in Julia Kelso's eyes. She wasted no time.

"I've spoken to the doctor treating her. She was hit by a car, a hit and run, near the hotel she was staying in. The girl she was with took the full force of the impact and died at the scene. Mel was resuscitated, first by the owner of the dive school she was at, then by paramedics. They kept her on CPR all the way here. She has a fractured skull, fractured pelvis, femur and a damaged hip, some rib fractures and a punctured lung as well as more damage to her arm and shoulder. It's the skull that's most worrying. There's a lot of pressure fluctuation and they keep trying to stabilise it."

He listened.

"Why do you think it wasn't an accident?"

"The doctor, Christos his name is, translated the police report for me. It said that the car was stolen, it was a hire car, open top. The car drove right at her, it had been waiting nearby. When she came out of a bar it drove at her at full speed. The driver was wearing bright conspicuous clothing, it's a distraction technique. The car was found on fire a mile or so outside the town less than 15 minutes later. No description of the driver, apart from his or her yellow tracksuit."

"Has anyone been notified, the British embassy or anyone like that?"

"I don't think so. No one's mentioned it. Christos phoned Mel's mum because it's the next of kin contact name in her diver's logbook. Her passport wasn't with her, or her mobile. They must still be in her hotel room."

"Do you know where she was staying?"

"No, only that the incident happened in a place called Elounda. It's in eastern Crete, about an hour and a half's drive from here."

"We can sort that out tomorrow. If it was deliberate, targeted, how did anyone know where she was?"

"I've been thinking about that," said Jake, "it was a last-minute thing. She booked her flight and hotel the day before she travelled, all online. I don't think she'd told anyone but me, her mum certainly had no idea she was here. Any ideas?"

"As a cop, I'd be using airline passenger lists and border control information to find out where someone was going to or from. It's unlikely that anyone in Elounda would be in contact with someone who wanted Mel dead, and we both know who *would* want her dead - the same person who wants you and me dead too. It would be a very long shot indeed if Dido Sykes had sources in a sleepy tourist town in Crete. If she is behind it, she must be able to get into airline booking systems. And if she can do that, she may know you're here, and may guess that I will be too. She may also know that Mel isn't dead."

"You're making sense, Alf, but you're also making me very nervous. She needs protection until we can get her away from here."

"So do you. Kelso's not a common name, nor is Demelza. I'd bet they're the names Sykes looks for. I'm currently Piet Kuyper, common as muck and almost untraceable even if she knows I'm using the name."

"I need to make a call. Do you have access to money?"

He nodded.

"Good. Wait here. She's in the room on the left, just her and a nurse. Go to her, look after her. I'll be back in a few minutes."

He went into Mel's room. It was cold and still. Mel was on her back, covered with a thin sheet, a sheen of sweat on her face. Her light brown hair had been cropped short; parts of her head shaved. A nurse dabbed at her cheeks with a cool towel. A monitor stood guard next to the bed, blinking and bleeping rhythmically. She was completely unconscious.

"How is she, nurse?" he asked.

"Sorry, very little English. She is very sick, but strong. We hope she will be OK."

He nodded and sat down on a plastic chair. His throat felt thick. The vulnerable girl in the bed looked like the vivacious, confident woman he knew and loved, who he'd slept with and laughed with and drank with, but she was different. He'd seen her asleep, but he'd never seen her look so small and alone. He stood and held her hand for a moment. It was cool; he squeezed gently. There was no response.

"We have given her strong sedative," the nurse said, "so she rests still. For the head."

Outside in the car park Julia took her work phone from her bag and turned it on. When it was ready, she scrolled through her saved numbers and found the one she was looking for. It would be nearly 9pm in Abuja, two hours behind Crete. She pressed call.

"Evans," a voice said.

"Justin, it's Jake. Sorry to bother you."

"Jake! *Quelle surprise!*" There was loud music in the background. "Sorry, I'm at the High Commission club, I'll move somewhere quieter."

"Not social, I'm afraid, and I need to be quick."

Military Attaché Justin Evans, Lieutenant Colonel, formerly of the SAS, was a friend. He'd been assigned to MI6 and Julia had met him then.

"Justin, do you know any ex-regiment guys who do close protection, civilian style?"

"A few, why?"

"You remember Mel Dunn? Well, someone's tried to kill her and may try again. I'm with her now, with a friend, but we're going to need help until we can get her somewhere safe. She's sedated in ICU, so we can't move her yet."

"Where are you?" He had become very professional.

"I'm in Crete, Heraklion, at the University Hospital. We have access to funds; I know this sort of thing doesn't come cheap."

"Keep your phone on. I know someone who's based in mainland Greece these days. He might be able to help. He'll call you unless you hear from me first."

Justin hung up. She paced up and down for a few minutes. After ten her phone rang. The number was withheld.

"Julia Kelso? Friend of Justin. You need some help, I hear."

"I do."

"Justin filled me in on what you'd said. I can't help with armed protection, but I can certainly sort you out some solid and capable support. I can just about make the last flight to Heraklion from Athens, so I'll see you around 1am at the University Hospital. Where will you be?"

"In the Intensive Care Unit. How will I know you?"

"Justin's described you and given me some information that'll mean something to you. You'll know I'm pukka when I speak to you."

The call was ended.

Julia took a deep breath. She cried quietly for a minute or two, then controlled herself. She wiped her eyes and went back to Alf and Mel.

"Cavalry's coming, a couple of hours," she said, gripping his hand, "but it's up to us until they get here."

"We'll need to get her somewhere safe," Alf was thinking out loud, "but she can't be moved yet. I'm going to look into chartering an air ambulance, but I really don't want Sykes to know where we're going with her. I need to think."

"I'll stay with her. Go outside and punch a wall or something. Come up with some ideas."

"I'd sooner stay here with you two," he replied. He lapsed into silence.

The next two hours passed slowly. He fetched water and tepid machine-made coffee for them. She went to the bathroom.

Shortly after one in the morning there was a gentle tap on the door. Alf was immediately alert and on his feet. He opened the door.

A stocky black man in his forties stood a short way back, a grin on his face.

"Easy, tiger," he said with a Brummy accent, "I'm the first instalment of the help Julia's asked for. Is she here?"

Julia came to the door.

"Name's Spike, Justin sent me. Said to mention a dolphin in December and ask how your scar is doing."

Julia nodded.

"You're pukka. Julia Kelso, and this is my friend Piet Kuyper. Actually, a friend of both of us." She nodded towards Mel, who remained unconscious.

"OK. I've rustled up three mates. They'll start arriving tomorrow morning. We can do shifts, two men, twelve hours each for up to four days to start with. I understand the threat is real, but we don't know where it's coming from. An attempt has been made with a vehicle driven by a single occupant. That's good because it means he or she probably doesn't have ready access to weapons. I checked Greek media before I left home and there's only a report of a bad traffic accident with a fatality in the Cretan papers. Please try to keep anything else out of the press. Hospitals are leaky and porters can make as much from journos as they can from the hospital. You both look bushed. Why don't you go and get a hotel for some sleep? Here's my number. Call me when you're settled somewhere."

"You're from the regiment, then?" It was the first time Alf had spoken.

"Correct. You don't sound very Dutch. I was in Evans's platoon, a sergeant. We had some fun. I've got a bar on a beach near Athens with my wife and kids now, and I do a few favours for old mates from time to time."

"We can pay, you know," said Alf.

"Justin said. We can discuss it later when we know the extent of what we're dealing with. But as far as I'm concerned, if Justin says you're cool, that's good enough for me. Now, go get some sleep. She's safe with me."

In a taxi to one of the chain hotels in the town he held her hand.

"What was all that stuff about dolphins in December?"

"I'll tell you one day," she said, kissing him gently.

Chapter 10

They slept fitfully, together but apart. Jake was preoccupied, clearly distressed about what had happened to Mel. Alf was worried by Mel's injuries, but his primary emotion was fury. Whoever had done this to Mel would pay a high price. As soon as day broke they were up. Alf set about getting hold of a hire car while Jake took a taxi to the hospital.

Spike was there with Mel in her room. She was still unconscious.

"I've been chatting to the nurse," Spike said, "they've put Mel in an induced coma to allow the brain swelling to ease. They're pleased with her progress and as long as there are no adverse changes they'll start waking her up the day after tomorrow. Once the brain issue is sorted they're going to reset the worst fractures and try to realign her pelvis."

"You speak Greek then?" Julia asked.

"Course," he replied, "I've lived here for six years, since I left the UK, and my wife is from one of the islands. I asked the nurse about the prognosis, for Mel I mean. The first hurdle will be any brain damage. They won't have any indication if there is any or how bad it could be until she wakes up, then they may have to do a scan. If that's all fine, she'll need a long time to recover from the other injuries. I've seen people bounce back from worse, but it's more luck than anything else. The nurse says if she was less fit and healthy your friend would be in the mortuary rather than intensive care. The nurse is very experienced, and she's saying that Mel has a good chance of a reasonable recovery, as long as the brain is OK."

"She said 'reasonable'?" Julia asked.

"Yes, just reasonable. There will probably be some lasting damage, but stuff she can live with. We'll have to wait and see. Now, the others are going to start arriving this morning. Like I told you last night, I've got three guys to work shifts with me, there'll be a Greek speaker on each shift. Overnight I had a think and I've asked two girls to come over as well. They're not SAS, but they're former combat medics. That's like super-trained paramedics, not exactly qualified doctors but better than most you'd find in your average emergency room, especially on gunshot, blast and trauma injuries. These two are among the best; I worked with them both in Iraq and a few other places. Mel's going to need some personal attention once she's awake, and Greek hospitals aren't exactly like your NHS. The staff are very good medically, but they don't tend to do personal care. That means that family and friends have to do it. The wards are more like railway stations in the daytime, there are that many people wandering about. Have you thought about where Mel's going to go when she's well enough to move?"

"No, not yet. We'll come up with something."

"I know you're worried, but I think we need to talk about the elephant in the room," Spike said.

"You mean the attempt?"

"Yes, that and the Cretan police."

"How do you mean?"

"Well, the police are either going to work out someone tried to kill your friend, and *did* kill the other poor girl, and put on a very public investigation. More likely they're going to try to say it was just a traffic accident, no more than that. It's nearly peak tourist season and they don't want to scare people off. Either way, it won't be long before it gets out that Mel has survived. As long as she's unconscious we're probably OK, but the nurse said the police instructed the hospital to contact them the minute Mel wakes up or dies. Sorry, but that's what she said. All this means that you need to have something lined up for her within a couple of days. Things could get very awkward for her, and us, if the police are all over her while she's in this hospital."

"What would you suggest, Spike?"

"First, get her off the island. I can help you arrange that. I've got a mate who runs a parachute club on the mainland. He's got one of those Cessna Caravan planes which he can fit out for casualty evacuation. Thing is, where to take her?"

"Let me talk to Alf, I mean Piet," Julia said. "Do you want a coffee?"

"I'll go get it. I need the lavvy anyway, so you stay here with her. Has she got any family?"

"Yes, I'll give her mum a call now. Thank you, Spike. I'm really grateful for your help. I'm sure Mel will be too."

"No problem, Julia," Spike said with a grin, "I never could resist a damsel in distress. And Justin said you're alright."

Spike went off to find some coffee, Julia called Mrs Dunn using her work phone.

"Mrs Dunn? It's Julia Kelso, I'm in Crete with Mel, at the hospital."

"Thank God," Mrs Dunn said, "is she OK? Can I talk to her?"

"She's asleep, Mrs Dunn. They've sedated her to help her recover. Mrs Dunn, she's badly hurt, but she's getting good care and the best treatment. I'm going to come to see you when I get back to England, and I'll explain everything then, but I think you ought to know that Mel was attacked - it wasn't an accident. She's out of harm's way now, but when she gets out of hospital she'll have to go somewhere safe for a while."

"What do you mean, attacked? Why? Who by?"

"I'm trying to figure all that out, Mrs Dunn. Let's focus on the good news that she's doing well, she's a fighter, your Mel. When she wakes up I'll get her to call you herself, but it won't be today."

"Should I try to get to Crete to see her? I can get my other daughter to take care of her dad for a few days. I'll need to get a new passport, mind, mine's run out."

"We hope to be able to move her somewhere else in a few days, so maybe it's best you sit tight until your new passport arrives, then we can arrange for you to see her. Is that OK?"

"Yes, I think. I'll get on to it. Will you call me again when you can?"

"Of course," Julia said. "I'll call you every day or two, hopefully with good news."

Julia ended the call and sat still for a few moments. She looked at Mel, motionless apart from her shallow breathing. A monitor beeped occasionally beside the bed. A drip was feeding fluid into her arm; she looked weak and helpless. For a second Julia felt frightened, frightened of losing her friend, frightened of what had caused her this pain.

Spike reappeared with steaming mugs of aromatic coffee and a plate of pastries.

"Sweet-talked one of the ladies and got us some real coffee," he said, his grin in place, "have you spoken to her mum?"

"Yes, she's a bit shocked but relieved, I think, that Mel's not alone."

"Your mate's downstairs, Piet or whatever you call him. He's having a bit of a barney with a parking attendant - the car park's mad at this time of day. I said he could abandon his car for ten minutes, but any longer than that and it's going to get towed. He'll be up in a minute."

Right enough, Alf walked through the door.

"Morning," he said to the room in general, "how's she doing?"

"No change," Spike said, "I told Julia I'd been talking to the nurse overnight and got a fair picture of Mel's situation."

"Spike's been wonderful," Julia said, "he understands the Greek system and speaks the language. The doctors are keeping Mel sedated until her brain swelling stabilises, then they want to fix the worst fractures. They're going to try to start waking her up in a couple of days, and as long as there's no brain damage they'll operate pretty much immediately on her pelvis and leg. We've discussed moving her as soon as we can, probably in three or four days. The threat hasn't gone away, and as soon as it gets out that she's alive the killer may well come back for another go. We need to get her away from here, off the island. Any ideas?"

"What about my place?" Alf said. "There's plenty of room and I'm sure we can arrange the right medical care."

"I can help with medical stuff," Spike said. "I told Julia I've sent for two girls, ex-RAMC combat medics I worked with in Iraq. They're good and capable. They'll be here later and I'm sure they'll be happy to tag along. Where is your place?"

"France," said Alf, "Charente."

"Neat."

"We need to get her there, though," Julia said. "If we use an air ambulance there'll be traces. For your information Spike, we think the person responsible for the attack, the one who ordered it, has access to a lot of information. We think Mel was traced to Crete through an online flight booking. We need to move Mel under the official radar."

"OK," Spike said, "getting her off Crete will be easy. Like I said, my mate can fly her out. If we get her to mainland Europe inside the Schengen zone she can disappear without trace. Which means if we're going overland it will have to be a hop from here to Italy, then by road up to Piet's place. You'll need a station wagon or van that she can lie in, or ideally an ambulance."

"Leave that with me," Alf said, "I'm going down to Elounda this morning. I want to find the rest of her things, and to see if I can get anything else on what happened down there. I've got the name of the dive school she went to from her logbook - I'll start there. I'm also going to book a flight back to France to fix the transport."

Julia nodded. Alf squeezed her hand briefly and shook hands with Spike.

"See you later," he said.

When he'd gone Spike looked at Julia quizzically.

"Your man Piet sounds a bit Belfast when he lets his accent slip. He's not Dutch at all, is he?"

"It's complicated, Spike, but he's genuine. He loves Mel."

"None of my business, really," Spike said, "I just like to know what's what when I'm on a job."

Spike's phone buzzed. He looked at it.

"The team's here. I'll go get them. Back in ten minutes."

In the relative quiet of the intensive care room Julia held Mel's hand. She felt it stir, but Mel stayed asleep. Impulsively, Julia stood and bent over her. She kissed her damp forehead and wiped the sweat back from her eyes. When she stood, Spike was in the doorway watching her.

"Julia, this is Steph and Tracey. The ugly one is Mike. He's my oppo. The other two have gone to find somewhere for us to stay. They'll be back to take over at midday. Steph will work with me; Tracey gets the other lot. I wanted to brief them both on Mel's condition together."

For the first time since she'd boarded the plane to Crete, Julia felt like she was starting to get a grip on the situation.

"I'll leave you to it, I need some air. I'll be back soon," Julia said.

She went down in the lift, quite crowded with people, some weeping, some silent. Outside in the warm sunshine she took a deep breath. For a passing moment she wished she smoked. She bought a bottle of cold water from the cafeteria and found a shady bench. She sat and sipped the cooling water, enjoying the chill as it passed her throat. She saw but didn't take any notice of the pale-skinned couple with a toddler in a push chair as they strolled past her. Had she done so she might have noticed the woman stare at her and whisper urgently to the man. They were speaking Dutch.

Chapter 11

It took Alf more than two hours to get to Elounda, once a sleepy fishing village towards the eastern end of Crete but now a developing tourist town. He parked his hire car near the waterfront, not far from the scene of the attack on Mel Dunn and her French diving instructor. He saw a wilting bunch of flowers tied to a lamppost, and on the road surface there were still traces of what looked like blood. The café bar on the opposite side of the road was closed with shutters fastened. He found the office of the diving school and went inside.

It was shady, cool and quiet. A young woman sat disconsolately in front of a computer screen, while in a back office a middle-aged man with a neat grey beard was visible. He looked tired and drained. Alf spoke to the woman in the outer office.

"Hello," he started, "my name is Kuyper and I'm a friend of Mel Dunn, Demelza, who was hit by the car outside. I was very sorry to hear that your instructor was also hit and did not survive."

The young woman looked up at him, her eyes moist, waiting for him to say more.

There was an awkward pause.

"What do you want?" This from the bearded man in the inner office.

"I've come to find out what happened, and to collect the rest of Mel's things. Her family asked me to come."

"Come in," the man said, "I am Fotis. I own the dive school. How is Demelza?"

Alf went in and shook the man's hand. It was rough and hard, weathered by a lifetime of working on boats.

"Demelza is very sick, but she's strong. We hope she'll pull through. I'm sorry about the other woman, your colleague," Alf said.

"Stella was a good teacher and a good dive guide. The students and passengers all liked her. She was an asset, and a good friend too. I think she was attracted to Demelza. We have a rule that instructors and guides must not interact socially with students and guests, not alone anyway. A beer after a day on the boat is fine, but not in private. Once Demelza had finished her training I think Stella wanted to get to know her a bit better. And now she is dead. I had to call her family to tell them. It was very difficult, they don't speak English or Greek and I don't speak French. I'm not sure they understand now what has happened. I called the French consul in Heraklion, he said he'd contact the family, but that was yesterday. I've heard nothing since."

"I'm sorry to hear that. Can you tell me what happened?"

"I saw it. I was in the bar, the one across the street. It's closed now, out of respect. Demelza left, she'd had two beers and said that was enough. She said she was going to get an early night to be ready for the next day's diving. We were going to go to an archaeological site just to the south of here. She was very excited. She had learned well; she was a good diver, very controlled. As she was leaving Stella went after her. The two of them spoke for a few seconds, then Stella came back for her bag; she looked happy. Demelza was a couple of paces in front of Stella crossing the street. Stella stumbled. She was wearing flipflops, Demelza waited for her to catch up. Then I heard a car engine. It was loud. I saw Demelza grab Stella's hand and start to run, but Stella was not quick enough. The car hit Stella and went straight on into Demelza. Both of them went up in the air, over the top of the car. It didn't stop or slow down. It was a small jeep, with the top down. One of the girls, I think it was Demelza, hit the windscreen and it broke. The driver was a man, I think, quite tall although he was seated, of course. He was wearing a bright yellow tracksuit and a dark baseball cap with sunglasses on. As the car went past I saw he had gloves on. It is my opinion he was waiting for them, or one of them. I don't know if it was Stella or Demelza. It looked like it was deliberate. I told this to the police, but they are not interested. They want it to be a traffic accident.

"The car, the small jeep, they found a short time later. It was on the road going north out of the town; it was on fire. Someone I know told me that the yellow tracksuit and gloves were on the seat, also burning. There must have been another car waiting for him. Back here, I went out to see if I could help. It was obvious to me that Stella was dead; her neck was broken, she wasn't breathing. Demelza was alive but not conscious. I did resuscitation, as a dive school owner and master scuba diver I have medical training for emergencies. Demelza's pulse was weak. I told the bar owner to call an ambulance, to say that it was urgent - cardiac arrest with multiple fractures. The ambulance came quickly - I kept up the CPR all the time until they arrived and took over. That's all I know."

"Was there anything about the driver? Anything that stood out?"

"I can't think of anything. One thing is a bit strange, though. The day after the accident a couple came into the dive school. They had a small child, not much more than a baby, with them in a pushchair. They said they were on holiday up the coast and had heard about the accident. They wanted to know if both the women who were hit were alright. The thing I thought strange was that they should come to ask me, not at the bar or one of the shops closer to the road. But they came here, to the school."

"What can you tell me about them?"

"Are you a policeman or something?"

"No, I'm just a friend of Demelza's. I want to find out as much as I can for her and her family."

"The couple with the baby were from northern Europe, I think Holland maybe. They looked Dutch. Tall, quite thin, they were dressed like they were on holiday. They wore rings on their hands, like wedding rings. We have CCTV in the office, there's a lot of expensive equipment here. I was curious about these two, so I printed pictures of them. I have them here."

Fotis rummaged in a desk drawer and pulled out a small folder. In it were three or four still pictures each showing the same couple, the woman holding on to the handle of a pushchair. The child could not be seen, but the faces of both adults were clearly defined.

"Did you tell the police about these two?" Alf asked.

"They still weren't interested," Fotis sighed.

"May I take one of these?" Alf asked.

"If you want." Fotis sounded resigned.

"Thank you. One more thing - can you tell me where Demelza was staying? She didn't have any of her things with her at the hospital."

"She was at a small hotel, just down beside the harbour. The owner has brought her stuff round - he wanted to re-let her room. Her bag is in one of the lockers."

Fotis said something in Greek and the young woman in the outer office went away. She came back a few moments later with Mel's sports bag, one that Alf had seen her with many times before. She put it on Fotis's desk. He nodded his head as an invitation for Alf.

Alf unzipped it. On top of Mel's clothes were her passport, phone and wallet, all seemingly intact. He didn't go through the rest of it. He checked the phone and saw a few missed calls, presumably from her family. There was also one from Jake's personal mobile.

"May I take this to her?"

"Please do. But you must sign a receipt for it."

"Of course. Thank you for looking after it."

"One thing, Mr Kuyper," Fotis said, "why would someone want to kill Demelza? I can't think of any reason why anyone would want to hurt Stella."

"I don't know, Fotis, I really don't. If I ever find out I'll let you know."

Alf took his leave and drove back to Heraklion. He took Mel's bag up to her room. He found Julia there, with another man he hadn't seen before, and a young woman.

"Piet," Julia said, "this is the late shift. Tracey is a trained medic, and Ricky is from the same lot as Spike. His colleague Ewan is downstairs. He called to say you'd arrived. Spike described you to the team. Spike and Mike have gone back to their digs, a guest house near here, with Steph, who's the medic on the other shift."

Alf greeted Ricky and Tracey.

"I've got Mel's things; her passport and phone are in there. I've also got this, but it's the only copy I have. It's a CCTV shot of a couple who were asking about the accident, but in an odd way. I think the dive school owner thinks that the man might have been the driver of the car that hit Mel and Stella."

Julia looked at the photo, frowning. She passed it to Ricky who studied it. He took a device from his jacket pocket.

"It's one of these new-fangled camera phones," Ricky said, "I got it in Japan a few months ago."

Ricky took a picture of the grainy image Alf had brought with him. He fiddled with the phone for a few seconds.

"There. I've sent it to Spike. He'll make copies for the whole team."

"Can I see that again?" Julia asked Alf.

He passed her the picture.

"I think I might have seen these two. Here, this morning, in the car park when I went out for some air. I can't be sure, but I think so."

No one spoke for a few moments. Then Ricky made a quick phone call. Thirty seconds later another stocky, middle-aged man, this one with short ginger blond hair and tattoos, appeared in the doorway.

"Show Ewan the picture, Piet," Ricky said.

Alf did so.

"Julia thinks she might have clocked these two in the car park earlier today. Have you seen them?"

Ewan shook his head.

"No, mate, but I'll keep an eye out. How sure are we that they're hostile?"

"We're not," said Ricky, "they're just possibles for now. I'm going to get Spike to run them past his contact in Intel to see if they're in the big book of bad boys. If they show up, treat them with caution, but unless they make a move first don't strike."

"Got it," said Ewan. Tracey nodded. She may have been a medic, but she was just as capable of striking as any of the men on the team; so was Steph.

******

In Montreal she awoke and stretched, aware of her own muscles and sinews, not needing or wanting anyone else's touch. After a shower, she opened her screens and checked the emails. Julia Kelso hadn't opened or sent any emails for at least 36 hours. On a whim she checked flight manifests from London to Crete, Heraklion in particular. She found the name quickly. Open return, business class, Gatwick to Heraklion, first leg flown the day before yesterday. Kelso was in Crete. Had she gone to get the body, or was there bad news?

She checked her own emails, firstly on the dark-web system the Dutch killers used. It was bad.

We think Dunn survived, they had said. We think she's in the University Hospital. They had seen Kelso in the car park, but no police. They were planning a second attack, this time in the hospital, but it would take some time to prepare.

"Just finish Dunn! Kelso can wait," she wrote back.

Chapter 12

Alf left that afternoon. That Julia and Mel were in good hands reassured him. He knew that Jake was not at her best; she'd been shaken, struggling to get on top of what had happened. She'd been distracted and almost distant when he took his leave - not that he was expecting an emotional departure. It was just that she seemed to lack her usual natural warmth. He sat back as the plane powered northward towards Nantes. He would be home by midnight, and tomorrow he'd start looking for transport.

He'd told Jake he'd phone her when he landed. She answered immediately.

"How's it going?" he asked.

"No change, but it's good to have the team here. Ricky's a Greek speaker too, so we're getting good medical information. Tracey and Steph can make sense of it, and they're getting an idea of what she'll need when we get to your place. One thing they say Mel will definitely need is an orthopaedic hospital bed. Apparently they're quite easy to get hold of. There'll have to be one there when she arrives or soon after. She's probably going to be in a cast from the waist down with her right leg straight, so she'll need to be able to lie down while travelling. The girls are going to keep her pretty much sedated on the journey, but they want it to be as quick as possible. Spike's parachuting buddy knows of an airfield in southern Italy near Otranto where he's done drops before. It's around two hours flying time from western Crete; it's about as far as he wants to take the Cessna. Otranto's probably best part of a full-day's drive to get to yours. We'll split the driving and do it in one hit. Ricky's planning to go over a day before and get transport for himself and Mike; they'll ride shotgun for us. Steph and Tracey will come with us, so whatever vehicle you get will need to be big enough."

"Got it. Now how are you?"

"I'm fine." She didn't sound it. "Call me tomorrow evening." Julia ended the call.

Alf retrieved his Peugeot and drove south. It was late when he pulled up outside his house. A few lights were on timers, so there was a welcoming glow in a few windows. Inside he had a hot shower and poured himself a large whisky. Another followed it, just to slow his racing mind and let him relax enough to sleep. He woke early.

On his computer he searched for hospital equipment suppliers. He found a medical wholesaler in Poitiers and called as soon as they opened. His French on the phone wasn't good enough, so he drove into town. At the wholesaler's he found a young assistant who spoke English, placed an order for delivery within two days and paid cash. They would put the bed in the main barn if he wasn't there to receive it. They hoped his elderly relative would find it comfortable when she arrived. Alf then turned his mind to transport. He cursed himself for not searching on the internet before he left home. The journey to the south of Italy would be long, almost 2000 kilometres each way, so the vehicle had to be good, reliable and comfortable, and it had to be an ambulance. A van, mobile home or station wagon wouldn't work because Mel would need to be on a stretcher.

At home he searched for second-hand ambulances. He was amazed how many there were. In France and several other European countries ambulances are operated by taxi firms, consequently there was a good supply of well used, and well maintained, properly equipped vehicles. Having an EU identity card and a Belgian bank account made such a purchase relatively straightforward; the French authorities had started to clamp down on tax dodging by making large cash purchases more and more difficult. He found a motor trader on the *Rocade* ring road near Bordeaux who seemed to have a few suitable vehicles available. He set off in the Peugeot, and by mid-afternoon he had shaken hands on a deal to buy a reliable, well equipped Mercedes Sprinter ambulance in good order but with a lot of kilometres on the clock. The dealer would service it and deal with the paperwork and, understanding that monsieur needed the vehicle rapidly, it could be ready for collection the following afternoon. Alf waited while his card payment was processed and verified. All was in order.

One last thing, Alf had said, he wanted to leave directly after he collected the ambulance, so would the dealer be interested in buying his old Peugeot? The dealer wasn't, but said he was welcome to leave it in the corner of the yard for a couple of weeks if he wanted to. No extra charge.

That evening, back in his own house and having been for a swim in the pool, Alf called Julia again.

"How's it going, Jake?" he asked.

"Good and bad, Alf," she said, "Mel's doing well. Her brain swelling's gone down sufficiently, and they did a scan. There are no apparent signs of brain damage, but they did say that with some caution. They're going to reset her pelvis and thigh tomorrow. Once she's out of surgery and has been under observation for 24 hours we can move her."

"And the bad news?"

"Spike's intel friend has had a look at the picture you got in Elounda. The couple in the picture are professional killers. They use the dark web to sell their services, which they term 'bespoke personal alterations'. In other words, any bodily harm from GBH upward, for the right fee. They don't know their names, but the suspicion is they're based in the Netherlands or possibly Scandinavia. Spike says it changes things and makes matters more complicated. He's gone back to Athens to get some 'kit' and he's coming back with his parachuting pal in the Cessna tomorrow morning. In the meantime, the whole team is spread out around the hospital and I'm sleeping on a chair in Mel's room. Red alert here."

"I'm glad they're there, Jake. When do they want some money?"

"I asked Spike before he left. He says he'll need some cash for expenses when we get to Italy. He hasn't given me a figure, but there's a team of six, the plane and pilot, and all their expenses. I'd guess Spike's rate is at least two grand a day, the others around 1500, Euro I mean, so a rough figure of 10 to 12 thousand a day. They'll have done four days by the time we get to Otranto. Bring at least 50 grand, if you can."

"I'll bring a hundred and get enough spare to cover the trip and any additional expenses, I'll sort it out tomorrow. I've got hold of a proper ambulance, by the way. It's in Bordeaux and I can get it tomorrow afternoon. I plan to set out for Italy immediately. On my own it'll take more than a day. Mel's bed's arriving tomorrow or the day after. It'll need to be put together but it'll be here. Do I need to get anything else?"

"Steph said we'll need to have access to a good orthopaedic specialist. She's trying to track one down in your part of the world. You might need to go and talk to someone before you set out tomorrow; I'll let you know if you do. Steph and Tracey will have a long shopping list of medical supplies, but they'll sort it out when they get there. Steph speaks French. Spike says we can discuss security at your place when he's had a look at it."

"Fine. Are you OK?"

"I've been better. I'll be happier when we're safely tucked up at your place, I'm feeling like we're a bit exposed here."

"Have you thought about getting the local police involved?"

"I've thought about it, and about getting the British Consulate on the case. I've decided it's safer to handle this ourselves. Spike knows the territory and how this place works. He says if we go official our problems will only multiply and I tend to agree with him. So, it's up to us for now. Are you worried?"

"I'm worried because we're needing to be responsive. In the past, we've been driving events, setting the pace and the agenda. This time we can't see who or what's out there, Jake."

"I know. I've been thinking about that too. Our first priority though is Mel. Once she's sorted, we can start thinking about going to war."

"Agreed." He paused. "I miss you."

"Call me again tomorrow morning," Jake ended the call.

******

In their family room at the beachside hotel in Malia the Dutch couple were arguing. They were doing it quietly because they didn't want to wake their daughter, and also because they didn't want the people in the next room to hear their heated conversation through the paper-thin walls.

"I'm telling you, it's too risky to try to get into her hospital room!" the wife hissed. "I dressed as a cleaner and went past it today, twice. She's never alone. There's always a man outside and two women inside, as well as any doctors and nurses. One of the women is Kelso, I'm certain of it."

"But we can't wait!" the husband protested. "If we leave it, they'll move her. We know where she is now. I agree a straight frontal attack is too risky. Let's think of something more subtle, or at least with a delay. If we're taken, I don't want the child growing up in a Greek children's home."

"She'll grow up with us, at home in Haarlem. Don't be so defeatist!" The wife was angry.

"OK, calm down. What are our options? We don't have a firearm with us."

"I saw in her room, just for a moment. There's a drip in her arm. Whether it's just saline or the sedative I don't know. If we can find out and get to it as it leaves the pharmacy, we can add something to it. I have a few chemicals in my wash bag, enough for one lethal dose in a litre of IV fluid. The only reason it might not work is if they notice before it's taken effect. She's on a monitor, so they'll see her pulse and blood pressure change."

"So, that's a no," he said, "what else?"

"A bomb? Outside her room?"

"She's on the third floor, not the top, there's no balcony or air-conditioning unit on the outer wall, so we'd have to put it in the corridor. With a man outside all the time?"

"We could take him, then leave a short-fuse device, just long-enough for us to get out."

"There's CCTV everywhere in there. If we bomb the main hospital in Heraklion our faces will be on every TV screen in Europe inside an hour."

"Well, you think of something then," she said.

"Gas!" he stated. "We can gas her, and anyone else in the room."

"What with?" she asked.

"CO2?"

"Too noisy, and we'd need too much."

"CO?"

"Better, but where do we get it from, enough to fill a whole room quickly?"

"Let me think about that. What about a flammable gas? There's already oxygen in there."

"That's it! A firebomb using hospital equipment! We can adapt an oxygen cylinder, put an ignition source on it and pose as hospital staff to take it in! Go to the hospital now. Find the tank store and get us an oxygen tank, a full one, on a trolley. I'll work out how to rig an ignition source and look after the child."

Chapter 13

Alf spent a while on the phone to his lawyers in Dublin. His friend Eugene Flynn had fully retired, but a younger partner had been briefed on the valued client known as Declan Walsh, another of Alf's identities. After the verification rigmarole, the lawyer undertook to send a cable to the main branch of the BNP Paribas bank in Bordeaux advising them that a Mr Piet Kuyper would be attending the branch tomorrow to withdraw €105,000 in cash from the law firm's Euro account with the bank. He included a description of Kuyper, and the number of his Belgian identity card. The transaction was all in order and to do with a property under development.

He'd decided to take a train from Poitiers to Bordeaux, go to the bank and then get a cab to the car dealer. He phoned Jake before he set out.

"How are things?" he asked.

"No change, which I think is good. Mel had a restless night - they're starting to bring her round, just enough to prepare her for surgery. It's going to be rough on her, Alf. We've been talking about her rehab and physio needs and it's going to be a long job. I've spoken to her mum again; she's getting more and more fretful at not being able to see Mel or talk to her. We'll need to do something about that when we get settled. The team's working well; they're a great bunch. How are you doing?"

"Fine. I've sorted the money and I'm heading off in a minute to Bordeaux to pick it up and get the ambulance. I won't leave there before 4 or 5 so I'm aiming for Lyon tonight. I'll be in southern Italy by tomorrow evening. You're planning to travel the following morning?"

"Yes, as soon as we can move her. God, I hope she'll be alright. Got to go." Jake ended the call.

He drove into Poitiers and parked near the station. The train to Bordeaux took two and a half hours and he got to the bank just before it closed for lunch. The cash withdrawal was surprisingly painless, and with a large envelope full of banknotes in his overnight bag he went for a leisurely lunch in a café near the Bourse. As soon as the motor dealership opened after lunch Alf took a taxi to collect his ambulance. By 4pm he was on the autoroute heading east towards Lyon and onward to Italy with a full fuel tank and a grim determination to make everything right.

******

In Montreal she wasn't happy. There was still a day to go until the deadline she had set, and when she'd opened the email replies nearly every one of them had started trying to bargain, protest or negotiate. Only three had paid up as directed. She composed stiff notes to the laggards making it plain that there was to be no negotiation, and they now had less than 24 hours in which to comply fully or face the consequences. She was tempted to inflict the consequences on two of the slimiest protestors anyway, but she'd controlled herself.

There was no fresh news from the Dutch couple in Crete. Kelso was still away from her desk and not attending to any emails at all. Some of her correspondents were getting quite pissed off about this, which must mean that she was devoting all her attention to the Dunn girl. Maybe, she mused, the red-top media in Britain might like to know that the holy Julia Kelso wasn't quite as conventional and hetero as people had always thought. Her plans to destroy Kelso were still taking shape; she wouldn't rush it. The Dutch couple had asked if she wanted Kelso dealt with in Crete. It would be relatively easy, they said, as she was with Dunn nearly all the time. She had declined, although she didn't really know why.

She went online again and spent a couple of hours lining up some stock deals. She was going to borrow stock in five major oil companies for two weeks, after which the same number of shares would be returned to the rightful owners, plus a borrower's fee. It was a common enough transaction. Once she had the shares, she would sell them. Then she would unleash phase two of her experiment on the five oil companies, and a couple of others just for the fun of it. The value of stock in the companies she had targeted would plummet, allowing her to buy back the appropriate number of shares at a far lower price than she had sold them for a few days earlier. It was called 'shorting', and she would make several million US dollars, the difference between her sale price and the price she paid to buy back the shares. The emails to the oil companies were already composed and ready to send when she decided the time was right.

Her final task that morning was to ruin someone's life. The someone in question was a good-hearted person, a screen actor as renowned for his charitable works and his long and stable marriage as he was for the wholesome parts he played in many family-friendly movies. He had never done anything to her, she had never met him, she just found his wholesomeness contemptible. Among her harvested data from the sycophants was his private email address, which she'd exploited to gain access to his personal computer. She'd placed some really obnoxious images on it and faked up numerous emails to and from choirboys and starlets. The sum of her parts was an almost irrefutable case that the wholesome star was in fact a dirty rotten low-life scumbag who exploited aspiring young people for his own deviant ends. If they did not cooperate and indulge him, he ended their careers. She wrote an emotional exposé of his disgusting deeds and sent it simultaneously to the LAPD, FBI, the Los Angeles Times and the National Enquirer. For added impetus she sent a further copy to Fox News. It was to encourage the others.

After all that, she made some green tea and rested for a while with her eyes closed.

******

In Malia the Dutch husband had returned in the early hours with an oxygen cylinder, fully charged with a pressure of over 130 bar. It stood about 150cm tall and came on its own small two-wheel trolley rack. The Dutch wife had spent the rest of the night mixing various chemicals she had in her washbag. Searching for a suitable container for her improvised detonator and combined ignition source, she selected a steel-barrelled ballpoint pen. When the detonator was assembled, complete with a small watch as a timer and a thin battery for power, she attached it firmly with thin wire to the valve mechanism. The detonator wouldn't be powerful enough to destroy the valve mechanism in its entirety, but with the valve cracked open just far enough it would easily destroy the sealing cap covering the outlet, allowing a fiery jet of ignited high pressure oxygen to escape into the room. Not a firebomb as such, more an unpredictable and uncontrollable flamethrower. By the time she had finished she was exhausted. She crept into bed beside her husband and slept until daylight.

Chapter 14

Mel was barely conscious when they came to take her for surgery early in the morning. She hadn't spoken and showed little sign of recognising anyone or anything. It was usual, Steph said. With Mel safely in an operating theatre it only took one team member to stand guard nearby in the corridor. Steph stayed in Mel's room on her own while the others took a break for a shower and a change of clothes. Julia was glad to get away for a few hours. Steph needed a bathroom break, so she closed the door to Mel's room and was gone for no more than five minutes. When she returned the door was ajar. She went in and checked the room carefully - everything seemed as it was, all in order. Steph made a mental note to get Ricky to speak to a nurse to see if the cleaners had been in. She opened a window to let in some fresh air, and then rested in a chair, thinking about everything and nothing.

They brought Mel back a little after 1pm. She was grey and cold, and breathing rapidly. A nurse plugged her back into the monitor and Steph could read the numbers. She was coming out of the anaesthetic. Instinctively Steph checked the oxygen cylinder resting in its stand beside and slightly behind Mel's bed. She was momentarily puzzled; something wasn't right.

Steph got her phone out and speed-dialled Ricky. He had just got back to the hospital.

"Get up here now, Ricky. Someone's been in her room - I think there's a problem. I'm going to get her out, but I'll have to fight off the nurse. Get up here now!"

Ricky arrived a few seconds later at a run.

"What's up?" he panted.

"The oxygen. Something isn't right. Tell the nurse we have to move Mel while we check it out."

Ricky took a look at the wire and the body of a ballpoint pen attached to the rear of the valve mechanism.

"IED," he said calmly.

He spoke rapidly to the nurse while releasing the brakes on the wheels of Mel's bed. Steph unplugged the monitor and between them they pushed Mel into the corridor. The nurse was protesting loudly.

She was silenced by a popping sound, followed by the roar of a jet of flame. Ewan had arrived and used a nearby fire extinguisher to shield himself as he approached the cylinder. He tried to turn the valve to stop the flame. It was stuck fast. He pushed the nurse out of the room and shut the door behind them, hoping that the hospital's sprinkler system worked. He punched a fire alarm glass as he passed it and bells began to ring,

Downstairs in the car park the Dutch couple in their hire car sat and watched, their daughter secured in a child's car seat. They watched smoke billowing from the window of Mel's room, then flames. The device had worked. If the Dunn woman was in the room there was no way she could survive the inferno. Sirens were approaching; people were starting to stream out of the hospital building, some in wheelchairs, some in beds, some walking or running. The Dutch couple decided it was time to leave. They'd try to find out later whether the Dunn woman had died.

Steph called Julia as soon as they were clear of the Intensive Care Unit.

"Julia," she started, "they've had another go. Mel's OK, but she's just out of surgery and not that stable. I've called Tracey and between us we can manage her, but we need to bring forward our departure. They've tried twice. If they find out she's survived again they'll go all out for a third attempt. You'd better get back here right now."

Julia was out and in her hire car within five minutes. She called Alf to tell him to get to Otranto as soon as he could. He started to ask questions, but she cut the call and drove. She found Steph and Tracey shielding Mel in a curtained-off cubicle in the emergency department. The hospital was in complete turmoil, and no one was taking any notice of them in the chaos.

"What happened?" she asked Steph, without any preamble.

"They managed to get a doctored oxygen cylinder into her room. It was wired to ignite around lunchtime when it's usually quiet and everyone's resting in their rooms. We clocked it just before it went off and managed to get her out, but only just. Ewan's got a few minor burns, but he'll be fine. Her room's been destroyed, and everything in it I expect. Good job you took her bag back to your hotel."

"Can she be moved now, right away?" Julia asked.

"As long as it's not too far and we can keep her as still as possible. Ideally, we'd have an ambulance, a van at least. I've called Spike, the Cessna is leaving Athens now. Spike said they were going to go to Chania but I've asked them to get to Heraklion instead. It would be too much to take Mel by road all the way to Chania. They'll be landing in about 45 minutes."

"Piet's nowhere near Otranto yet."

"I'd rather have her stretched out in the back of the Cessna on the ground in Italy than keep her here in Crete. I'm saying we move her now. Ricky's gone to see what vehicle he can get hold of. Why don't you take Ewan, get yours and Mel's stuff from the hotel and get your car back to Heraklion airport. Meet us in the private aviation area as soon as you can. The Cessna will be down only long enough for fuel and to get Mel on board. Spike and Ricky will need to talk us through all the officials."

Julia did as she was told. Forty minutes later she handed her car keys in at the returns desk and followed Ewan to a taxi rank. They paid a large fare for a short ride, but the driver was happy enough in the end. As they waited at the private aviation terminal an ambulance arrived on blue lights. Ricky was driving it. He pulled up beside the ungainly Cessna as it came to a stop. Spike hurried to open the large rear door. Steph and Tracey supervised Mel's transfer from the ambulance to the aircraft. Julia got a glimpse of Mel's face, just about awake now, and obviously confused and in pain.

Ricky got back in the ambulance and drove it quickly to the terminal gate. He left the keys and a €50 note with the gatekeeper, saying someone from the hospital would be along to collect the ambulance soon. He jogged back to the Cessna and was the last one on board.

"Let's go," Spike ordered.

The pilot spoke into his headset mike and pulled on the throttles. The aircraft taxied to take its turn in the take-off queue. There was unspoken tension in the cavernous rear cabin. Steph and Tracy busied themselves with Mel. They were inserting a drip tube into her canula.

"We managed to nick a load of stuff from the hospital," Steph said, "so we can keep her comfortable for a day or two."

Mel's eyes closed, and she slept.

"Where did you get the ambulance, Ricky?" Julia asked, almost shouting above the engine noise.

"A sort of informal hire, Julia. I bunged an ambulance driver a few Euro, more than a few, and said he could pick it up in an hour at the airport. I did have a knife to his throat, so he wasn't going to say no, was he? He's happy enough now."

Julia slumped back against the side of the aircraft. She was sitting on a canvas bench.

"Seatbelts!" Spike shouted as they accelerated down the runway.

They climbed slowly for more than ten minutes before levelling out at a low cruising altitude of around 2,000 metres, far below the busy air traffic lanes across the Mediterranean.

"Well done everyone," Spike said to them all, "we'll be in Otranto in a couple of hours, so a quick nap is in order."

He passed round bottles of cold water and pre-packed sandwiches. Julia drank and ate in silence, her eyes on Mel's sleeping face all the time. She looked tired and vulnerable, not like the vivacious, curious woman she really was. And hopefully would be again.

Spike came back and sat next to Julia.

"What time do you think Piet will get to Otranto?" he asked.

"He said he left Lyon at 5 this morning. It's about 1500 kilometres, with fuel stops and some very strong coffee it's going to take twelve hours at least, I'd think."

"That's OK. We can wait quietly on the airfield until he gets there. Ricky needs to find us some transport anyway, and the plane isn't going anywhere tonight. The pilot will be out of hours. Are you OK, Julia?"

"I'm fine, thanks. And thanks to you and the team for everything, they've been marvellous."

"We're not done with this, Julia. Nor are you, I suspect."

"You're right, there's a way to go yet."

"What are you thinking, long-term I mean."

"I'm thinking I'm going to eliminate this threat to Mel, and to us - Piet and me. It's a long story, but I need to fix it; I'm going to."

"I think you will, Julia," Spike said, squeezing her hand for an instant.

"Call me Jake," she said.

"OK, Jake. Justin said that's what he calls you. Rest now; we'll be landing before you know it."

Chapter 15

As the Cessna left Crete Alf was piloting his ambulance down the E55, the *autostrada* skirting Italy's Adriatic coastline. He'd made good progress through the north of Italy and was now approaching Pescara. He needed fuel and coffee, and a good stretch. Fatigue was starting to set in, but he needed to keep going. He stopped at a service area, used the unappealing toilets, drank a ferociously strong *espresso* and brimmed the fuel tank. In less than twenty minutes he was on the road again, heading south. He thought he'd get to Otranto around 5pm, assuming he could find the airfield. He wished he'd taken the time to buy a satellite navigation gadget, but it was too late now.

As he neared the seaport of Bari Jake called. They'd just landed, it was a little after 3pm. He was glad to hear her voice. All was well, they were safely on the ground, waiting for him. Steph and Tracey decided to keep Mel inside the plane; she was still sedated and sleeping. They wanted it to stay that way as long as possible.

"I'll be a couple of hours yet," he told her. "The traffic's building up and the toll queues are getting slower. I'll need to have someone talk me in when I get near to the airfield."

"Hang on, here's Spike," she said.

"Piet? I've sent Ricky into town to get a hire car. Jake will send you the car details. I'll have him wait for you at the Otranto exit off the SS16 and he'll guide you to us."

"Thanks Spike," Alf replied, "see you in a while."

He ended the call, Spike's use of Jake's intimate nickname ringing in his ears.

******

The Dutch couple hadn't seen the Cessna take off. They had arrived at the airport later having spent their last morning in the pool with their daughter, who was now pink and sleepy in her pushchair. The TUI charter flight back to Amsterdam was due to depart at 16.30. They had seen the TV news at the hotel that morning and had asked the receptionist what the main story was, the one showing a major fire at the hospital.

"It is terrible," the receptionist said, "an accident at the hospital, a fire. They say at least three people are still missing, unaccounted for. They are searching for bodies now."

"That is terrible," said the wife, "how did it start?"

"They don't know. Maybe an electrical fault, they think."

"Who are the missing people?"

"The news does not say, but my cousin works at the hospital. She said that three patients in the Intensive Care Unit are missing, two local men and a foreign woman, a tourist who had a car accident. Their rooms are where the fire started, so there is not much hope for them. It is so sad."

"Yes, very sad," the wife said.

She walked away from the reception desk smiling. They had some good news for their employer. She went back to the room and sent a quick email from her laptop computer before joining her husband and their daughter at the pool. They all spent a couple of hours splashing and playing before it was time to get out, get changed and pack up to go home.

Their flight back to the Netherlands was uneventful and their daughter slept all the way. They took a local bus from the airport to Haarlem and walked back to their houseboat. He carried their bags; she pushed the pushchair. It was still light, so they sat on the deck with a cold beer each. Their daughter was in bed. She checked their emails.

"Good!" was the reply from their employer.

******

Julia got out of the plane to stretch her legs. She took a moment to call Mrs Dunn, just to tell her Mel was OK and they had moved her from Crete. Julia said she would travel to Yorkshire to talk to Mr and Mrs Dunn when she got back to London in the next few days. She felt tired but exhilarated. They had extracted Mel; Steph and Tracey said her sats and blood pressure were good, her pulse strong and regular. Now that the plane was on the ground they'd been able to examine Mel's arm and shoulder injuries, the ones the surgeons had not yet attended to. The shoulder was still dislocated, so Steph popped it back in while Mel was sedated. They didn't think there were any fractures in the arm, just bad bruising. They checked the reflex dilation of Mel's pupils, which seemed fine. They were concerned about possible undetected brain damage which would not become apparent until Mel was fully conscious, and that would not be until she was nicely tucked up in her new hospital bed at Piet's place in France.

The surgeons had stabilised Mel's pelvis fractures with internal metal plates and screws. Her right leg was in a cast from her hip to her ankle; luckily the hip joint had escaped major damage despite the initial fear that it had been broken. The pelvis injury could have been life threatening, and she had lost a lot of blood at the time.

"If she hadn't been as good as combat-fit," Steph told Julia, "she wouldn't have survived the injuries. That other girl being between her and the car probably helped save her life too. I wouldn't tell her that though, not for a while."

Julia had got back in the plane to stay out of the bright sun. In the aircraft cabin Tracey gave Mel another shot of something.

"Morphine mixed with a sedative," Tracey explained. "It'll keep her still and pain-free for a few more hours. We're going to keep her topped up all the way, which is why we need to get there as quickly as possible. There's only so much of this junk a body can take. We'll start to take her off sedation tomorrow afternoon, but we'll keep the pain management in place until we can see what state she's in. My main concern at the moment is keeping the surgical wounds clean and free of infection. I've given her antibiotics and we've cleaned her up, but the sooner we get her settled in hygienic conditions the better."

The wait for the ambulance seemed interminable. Shortly after 5pm a small convoy comprising a red Alfa Romeo saloon and a fly-splattered white ambulance with a large blue cross painted on the front and French licence plates drove up to the aircraft.

Alf / Piet stretched as he got out of the ambulance, his shirt sweat-stained, two days stubble on his cheeks. Julia was so glad to see him. Steph and Tracey went immediately to the back of the ambulance, armed with disinfectant sprays and sanitary wipes.

"Not bad," Steph said, "there's enough space and the bed's good. I'm glad we pinched enough bedding in Heraklion. Shall we get her loaded?"

The two girls, helped by Mike and Ewan, carefully lifted Mel's stretcher from the aircraft and carried it to the ambulance. They placed it on the ambulance bed, and on Steph's command they lifted her sleeping body while Ricky carefully withdrew the stretcher. Steph and Tracey arranged Mel on the bed, covered her with a light blanket and adjusted the straps that would hold her in place.

Outside, Piet and Spike went into a huddle.

"Jake said you'd need some cash for expenses and the like," Piet said, "I've brought some with me. How much do you want?"

"I've done an invoice for you," Spike said. "As it's a favour for Justin, we've all agreed to do mate's rates. It's full whack for the plane and pilot though, and all the other outgoings like flights and car hire are at cost. It's all down here."

Spike handed Piet a sheet of paper folded in half. Piet opened it and was pleasantly surprised. The bill to date was under €23,000. Piet peeled off two slim bundles of €200 notes and counted out a further thirty €100 notes.

"Glad you've avoided the €500 notes, you can't spend them anywhere. Now, here's an outline plan for the next week or so. Ricky and Ewan will follow the ambulance in the Alfa. Mike and I are going to get another vehicle and follow on. We've brought some bits and pieces with us and it's best we're not all in convoy together. Steph and Tracey will be sticking with you as long as Mel needs them. The four of us are going to take care of your perimeter and help you set up something more permanent if that's what you want longer term. I need to get back to Glyfada in a couple of weeks, and we can regroup once we're all settled in at your place. What accommodation have you got?"

"I've got plenty. There's a spare downstairs room in the main house for Mel, close to a shower and toilet. Jake and I can stay in the main house, and there are rooms for Steph and Tracey too. Outside there are a couple of two-bedroom cottages which were used as holiday lets, so with their own bathrooms and cooking facilities. There's around four acres of land, and there's a decent sized swimming pool for exercise and I'm guessing some rehab and physio for Mel."

"Sounds good, better than we usually have to put up with. OK, let's get going. Mike and I will ride with Ricky and Ewan as far as town, so they'll be stopping for a moment. Don't lose them."

"I won't, Jake's going to have to drive for a bit. I'm done in and I need a sleep. I'll tell her about the stop, and not to lose the Alfa."

With that, Spike went off to talk to the pilot for a few seconds, and to pay him for his efforts. Then the small convoy left the airfield. Jake got used to the ambulance's unfamiliar controls quickly. The Alfa stopped for a few moments and Spike and Mike got out, then they were off. Steph and Tracey were in the back with Mel, each settled in one of the comfortable attendant's seats. Mel was sleeping soundly, as was Steph after a few minutes. Once they'd reached the *autostrada* and were pointing north Alf / Piet closed his eyes in the front passenger seat, and he didn't stir until Jake stopped for fuel four hours and almost five hundred kilometres later.

They drove in four-hour shifts, stopping at each change over to refuel and drink copious amounts of water and strong coffee. Darkness fell and they drove on relentlessly. Dawn was beginning to break as they passed Monaco, the Mediterranean glistening off to their left. A thousand kilometres later they left the *autoroute* network near Poitiers and Piet guided them home.

It had taken almost twenty-four hours of continuous driving, over two thousand kilometres, but there had been no border crossings, no airports, no credit card transactions, no computerised bookings, nothing that Dido Sykes could latch on to. They were home.

The team quickly assembled Mel's bed in her downstairs room; Steph and Tracey set it up as it should be and made it with fresh bedding. Spike and Mike arrived in the second car an hour or so later, by which time Ricky had rustled up a meal for everyone, Piet had no idea where he'd found the ingredients. Piet had swum twenty lengths of the pool to release the tension of the long drive. Ewan stood guard while everyone else slept. Steph took first watch with Mel.

Jake had followed Piet to his room uninvited. She showered and slipped into his bed, cool and naked. She was fast asleep in moments. Alf / Piet stroked her damp hair, kissed her gently and felt his tired eyes close.

Chapter 16

Despite their lingering fatigue, Jake and Alf were up early. She was business-like, and there were no intimate vibes in their bedroom that morning. By the time he'd got up and showered she was downstairs at the large kitchen table with Steph making shopping plans. Jake was listing food and provisions, Steph medical equipment, drugs and dressings.

"Morning Steph," he said, "how's Mel?"

"She's had a good night, didn't stir," Steph said. "It means we've got the pain under control. We're going to ease off the sedation and she should start to wake up after lunch. She'll have a cow of a hangover, I expect."

"She's had a few of those in her time," Jake smiled for the first time that day. "I'd like to be there when she wakes up."

"What's the plan then?" Piet asked.

"Spike and Ricky are going round the place, checking out the perimeter," Jake said, "you and me are off to the shops. Steph's going to phone an order through to that hospital supply place you got the bed from, we can pick it up in town."

"So we're going into Poitiers?"

"Yes, and we'll hit a supermarket on the way back. I'm going to stock up with enough for all of us for a week or so."

"OK. I'd like to get my car; it's by the station." Piet said.

The conversation felt awkward, almost like Jake was putting on a show in front of Steph.

"I'll make some coffee first. We can go after breakfast," Jake said.

Thirty minutes later they left, Jake driving them in the borrowed Alfa. Alf gave directions to the main road into Poitiers.

"Are you OK, Jake?" he asked her. "You seem distant, a bit off."

"I'm fine, I'm sorry. It's all been a massive strain; I'll feel better when she's back with us."

"Is that all?"

"What do you mean, 'is that all'? Someone's tried to kill our friend - my best friend - twice! They nearly succeeded, too. And we could do fuck all about it."

"I didn't mean it like that," he said. "I'm not trying to belittle what's happened, I was just talking about the way you seem to be because I care. You seem so different to how you were in Boulogne."

"We change all the time, don't we? You don't have to worry, though, I haven't gone off you or anything if that's what's really bothering you."

"It's not that," he lied, "like I said, I care about you."

"If you do, care about me that is, come up with a way we can neutralise that bitch Sykes. All I've got so far is the blindingly obvious - find out where she is, what she's doing, and stop her. Which is no fucking good to anyone."

"What do you mean, neutralise?"

"Not how you think, but if I find myself alone with her I might change my mind. I want her out of the running or locked up where she can't do any more damage for a very long time, ideally forever."

"I'll put my mind to it. Let's hope Mel is still Mel when she wakes up; she can help us think. Take the next right. We'll go to the hospital supplier first."

Steph's order was ready, all packed up. Alf paid cash and the assistant helped them put the packages in the car. She started talking rapidly in French. Julia intervened.

"She's just cautioning us about some of the equipment and some of the pharmaceutical stuff. Steph's already told them she's a nurse, and everything she's ordered is at the strong end of non-prescription. They're happy."

Julia spoke briefly to the assistant in her fluent French, and they parted with a handshake.

"All done," she said, "let's go get your car. I bet it's a *bagnole*."

"A what?"

"*Bagnole*, it means the equivalent of an old banger."

"Of course it is. You should know me well enough by now to think otherwise."

They collected Alf's old Peugeot and he led the way to a large supermarket on the southern edge of town. Alf pushed the trolley while Jake loaded it. He was pleased to see she bought his favourite whisky as well as her preferred gin without him having to ask. At the checkout she packed it all proficiently and all he had to do was count out a lot of banknotes. They were back at his place by late morning. They saw Mike busily pretending to do something near the gate; he was the sentry.

"Hiya Piet, Julia," Mike called as they drove in.

Spike was in the kitchen with Ricky. He was writing out a duty rota, deciding that a daily pattern of three men on four-hour shifts with the fourth resting and in reserve was the best use of their resources.

"Hi Jake, Piet," Spike said as they entered, laden with shopping bags. "Let me help you put that away. We're just mapping out duties. Just so you know, we've obtained some weapons in case we need them. I brought them from Athens on the plane. We've got a sidearm each, all six of us including Steph and Tracey, and a couple of spares if either of you want one. Mike's building a shelter near the gate, it won't look like a sentry box but that's what it is. There'll be an assault rifle in there, and another here in the kitchen. It's in the cupboard beside the cooker. We've also got smoke grenades. It's all defensive, and we won't be taking anything off the premises until we leave for good. Are you OK with all that?"

"I am," Jake said, "Piet?"

"Sure. I'd like to have a pistol and get to know the assault rifles - just in case."

"I'll take you through one in a while. I don't propose any practice firing though, not unless you want a visit from the gendarmes."

At that moment Tracey came in.

"Mel's sedation is wearing off and she's starting to come round. Steph said Julia wanted to be there when she wakes up."

"Thanks," Jake said, getting up from the table and following Tracey.

There was a moment of silence between Spike and Alf / Piet at the table.

"She's quite a girl, your Jake," Spike broke the silence.

"My Jake?"

"She doesn't hide it, mate, you're a lucky guy. Let me show you how the rifles work. They're not new, but they're good, Swiss-made SIG 550s."

In Mel's room Steph was busy applying a fresh supporting bandage to Mel's shoulder.

"It'll be painful when she wakes up. I don't want her to try to move it just yet," she explained.

Mel's eyelids were fluttering, she was making small sounds and her left arm was twitching slightly. Jake was feeling incredibly nervous and very emotional. After another twenty minutes Mel's eyes opened. She blinked and squinted against the bright sunlight. Tracey got up and drew the blinds. Mel looked around, confused. Her eyes stopped on Jake's face; she looked puzzled. She tried to speak but no words came out. Steph wet Mel's lips with cool water, repeating the motion a few times."

"Your throat will be a bit sore for a day or two, Mel," she said, "how are you feeling?"

Mel continued to scan the room until she found Jake again.

"Have you been giving me gin again, Kelso?" she croaked. "My fucking head!"

"Welcome back, Dunn," Jake said, "I've missed you."

"What happened?" Mel asked. "Where am I?"

"What do you remember?" Jake asked.

Mel thought for a moment.

"Nothing. Everything's foggy."

"Who's the Prime Minister?" Jake asked.

"Not that fucking foggy!"

"She's feisty," Steph commented.

"You'd better believe it, Steph," Jake said.

"What's going on?" Mel asked. "Who are they?" She was indicating Steph and Tracey.

"Do you remember being in Elounda, in Crete?" Jake asked, "on a diving course?"

Mel thought for a minute.

"I think so. On a boat, then in a bar. Having a beer. Fotis, and the English lad, the shy one. And Stella, one of the instructors. I remember that. Why?"

"Do you remember leaving the bar, leaving with Stella?"

"Don't think so. Why? What happened?"

Steph interrupted gently.

"This is very common, Julia. Memories of an incident may or may not come back in time. Mel, my name is Steph, this is Tracey. You've been in an accident and you've been hurt. We are trained medical personnel, and we are taking care of you to help you recover. Is that OK?"

"Accident?" said Mel.

"You were hit by a car, Mel, in Crete. You've been in hospital," Steph said calmly.

"Is this a hospital?"

"No, it's Piet's place."

"Who's Piet?"

"It's Alf's, Mel, Alf's place," said Jake.

"Who's Alf?" said Steph.

"Long story," Mel said, "is he here?"

"Yes. He's next door, in the kitchen. I'll call him."

Alf came in. Mel gave him a warm, wide smile, but she winced almost as soon as she did it. He moved to the bedside and held her left hand.

"Take it easy, Mel," he said, "everything's going to be fine."

Mel squeezed his hand. She looked around again for Jake.

"You still won't beat me in a race Kelso, no matter what you've done to me." She tried to smile again but slumped back on her pillows.

"We'll see about that, Dunn. Your mum says hello, by the way. Get some rest now, we'll be next door."

Mel was already asleep.

Steph followed them into the kitchen.

"That went better than I was hoping," she said. "It's a good start but there's a long way to go. Some people never have any recollection of what caused their injuries, nor of their time in intensive care. Some people are OK with that, but it can drive others round the twist. Mel seems strong and focussed. I don't think she'll like not knowing what happened to her, and when she finds out what - and more importantly why - she might need some professional help. Right now, the painkillers are relaxing her, but we won't use any more sedatives unless she gets agitated. Her 'fog' will clear over the next couple of days. I'm not sure what your plans are, but I think it would be best if you both stay here for now. She's going to need familiar faces and a friendly touch. She'll get to know us soon enough, and get to trust us, but for now you're all she's got to hang on to."

"Sure," said Jake, "I do need to get back to London quite soon, but another couple of days will be fine. I'd like to be here for her."

"I've no plans," Alf said, "I'll be here. I'd like a swim. You coming Jake?"

"Good idea," she said.

They did lengths. He had swimmers on, she swam in her underwear.

"I'll get a matronly bathing suit in town later," she said.

Afterwards, she wrapped one of his towels around herself and they both relaxed on loungers by the pool.

"It's a nice place, Alf, I just didn't imagine I'd get to see it for the first time under these circumstances, with a squadron of SAS guys and a pair of gun-toting Florence Nightingales. Thank God for Justin Evans!"

"What was that message about? The one that Spike passed when we first met him?"

"If you must know, Justin Evans and I had a one-night stand. Once, that's all. It was one December at Dolphin Square. We've stayed friends."

He wanted to ask which December but knew better than to pursue it. There was silence for a moment.

"Fine," he said, eventually. "I've been thinking. About Dido Sykes. You think she found Mel in Crete through an online flight booking, and if you're right it means she can do tricks with computers and the internet. And that means she must have an internet presence. It's her strength, how she does things, but it could also be a weakness, possibly. Mel's quite good on the internet, but we need a real expert, one who's on our side. Any ideas?"

"As it happens, yes, but it would come with a risk. If I ask her for help, and it is a her, she'll need to know about us. I hardly know her, and I certainly don't know if we can fully trust her or if she'd be up for our sort of thing. I'll need to get to know her better when I'm back in London. You're right, though, if Sykes is doing whatever it is she's doing using the internet, we have to use it against her. What do you want to do now? We can have lunch, or we can go upstairs, your choice."

He looked at her for a second. She was lying back, her eyes closed, her face relaxed and beautiful. The towel had come loose and he could see her breasts beneath her damp bra.

"Lunch only makes you fat," he said, "let's go up."

He stood up. She took his hand and they walked together towards the house.

"I do love you, Alf. Don't doubt that" she said.

He didn't know what to say, or what she meant, and for now he didn't care.

Chapter 17

A week past, a routine developed; Mel showed improvement day by day, but she still slept most of the time. Jake put off her return to London one more day at a time.

"We need to make sure there's no weight on her pelvis, so we keep her feeling a bit droopy to ensure she doesn't try to get out of bed. She's not good at staying still, is she?" Tracey commented to Jake over breakfast one day. "I think we can keep her as she is for another week, but then we'll need to give her something to keep her mind occupied. Steph's going to that medical place in town to get her a suitable wheelchair, and Mike and Ewan are keeping fit by building a ramp from the terrace to the garden."

Tracey wasn't really expecting any responses, she was just chatting away.

"I've got to go back to the UK soon," Jake said to Alf, "possibly as early as tomorrow. There are things I need to do there, not least going to see Mel's mum, and her boss at NCIS. Everything seems fine here."

"How long will you be gone?" Alf asked.

"Don't know, not too long I hope, no more than a week or two maybe. I'll need to have a long talk with Mel when she's up to it; things were a bit up in the air before she went to Crete. What are you going to do?"

"I'm a bit spare. I'll be taking turns with the guys on security once Spike goes - he's leaving at the end of the week. The thing is, we don't know if the threat's gone away. If we had an inkling that Sykes believes Mel's really dead, we could relax a bit. Even if she doesn't, I'm pretty confident we've left no traces to point to where we are. When you go back use the Belgian ID card to travel. Do the same as the Boulogne trip, use the trains and get a ferry as a foot passenger with no advance booking. In my spare time, I'm going to try to think of a way to get a handle on what she's up to."

"Sykes?"

He nodded.

"If her paid killers were around the hospital, they probably saw one or both of us. You were there in her room nearly all the time. I left after a day or so. It could be the second attempt was meant for you too, as well as Mel. And if it wasn't, why not?"

"It hadn't crossed my mind," Jake said, "but it makes sense. If they found Mel they must have seen me, and probably told Sykes if they're in contact with her. I think I get where you're coming from."

"If she didn't send her killers after you, she's got other plans. I can't imagine she's just decided to let it go, can you? If she does have something in mind for you, something she wants from you, it gives us a chance. Not that I like the idea of you being bait."

"It's not my natural tendency, I'll admit," Jake said, "but it's logical. She'll probably try to get to me one way or another. We need to get a handle on her, Alf. You see if you can get any inspiration here, I'll do the same in London.

Alf drove her to Poitiers the next day. Neither of them spoke much. She'd left quite a few of her things at his place so had only a light travel bag. At the station she kissed him quickly.

"Turn your phone on this evening; I'll call you from London. Take care."

With that she was out of the car and he watched her walk quickly towards the ticket office and the TGV to Montparnasse. With changes in Paris and at Lille she would be in Calais in time for a late afternoon ferry to Dover. He was reflective as he drove slowly back to his place, stopping in the village for a coffee in the square. He felt drained.

******

Julia's first call the next morning, as soon as she got to her office, was to her boss, DAC Connaught. She made an appointment to see him as soon as she could. He was a huge improvement on her last boss, the late unlamented DAC Savernake - another of Dido Sykes's pawns. He had covered her absence with their seniors, but he deserved some sort of explanation. Julia had decided on a version of the truth.

"Julia, good to see you," he said once they were alone in his office.

"You too, Will, thanks for covering for me," she said.

"It was quite a mysterious disappearing trick, Julia. Not prying or anything, but you've been away for quite a while with barely any contact with the mothership."

"I know, Will, and I'm sorry. My friend, Mel Dunn, had a serious accident in Crete. I was concerned for a moment that it might have been related to the business with the private investigator and the photographs from the Americans; I thought someone may have tried to kill her. That's why I went to her on the hurry-up and without explanation. I thought if it got out that she'd survived they might go back for a second try. I went to get her to a safe place where she could recover in peace."

"And have you?"

"Yes, she's safe now. I'll not say anymore. Her injuries are quite bad, but she should be fine eventually."

"And are you OK, Julia? I mean personally."

"I'm fine, Will, but I'm going to have to ask you for a leave of absence for a while. I'll need to see Mel's family and speak to NCIS on her behalf. Then there are loose ends to be tied up, for Mel and me that is. I'd like to take some time to do that."

"How long, Julia? How much time do you need?"

"Three months tops, Will. If I can get back sooner I will, but if we can call it three months I'd appreciate it."

"I'll take it to the Commissioner. He won't like it, but I'll call it study leave. All I need is a way to contact you if I need to."

"Thanks, Will. I appreciate this. I'll be checking my email periodically if you need me to get in touch. I'll hand over anything pressing to my department heads and I'll send you a brief on outstanding matters before I go."

"Which will be when?"

"Tonight, when I'm done here."

"OK. Just take care of yourself and think carefully about what you're doing. You could have a great future here - I'll leave it at that."

"Understood, Will. Thanks again."

Back in her office she made another call, this time to Tanisha Chakrabarti, arranging to meet her that afternoon in her office. Her next calls were to the Director General of the National Criminal Intelligence

Service and to Mrs Dunn. She would see the DG tomorrow morning, and drive to Yorkshire immediately afterwards. Then she set about attending to outstanding police business, delegating what she could and passing other matters to fellow Commanders. She wrote it up for Will Connaught and sent it all to him in the internal post. Then she sent him a quick email confirming she would be away for a while, as discussed.

******

In Montreal, she had been out for an early-morning walk in Mount Royal Park. She liked it best when not many other people were there. Back in her loft apartment she made breakfast and turned on her screens. All but one of the fifty subjects she had chosen had paid up on time and as directed. One hadn't, and she had been exposed in the prurient media and was now an object of cruel ridicule. Her fake charity was richer to the tune of almost six million sterling, other genuine and deserving charities by far more. The screen actor in Hollywood had collapsed when the sordid life he knew nothing about was displayed to the public. His protestations of total innocence were at once disbelieved, and all his current and future engagements were cancelled. He was now in a special rest home for old actors in the hills above Santa Barbara, a broken man. News from Crete confirmed that at least three people had died in the tragic fire at the University Hospital in Heraklion and a few more were still missing. The fire had been ferocious enough to make identification of human remains very difficult, and it was assumed that the missing had been lost in the inferno. Among those listed as missing without trace, and presumed dead, was a 34-year-old British tourist named Demelza Dunn. Life was good.

She looked at Kelso's emails. She smiled.

"The bitch is back," she said out loud, "but it looks like she's not staying!"

Chapter 18

Raj was not happy. His boss was going away, leaving him high and dry for three months. She had 'lent' him to the computer crime team in her absence to help them catch up with their paperwork. He knew nothing about computer crime, and he didn't like working with other people. He liked working for his boss, even if she always got to the office before him and refused to drink his coffee. As he was packing up to leave just before 5pm a shortish and very pretty Asian woman appeared at the office door.

"She in?" was all she said.

"Who?" he replied.

"Your boss, Julia. She said to come and see her."

"And who are you? There's nothing in the diary."

"Tanisha," she said. "Actually, I'm your new boss as of tomorrow, in computer crime. You'll be working on my team."

"She's in her office," Raj said sourly.

"Thanks. See you tomorrow - don't be late."

Tanisha Chakrabarti knocked on Julia's door. It was ajar, so she pushed and went in. Julia had just finished changing and she was now wearing jeans and a cotton shirt. She was doing up a pair of trainers.

"Hi, Julia. You asked me to come by."

"Thanks Tanisha. Excuse me getting dressed. It's been a long day."

"I'm glad you're back, I wanted to see you anyway. I had a call from Amelia Armstrong, the lawyer. She didn't like what I had to say to her, but she was OK about it in the end. Resigned, you might say. She's heard on the legal grapevine that a bunch of other lawyers and their clients have had threatening emails from an anonymous sender saying they'd get the same treatment as her if they didn't make sizeable payments. I asked her how she knew, and she told me that one of her friends was on the receiving end of one of these emails and had called her about it. She's seen it. I got her to call the friend and get him or her to send me the email as an attachment, not to forward it, and I've got it tucked away. I've printed a copy so you can see what it says."

She handed a sheet of paper to Julia.

"You can see it's an explicit demand for money in exchange for not disclosing material the sender has. That's straightforward criminal blackmail. You've been away, but if you hadn't you would've definitely seen the tabloid sleaze-fest last week about that cabinet minister's ex-wife. According to Amelia she got an email too, discussed it with her ex who told her to 'brazen it out and not send a fucking penny to anyone' - her words, not mine. Anyway, the blackmailer was as good as his or her word and carried out the threat. The poor love's had to check herself into one of those posh clinics until the smutty articles stop. What I find interesting is the instruction to send donations to charities. Makes a change from suitcases full of cash."

"So, there is a blackmail campaign going on?" Julia asked.

"Looks like," said Tanisha. "I've examined the email that was sent by the blackmailer. There's all kinds of information contained in what they call metadata that can lead back to the point of origin, that's why I wanted the original, not a forwarded copy. The metadata would be lost if it was forwarded. I've started unravelling it and I've got so far, but I've hit a wall. The sender's used cut-outs and hijacked VPN servers which I can't get past, not with just one example. I called Amelia. She's going to ask her friends if they've got similar emails and if they do to send them to me. I've said they don't have to report them officially. Hope you don't mind."

"Why wouldn't they report them?"

"Because they think they'd get the Amelia treatment, even if they've already paid. If I can get more examples, I get more chances to trace the sender, get their pattern."

"How many do you need?"

"The more the better, it's an analytical thing. The way it works is that if it's one sender they can only be in one place at a time. If the sender wants to make sure that what he or she's demanding is being done there has to be a return mechanism for answers to get through to somewhere. It doesn't have to be straight to the computer they're using, but it's got to be somewhere they can contact. So, if I have enough originals, and if replies get or have been sent, I have a good chance of tracking enough of them to where they eventually end up. When the sender comes to get them, well, we can see where they are. That's the theory anyhow."

"What else have you got from this email?" Julia asked.

"A flavour of the character of the sender, I think. They're not your average blackmailer, not the ones who use the internet anyway. I'd say this one's intelligent and articulate, seemingly very confident but basically quite insecure. The way they lashed out at the cabinet minister's ex shows a petulance. A pro would have reissued the demand, given her a second chance, but not this one. Do as I say or else, no discussion. That suggests he or she doesn't *want* a discussion, doesn't want to get exposed to opposition or reason, or go up against a skilled negotiator.

"Next, the language. I think it's a native English speaker, I mean British English. I also think they probably haven't had any formal higher education, so as far as the internet and computers go probably self-taught. Also, they're not as young as your average internet nerd. You get hackers and blackmailers who are barely out of short trousers these days. I'd put this one a bit older, more experienced. The material they've chosen to use is effective, powerful. It's just what the smutty press want; it thrills and outrages at the same time. I'm no innocent, but I had to look up some if the stuff mentioned in Amelia's cases - I had no idea people did that sort of thing! I didn't know they could. My internet access was blocked for two days after my 'research' until I could explain to CIB that what I was doing really was for work. Now, what was it you wanted to speak to me about, Julia?"

"This sort of thing. It's helpful. I want to know more, though. Do you drink?"

"I don't not drink. Why?"

"Just wondering if you'd like to continue this over a glass of something. You'll be doing a lot of talking."

"Sounds good. I'll get my jacket and see you downstairs."

In the bar at St Ermin's Hotel Julia ordered drinks. Her usual gin and tonic, and for Tanisha a lager.

"I'm still an impoverished student at heart, Julia. I'm more at home doing happy hour in a Wetherspoons than being in a place where you don't even stick to the carpet."

"We can go to a Wetherspoons, or I can spill your drink on the floor to make it sticky if you prefer," Julia said.

"It's OK, I'll try to overcome my prejudice."

"Going back to our blackmailer, you still think it's just one person?"

"I do, even more so now. I've no idea where they are though, at least not yet."

"Do you have any thoughts on their motivation, why they're doing it?"

"Interesting. It's not money, or at least not *just* money. I've checked out the charities named, four are established, mainstream and well known. Number five is properly registered and all that, but it's pretty niche and based in a dodgy place. Most of the money demanded went to the mainstream charities, over 85%. That could add up to an awful lot of money. Even charity number five getting ten to fifteen percent could be a lot. But if it was just money, why not grab all of it? The victims we know about so far, Amelia's client, the cabinet minster's ex, Amelia's friend who sent us the email, are all rich and mostly famous, or at least high-profile. So, is it bitterness, envy, class-war, just malice? All of the above? None of the above? Who knows? Cheers."

Tanisha downed half her pint in one go. Julia was already half-way through her gin. She signalled for more.

"Time for a stupid question, Tanisha. Two stupid questions, Julia said. "First, are you OK with me calling you Tanisha?"

"I prefer Nisha. People who call me Tanisha also tend to call me Inspector Chakrabarti. When I was a kid it was Tani, but I'm not that keen on it to be honest. There weren't that many Asian kids at my secondary school - my folks moved out of London when I was ten - so everyone kind of struggled with my name and thought it was funny. First of all Chakrabarti became 'Shags Rabbits', and if you put Tanisha in front of that, well, you get Tani Sha-Shags Rabbits. I was called the Stutter Bunny for at least a year by some big bully in the fourth form. In the end I took him behind the bike sheds for what he thought would be a good time; what he actually got was my knee right in his plums, with all his mates watching. The bullies left me alone after that. Long story short, I took to Nisha instead of Tani. What about you? Is it always Julia, never Jules or anything?"

"No, never Jules. Close friends call me Jake," she said, suppressing a laugh.

"Why?"

"Just J K. Ever since I was a kid I've been Jake."

"Are we going to be friends?"

"I hope we will be. Stupid question number two: how does the internet work?"

"Blimey, Julia! How long have you got?"

"Just the overview, nothing too technical and none of that peculiar geeky language."

"I'll try, but if you don't mind I'll stick to how criminals are starting to use the internet rather than going through the whole thing in detail - you'd die of boredom. In a nutshell, the internet was invented and organised to enable a lot of information to whizz around the world very fast. It didn't happen by accident, and although everyone says it's revolutionary and joyfully anarchic there are a shed load of fixed, old-fashioned rules that make it work. There's a network of servers, that's big powerful computers to normal people, all tied in by these rules so they can operate together. People own the servers, agree the rules with owners of other servers and then they can all make people pay to use them. They're known as Internet Service Providers or ISPs and they are the really big business of tomorrow. Soon there'll be a computer in every home, maybe more than one, and each one connected to the internet and paying an ISP a few quid a month. Multiply that by billions of computers around the world and before you know it you've got a new clique of super-powerful billionaires.

"Governments both like and dislike the internet. They like it because it can make business easier, quicker and a lot cheaper; they don't like it because they don't have control of it. They didn't want to design, build or pay for an internet themselves - if they had done every country in the world would have a different one, thus defeating the object - and letting other people do it has cost them their control. They're frightened of it too because they can't keep up with it. In the old days, governments controlled the means of communication, telephones, TV and radio, the mail. They controlled access and use, and they could listen in or read your stuff as and when they wanted. International communications with telex and telegrams and phones were the same. Governments made operators give them the means to listen. If they used codes, they had to give governments the means to decode, the decryption keys.

"With the internet that's all changed, and it's going to keep on changing. Covert use of the internet is on the up. It's getting harder to intercept computer communications; it's getting harder to read encrypted communications; there are more and more different encryption systems, some virtually or actually impossible to break. And it's going to keep getting harder as technologies like broadband and fibre optics come into play."

"What are they?" Julia asked.

"Life's too short, Julia," Nisha said. "Just think of using the internet like you're driving your car. You need to know a bit about how it works, and someone needs to know boring stuff like the chemical formula of the fuel that it runs on, but you don't. You just have to get in and go, so forget about things like broadband and fibre optics and all that for now."

"OK, sorry to interrupt."

"There's only one internet," Nisha continued, "but in effect it has lots of layers. The bit that ordinary sensible people use to email their aunty or check the weather is called the Surface Web, it's at the top. Everything on it is formatted so it can be indexed and retrieved quickly by anyone using search engines like Google and Yahoo and what have you. But not everyone wants their stuff to be found, often for good reasons. Banks, for example, want to send money round the world and make zillions of payments and they want to use the internet to do it. But they don't want you and me being able to watch all that, so that sort of thing goes on using the same internet, but it's not indexed - you can't just find it. You can only see it if you're meant to and have logged in to the exchange of information, or if you know the correct unique reference for it. That's called the Deep Web, but like I said it's the same internet, just formatted so it can't be found on public search engines.

"Then there's this new thing. For a few years now some people, mostly in America - in fact mostly the US government - have been playing around with being anonymous on the internet. Like I said the other day in your office, everything on the internet has a specific IP address which can be used to trace a device or a user. The Americans have come up with this thing, working with some mathematician people, which they're calling The Onion Ring Project, or just the TOR Project. It assumes that the layers of the internet are like an onion and can be peeled back one at a time. They think it should be possible for two or more users in the same layer to be able to communicate directly and privately together without being identified or located. It kind of makes sense, but as a copper I can't help thinking they'll be sorry one day. Some people are already calling this the 'Dark Web'. It opens up all kinds of opportunities for armies and spies to do stuff secretly and quickly and cheaply, but it also gives opportunities to fruit-loops and criminals and terrorists to do the same.

"It's like Pandora's Box, Julia. It's there, it's open, everything's got out and there's no going back. We have to live with it. The crims and bandits are already exploiting the internet. You don't need to be a university graduate to make use of it, just have a mind wired in the right, or maybe the wrong, way and an aptitude for thinking quickly and ruthlessly logically. It's a social equaliser, or should I say it's a way in which social order is being completely and radically realigned. Old money and breeding and class and the right school don't mean diddly on the internet."

Nisha paused to finish her beer and start on the second.

"So, our blackmailer will be using the Surface Web, mostly, to communicate with the victims?" Julia asked.

"They have to. Both ends of the communication have to be on the same layer. They've set up ways to obscure who and where they are, but nothing on the internet can be totally anonymous, at least for now. Users can make things more difficult for people like me, but essentially if you want complete anonymity or privacy, don't use the internet.

"The blackmailer will have exploited the Deep Web too. Some of the material in Amelia's case and the other two, particularly financial transactions, most likely came from hacks on Deep Web traffic. It's not really much harder than hacking the Surface Web if you know what you're looking for. It's going to get easier as time goes on and more ordinary people start using the internet for things like shopping and banking and buying porn and stuff. It's already exploding. People do like a novelty."

"Do you think you can find her?" Jake asked.

"Her? You mean the blackmailer? Are you saying you know who it is?"

"Possibly. It's a long shot and a long story. Not one for right now at any rate. Nisha, when we met in my office the other day, I asked you if you were a white-hat hacker. You said you'd only just met me and took the fifth, you chose not to incriminate yourself. What would you say if I asked you again, right now? Are you a white-hat hacker?"

Nisha drank her beer.

"I'll answer you, but only if you tell me why you think you know who the blackmailer is. I'll show you mine if you show me yours."

"You're very sure of yourself, aren't you, Nisha?"

"Only on the outside, and only because I'm doing a job that I don't need to do and I don't mind if I get fired."

"Alright, I think the blackmailer may be, and it is only *may* be, someone I know. Someone who regards me as her enemy. I know her by a certain name, which she no longer uses. I met her when I was a student, she was in Oxford at the same time but she wasn't at the university. She's bright, cunning, and incredibly ruthless. If it is her, she's not just a blackmailer, she's a human-trafficker, a sadist and a killer. She has a contract out on my life and just a few days ago she almost succeeded in having my closest friend murdered. I want to get her, and I'd like you to help me. Now, are you a white-hat hacker, Nisha?"

Nisha thought for a while, her face set, tight lipped, suppressing her emotions.

"She almost murdered your best friend? She has a contract out on you? Julia Kelso, I am telling you that I am a white hat hacker. There, I've said it; you can arrest me now if you want. You've told me a bit about who you think it could be, and even if she isn't the blackmailer, I want to help you get her. Can I do that for you? Will you let me help you?"

"Thank you, Nisha, yes. Yes, please. There's a lot more I need to tell you. Let's have one more for the road, shall we?"

"Why not? Jake."

Chapter 19

Early on Friday morning she packed a few things in an overnight bag before checking her screens. Kelso's email was quiet and she wondered if she had already gone away again. Although all the signs pointed to the success of the Dutch couple's second attempt, if Kelso had vanished so soon it could mean that Dunn was improbably still alive. She had been scanning airline reservation systems and hadn't been able to find any trace of Kelso or Demelza Dunn leaving Crete. She hadn't been expecting to find Dunn, but there should have been something for Kelso. She made a mental note to check out private charters and air ambulances when she got back.

She had instructed several brokers to arrange to borrow stock in four different oil and gas majors, some US based, others not. Now that she had confirmation of possession, she put in place an array of sell orders over a few days, starting after the weekend, not too many at once, at the market price. She would deal with the next phase of that piece of business after her trip down to San Francisco. She shut down her screens and left the apartment. The day was going to be warm again, although it was still early - not yet 6am. She walked the silent streets towards the Latin Quarter and Berri station to get the airport bus. She could have taken a taxi or used her limo service, but she was getting into the role. The bus was more appropriate. She got to Montreal airport around 7am and checked in for the first flight of the day to Vancouver, economy on Air Canada.

The plane was less than half full. She deliberately left her laptop in her bag and instead read a couple of magazines and dozed for a while. The flight took almost five hours, but with the time difference it was still not yet 11am when the plane touched down on the West Coast. She had a couple of hours to kill. She was going to meet him at the boarding gate for the San Francisco connection at around 1pm, and she didn't want to see him before then. She broke cover and used her Air Canada frequent flyer card to get into the business lounge where she found a quiet corner, a fresh green tea and a spare desktop computer. She busied herself until it was time and then went to the departure gate. He was waiting nervously. He smiled when he saw her.

"Hi," he stammered, "I'm glad you could make it. How was your flight?" he asked.

"It was fine. Is everything ready?"

"Yes, all set. I've got the conference passes, and I booked rooms for us in the residence halls at Berkeley. I think you'll find it interesting."

She didn't reply. She'd found him a couple of years ago at a closed meeting of a hackers' group she knew. He was on his own, bulky, shy and ungainly, wearing a stained tee-shirt, old jeans and smelly basketball sneakers. She had seen something in him, smiled at him once and had him in the palm of her hand forever. She told him her name was Leah, he said his was Sammy. He was originally from the States but had moved north to British Columbia to escape the bullies, thugs and drug dealers of his native Bakersfield, where his dad worked in the oilfields. As a quiet, clumsy, studious kid he had been picked on relentlessly, and when he went away to college he vowed he would never go back. His parents had seemed relaxed about his departure, and although his mom had tried to get in touch once or twice she had now mostly given up. He hadn't been home in over three years.

Sammy had told her everything about himself, almost all at once. How he had supported himself through college by fixing people's broken computers, building or upgrading machines for people who wanted to develop games or download movies, and eventually by hacking. He hacked the smaller banks at first, finding a way to sweep up the tiny fractions of cents left over in interest calculations and bundle them together to make whole cents and dollars to put in his own account. It was money from nowhere, money the banks' customers would never see, and which the banks' accounting systems would never miss. He kept it modest, never exceeding what he needed for his basic requirements, which were very basic indeed. A room, some food, computers and electricity. He replaced his jeans and tee shirts when they fell apart. He had no social life, apart from seeing the temporary friends he made at hacking groups when they needed his advanced skills. She was the first person he wanted to call a friend, and the first girl he had had a conversation with since he was in grade school. He had no idea that the girl was actually a woman in her midthirties; he knew next to nothing about her, not where she lived, what movies she liked, where she came from. Only that she was the loveliest girl he had ever seen, and the only one who had ever spoken to him like he was a person. Now he saw her every few months when they went to unpublicised conferences with their sidebar meetings of small groups of lawless radicals of the computer age.

She took the window seat, he took the aisle, leaving the middle seat empty. The flight wasn't full, and he knew she didn't like to feel hemmed in. She was unmoved by the sight of the Golden Gate Bridge as they banked over San Francisco on the approach to SFO. Coming into the USA from Canada was virtually like a domestic flight, and a mere thirty minutes after touchdown they were on the BART subway train, first the line towards Antioch, changing to the Richmond line at Embarcadero. They alighted at Downtown Berkeley a little after 5pm and walked towards the university campus.

More people tried to speak to her than to him, which he was used to, and she responded coolly to almost all of them. Small talk among the geek community was not a big deal, and no one seemed to mind. There was an evening session for the mainstream conference about the future of cyber security, as it was becoming known, and the prevalence of new, continually evolving viruses that would keep the industry in work and funds for years to come. The speaker, who was from one of the emerging market leaders in anti-virus software, ended with an undiluted pitch for anyone with interest and ability in the virus arena to come and see him about a job.

Afterwards Sammy and Leah went to a side room to meet with a handful of others in a closed meeting with no agenda. They were there to talk about the latest developments in hacking and anti-hacking techniques; to discuss the measures being adopted by governments, corporations, political movements and the banks to deter intrusion by people like them; and to toss around ideas about how to keep on top of their opponents. There would be a session like this on each of the three evenings of the conference, which was why she was there. The mainstream stuff in the main auditorium and the smaller meeting rooms was barely interesting enough to keep her awake.

On the last evening, the Sunday, emboldened by a couple of beers, Sammy tried in his usual hapless way to make a pass at her. She found him physically repugnant, but he was useful to her. She resisted as always but left him enough of a glimmer of hope to try again the next time they met. She might even let him succeed one day, but then again she might just kill him instead - once he was no longer useful to her.

The time difference meant she didn't get back to her apartment in Montreal until late on Monday evening. Although tired and stiff from sleeping in an unfamiliar and decidedly student-ish bed she opened up her screens and checked on developments. Kelso was clearly not at her desk. Her name did not appear on any flight or ferry manifest leaving Crete, nor on any lists of passengers on private charters or medical flights. There was also no trace of her arriving in or leaving London. She started to trawl through other passenger manifests, hoping she might get a sniff of Silva. There were just too many flights to and from too many places, and she gave up. Without a name or date of birth, or anything concrete, she could do nothing. For now.

She turned to the latest phase of her project, her plan to shake the planet's faith in the handful of titanic energy companies that underpinned their fuel, electricity supply and pension funds. First, she checked on the progress of her stock sales. Satisfied that the money was rolling in, she composed an email for identified executives in four of the giant corporations, starting each with the designated codeword she had told them to look out for. The emails were short. In a few days, she told them, something would happen. If the recipient didn't want to experience the same type of event, they must set up a regular payment to five nominated charities. She specified the amounts and the regularity of the payments, which would continue until further notice. Any attempt by a recipient to avoid their obligations, or to alert the authorities, would result in devastating consequences for the corporation concerned. That was all. She sent the emails. The corporation she had dealt with when she opened her campaign was not on the list of recipients.

******

Modern oilfield design and development is efficient, safe and integrated. It has not always been so. Many fields have a production life expectancy of many decades, decades in which technologies can change or even get invented. Some of the oldest oilfields still in production are in the Caspian region, in the several states surrounding the vast inland sea at the western end of the Eurasian plain. Over time, new bits have been added, new processes, new wells, new monitoring and data collection mechanisms. When the wells were initially designed and drilled there was no such thing as the internet. Data was collected on site, transcribed into lengthy telex messages and sent back to head office to be crunched by the engineers and accountants. Then it all went online.

In a control room somewhere near Baku a process control engineer was watching the graphs and dials and screens. Everything seemed in order until it suddenly wasn't. Well-head pressure on one of the production platforms started to climb rapidly, too rapidly and for no apparent reason. The engineer's initial thoughts were that it must be a fault on the pressure sensors, and she was right. A simple coded electronic message sent over the internet to the process control valve sensor telling it to double the pressure reading every three seconds was all it took. However, the more modern blow-out prevention devices on other wells linked to the production matrix did not think it was a sensor error or think anything at all. Suddenly, the massive mechanical blow-out prevention valves started slamming shut, instantly creating enormous backpressure across the matrix. The remaining couple of older wells didn't have sophisticated devices to prevent explosive disasters. Their well-heads and well casings weren't built for this eventuality, and they blew. Violently, explosively. Boiling hot, highly pressurised crude oil exploded through shattered wellheads in roaring fountains of liquid fire. Alarms sounded, fire suppression systems were activated, orders were barked. None of it made any difference. This was a massive blow-out, with plumes of smoke and flames that could soon be seen many miles away, under which were infernos that could burn for months and months and months, spewing destruction and environmental carnage.

She saw it on the news, and as the stock prices of not just the affected corporation, which was based in Houston and which was currently the subject of a very public investigation into corrupt payments, but of all major oil and gas companies, began to plummet.

Once a predetermined price level had been passed, her buy orders kicked in and she bought back all the shares she had sold the previous week for less than half the price she had got for them. The stock was returned, with the borrower's fee, to the previous owners who promptly tried to sell it on again before any residual value disappeared altogether.

A week later, four charities were surprised to see large donations from the stricken oil majors. Their ethics committees met and eventually agreed that just because a gift-horse has bad breath that's no reason to kick it in the teeth and turn down its very significant donations. The fifth charity had no ethics committee. She would start to move the money tomorrow.

Chapter 20

Their French was improving. Mel and Alf sat together most lunch times to watch the news on TV and try to make sense of the adverts. Mel was transfixed by the images of the Azerbaijan oilfield disaster, still burning fiercely a week after the initial blow-out. The commentary suggested it would be at least another couple of weeks before the oil fire experts were ready to have a first attempt at getting it under control. The corporation which operated the field, and owned most of it, had gone from one of the most stable and sought after of companies on the stock market to one of the most volatile and least desirable. The graph on the news showed that its market value had dropped by over 60% since the blow-out, and already packs of slavering attorneys were lining up to start the lawsuits.

"How does something like that happen?" Mel asked. "I mean, there must be safety systems all over oil wells."

"Search me," Alf said, "human error, sabotage, shit happens. It's going to take years for the operating company to recover, that's for sure, not to mention the environment. The smoke's disrupting flights right across the region."

"Turn it off, Alf, "Mel said, "it's depressing. Can we go outside? It's so warm in here."

He unlocked the wheels on her bed and with Steph's help he manoeuvred her through the double doors to the terrace. They set up a parasol to give her some cooling shade.

"Only a couple more weeks, Mel," Steph said, "the orthopaedic guy says your pelvis is healing well and it will be able to bear some weight soon. Then we can put you in the chair; it'll make it easier for you to move around."

"God, I hope so, Steph," Mel said, "I'm going nuts in this bed. When does the cast come off?"

"That'll be another four weeks or so yet."

They had taken Mel in the ambulance to a polyclinic in Poitiers to see the orthopaedic specialist Steph had found. He had arranged X-ray and CT scans and had been grudgingly complimentary about the quality of the repair job carried out by the surgeons in Crete. He consulted a colleague about Mel's brain CT - there was too much metal in her to do an MRI - and between them they declared that if you disregarded the fact that she had been mown down and almost killed by a speeding car, Mel was very lucky to be recovering as well as she was.

"Of course," Steph said, "we'll have to start your rehab once the cast is off and your legs and pelvis are working again. You'll have lost a huge amount of muscle mass which we'll have to start rebuilding."

"You mean which *I'll* have to start rebuilding," Mel said, "you'll just be standing there shouting at me. My arse has gone horribly bony, I can feel it."

Alf was pleased by Mel's outward attitude. Her spirit was still there; the intimate banter she did with Steph and Tracey seemed to lift her, even though he had sat on the terrace some evenings listening to her crying, either out of pain or frustration. She never complained, at least not seriously, despite being robbed of her privacy and dignity by her injuries. Steph and Tracey had to take care of all her personal needs, something which Alf knew must be incredibly intrusive for Mel.

After a long discussion with Spike and Ricky, Alf had agreed that the boys should stand down. They had wired the place with sensors, automatic alarms and CCTV cameras, and the dining room was now the security control hub. Steph and Tracey carried pistols while they were in the house, as did Alf. There was a spare one for Jake, who was due back soon, kept in a locked drawer in the kitchen. The SIG assault rifles were also stashed in a cupboard in the kitchen. Alf had never fired one, but both the combat medics were familiar enough with the weapons and said they could use them in the unlikely event that they were needed.

So, a routine was becoming established. Days passed, and as they did Alf's need to do something active about their situation grew. He wanted Jake to return, soon, so they could start working out what to do. She had phoned a few times but kept the calls short. She'd been to see Mel's mum, apparently quite a difficult encounter, but everything seemed OK now. He'd asked her when she'd be back, but she had changed the subject. She didn't make any mention of Dido Sykes. All he could do was keep waiting.

******

In England Julia Kelso had not been idle. She hadn't been into the office since she started her 'study leave', but she had been spending a lot of time with Nisha Chakrabarti. After their first social meeting in the St Ermin's Hotel, Nisha had launched herself into Jake's quest with gusto. She spent a few days tidying up her case load and giving Raj lots to do while Jake drove up to Yorkshire to see Mrs Dunn, and by the time she was back in London Nisha was ready to start a few weeks leave.

"How did it go with Mel's mum?" she asked Jake. They were in Jake's borrowed flat.

"She was very suspicious at first," Jake said, "understandably so. A stranger turns up at her door saying that her daughter's been seriously hurt and is being kept in hiding at a secret location. Reason: someone probably tried to kill her twice and may do so again. Stranger says trust me; I'll look after her, and by the way the British police, of whom said stranger is one, are not investigating it as attempted murder because they don't know it happened. As far as Mel's employer is concerned, she's been in a car accident and is convalescing with friends. So, it was all a bit tricky, Nisha. I told Mrs Dunn that I'd make sure she could see Mel as soon as it was safe, and that I would get Mel to write to her.

"She was very upset for a while, but in the end I think I got her to trust me a bit. I told her stories about things that Mel and I had done together - things I knew Mel had told her about too. I told her the bare bones of what had happened, and that I had arranged with friends to get her out of Crete to somewhere no one could find her. I wouldn't say Mrs Dunn trusts me fully, but at least she isn't totally hostile anymore."

"I'm not surprised. I can't imagine what my mum would say in similar circumstances. How do you know Mel? You said she's your best friend."

"She's a senior intelligence analyst over at NCIS. We worked on a case and got to know each other. We just sort of clicked. I've not known her that long, less than two years, but it seems like forever."

"I can't wait to meet her."

"She has some interesting ways," Jake said, "and she's complicated."

"Do you think about her a lot? You said you've been living together. Is there….."

"We've been sharing this flat, Nisha, not exactly 'living together'. Look, like I said, it's complicated; let's leave it for now. Are you sure about coming with me?"

"I'm sure. I've booked three weeks leave 'to go travelling'. They've got my mobile number if they need me. How are we going? I've got quite a lot of stuff."

"How much stuff?"

"Four laptops, some boxes of electric tricks, a few upscale modems, and a server tower - I can use one of the laptops as a monitor so I don't need a separate screen. I wouldn't fancy getting it through an airport security check, not since 9/11."

"Will it fit in the boot of a car?"

"Yeah, easy."

"Then I'll go get a car."

"Where are we headed?" Nisha asked.

"France," Jake said.

"I'll need some adaptors, then. Rural or urban?"

"Rural, very rural."

"I hope there's a good enough phone line. French phone lines in the countryside are pretty crap usually."

"What if there isn't a good phone line?"

"If I can't use the internet as I want to, we'll never find her. No phone, no internet, bad phone line, bad internet. Bad internet is as good as no internet. Is money an issue?"

"Not really. Why?"

"I'll get hold of a satellite phone. They cost a packet, but at least I'll be able to get online. I'll have to do some messing about to disguise the sat phone's location, which could take me a day or two. Is that OK?"

"Fine. I'll head off in the morning and get the transport sorted out. We'll aim to leave the day after tomorrow, or maybe the day after that depending on how we do."

"Sounds good, Jake. Can I crash here? I don't fancy flogging all the way out west, not at this time of night. I've got a toothbrush."

"Sure, you can have Mel's room. Shall I get us a drink?"

The following morning Jake left the flat soon after Nisha had departed. She had enjoyed her company but was still trying to fathom her out. Nisha had the skills and knowledge she and Alf needed to try to get an angle on Dido Sykes, to use the internet and all its subsurface alleyways and shadows and darkness against her; to take the fight to Dido's door and beat her at her own game. They couldn't do it on their own. She had to take Tanisha Chakrabarti at face value, and hope that that she really was who and what she seemed to be.

Jake took the train to Dover again, made the crossing to Calais and took the bus into town. She found the Hertz office and took her place in the queue. When she got to the desk she spoke in fluent French, with what she hoped might sound like a Flemish accent. She needed a car for a week; she had a Belgian ID card and driving licence, but her credit card had been stolen. Could she pay cash? The answer was yes, as long as she left a big enough deposit. She counted out a pile of Alf's Euros and said she'd return the car to La Rochelle in a week. The clerk said fine and handed her the keys to a nearly new Opel with French number plates.

Jake drove back towards the ferry port but changed her mind. Instead, she took the A16 autoroute to the Shuttle terminal and bought an open return ticket for the next day. On a whim, she drove to Boulogne, to the hotel where she'd spent those nights with Alf just a few short weeks ago, but also another life away. She booked a room for the night, hoping they'd give her the same one as they had used. They didn't, but it was close enough. She left her overnight bag and went out to find something to eat. She was back in the room in a little more than an hour and it was still light outside. She had some gin in her bag and got ice and tonic at the small hotel bar. She made a drink and called Alf.

"I'm in Boulogne again, same hotel," she said when he answered. "How are things?"

"Good, the same. Are you coming back?"

"In a couple of days. I miss you. Both of you."

"We miss you too. Come back soon."

She hung up, sipped her drink, and cried.

Chapter 21

Julia Kelso pulled up outside Tanisha Chakrabarti's small but neat house in Teddington, a suburb west of London. It was just 7am. Jake knocked on the door and waited. A few minutes later the door opened. Nisha stood there, bleary-eyed and wrapped in towels, one round her head and another just about covering her torso. She waved Jake in without speaking, gestured towards the tiny kitchen and staggered upstairs.

Jake overcame her coffee snobbery and made herself a mug of instant. Twenty minutes later Nisha came back downstairs, her hair still wet but now combed. She had pulled on a pair of jeans and a tee shirt. Her feet were bare.

"Not a morning person, Nisha?" Jake asked.

"No. What time is it?"

"Almost seven thirty."

Nisha groaned.

"Sorry, I was up nearly all night on the web, trying to find your mad cow Dido. I'm knackered. When are we leaving?"

"Whenever you like. The ticket's open, we can turn up when we want."

"OK. Must have coffee, then we'll put the gear in the car. You have got a car?"

"Why else would I be here?"

"Good point."

After another twenty minutes the women loaded the car. A soft bag full of Nisha's personal things, several computer bags and a few boxes, a sack of cables, and a new satellite phone still in its packaging.

"I didn't get a subscription yet; it would have cost a fortune and my credit card would have broken. We can do it online if we need to, and if we don't I can take the phone back."

"Are you going to be this entertaining all the way?"

"If you're lucky. Is there a pool where we're going?"

"Yes."

"Back in a mo."

Nisha went back upstairs and came down a few seconds later with a small and very colourful bikini, which she shoved into the top of her bag.

"Let's go," Jake said.

Nisha slept as Jake negotiated the M25 and M20 towards Folkestone. It took almost two hours in the heavy morning traffic and they got to the terminal just after 10am. Nisha woke up, but only long enough to have her passport checked. Boarding the train was easy and swift, and less than an hour later they were on the A26 autoroute heading south away from Calais towards Paris. Nisha had woken up again.

"Where are we, Jake?"

"In France, we've just left Calais. It's going to take around six hours to get where we're going, a bit more if we need to stop more than once."

"Do you want me to sing you a song, then, to keep you entertained?"

"Can you sing, Nisha?"

"No, not really, more of a pained wail."

"I'll pass then, but you can talk to me if you like. Why do they do it?"

"Why does who do what?"

"Hackers. Why do they hack?"

"You do like big questions, don't you? The simple answer is because they can. It's easy if you know how and you've got the weird brain needed to do it, but not many people know how and even fewer want to. I've thought about it a lot. My theory is that hackers do it so they can win at something. I've been to lots of hacker get-togethers and they're an odd bunch, not big on social skills, not physically impressive, strange footwear. It's hard to picture them as life's winners, not in the generally accepted sense. But give them a keyboard and they transform. They're in their element.

"So, when you're online you can do what you want, go where you like. There are no locked doors; no one's laughing at you or kicking sand in your face. In fact, no one can see you, you're like something unworldly. You can say what you want and people can't touch you; they can't shout back, can't argue. A hacker can win a battle against someone who doesn't even know they're in a fight. It's not just hackers, though, a lot of ordinary people get the same sort of kick out of the internet. It's remote, separate.

"You're safe at home in your bedroom but you can be having sex with beautiful people - or at least watching beautiful people having sex with other beautiful if unusually formed people - you can be a superhero, a football star, a rock god, anything. And you can be rude to people who can't punch your lights out because they don't know who or where you are."

"You make the internet sound like a bad thing," Jake said.

"What do the gun nuts in America say? Guns don't kill people, people kill people. The internet isn't a bad thing *per se*, but it's designed in such a way as to make it very easy for people to do things on and with it, good things and bad. It's changing the world, no doubt at all about that, and it's going to change the way everyone lives in the next few years. If you think about the way life was before trains and cars, when a person's world was only as big as the distance they could travel in a day or a week. If you were rich and glamorous and could afford it, you could get from York to London in a couple of days. Most people never got from York to London, ever.

Then the train came along and it was a few hours and a few shillings; and in a car you could take the wife and kids along too for the same price and just as fast. Now everyone's flying off to Florida and Turkey and Spain on their cheap holidays, and to Australia to see their cousin who only went there in the first place to get away from them. And you can get fresh asparagus all year round instead of just for a few weeks in May. Before planes who'd ever even heard of an avocado? It's progress, and once it happens you can't make it unhappen, whether the consequences are good or bad."

"Tell me about good and bad hackers, Nisha. You're one of the good guys who do it. What about the bad ones?"

"We're all a bit weird, but good ones do it because if they don't there'd be no one to stop the bad guys. They also do it to make the internet safer, to find flaws and vulnerabilities and fix them. Bad ones do it to cause harm by finding and exploiting other flaws and vulnerabilities. The skeleton of the internet is properly organised, but all the fleshy bits are stuck on by any old Tom, Dick or Harry. There's no set standard or master plan, so you're bound to get cockups and weaknesses.

You've come across lots of criminals, haven't you? Would you say there's a common factor? I don't mean between one-off crime-committers, I mean between regular criminals?"

"I've never really thought about it, but I guess there is a common thread. Regular habitual criminals don't care about other people; they just don't give a fuck. There's no empathy. Maybe they all love their mums, but everyone else is fair game."

"That's my conclusion too. No empathy. With hacking that lack of empathy is multiplied. They don't even have to look their victims in the eye when they rob them or humiliate them. They're cruel, Jake, the bad hackers. Like people who torture cats and pick on people who can't fight back. I hate them, Jake, I hate hackers. Bad ones, I mean."

"So, someone like Dido Sykes. Why does she do it? I knew her at Oxford. She was a bit strange, but she wasn't short on people skills. She could get people to do whatever she wanted."

"Lack of empathy doesn't necessarily mean short on people skills. It's more about not caring about the impact of what you're doing or saying, not caring about the consequences of what you do to other people. Your Dido is a manipulator, judging by what you've told me. I said that most hackers are as good at psychology as they are at mathematics, didn't I? Even the sad sick ones know which buttons to press to inflict pain. Dido Sykes knows which buttons people have, and which ones will make them do what she wants. She knew your ex, Drew was it? His buttons were his sense of arrogant entitlement and his penis. The Shah woman had self-delusion, your ex-boss Savernake a total lack of self-esteem. She'll have worked out what buttons you have too, Jake. She couldn't get to you at Oxford, except through using Drew and knowing that you didn't know. It satisfied her to know that she was having you over, up to a point. If she's tried to have your best friend killed, it means she thinks that Mel Dunn is one of your buttons too, Jake, a weakness she can exploit to get at you. The fact that she thinks Mel is dead doesn't make her any less of a button, I'm afraid. She'll still use her against you, somehow. I expect she'll have identified other buttons, ones you haven't already revealed to me yet."

"You saying I've already revealed weaknesses to you, Nisha?"

"Course you have, same as I've shown you some of mine. It's what people do when they get to know each other, want to know each other as friends. It's a standard human transaction, a subconscious 'I'll show you mine if you show me yours' one, like I said. It's how relationships work. As Commander Julia Kelso you keep a lot of things concealed from everyone, just as I do when I'm Inspector Tanisha Chakrabarti. When you're Jake and I'm Nisha we're different, more open with each other. We've seen each other first thing in the morning when we've just got out of bed, had coffee in each other's kitchens in our towels or dressing gowns. Yours is much better, by the way, your kitchen and your coffee. Where are we now?"

"Still in France," Jake said, thinking things through.

Nisha reached over and held Jake's hand on the steering wheel. She squeezed it gently.

"It'll be fine, Jake, we'll get this over with and you can get your life back. Do you want me to drive for a bit?"

"Are you a good driver?"

"Bloody awful. Especially when everyone's on the wrong side of the road."

Jake threw her head back and laughed out loud for the first time in weeks.

Chapter 22

In Montreal she was getting bored. The oil companies had all paid up, as had the lawyers and their clients. She wasn't sure if she wanted to go after all the glitzy people, at least not yet. There was a risk of the media overdosing on scandal, and the sums of money to be made from individuals, even Hollywood movie stars, wasn't enough of an incentive to motivate her. A lot of work would be needed, and she already had more money than she would ever need or could ever spend. No, she thought, I'll just throw the odd one to the wolves every now and then.

She spent the rest of the morning going through her profiles of film, TV, sport and music people, eventually selecting a short list of five. Each had tiny grains of embarrassing truth which could be exploited and amplified to become landslides of scandal. Drugs, perversions, cringe-making personality traits, addictions, all enough to fuel career-ending deaths by media. She chose one, a global name in sport who had once inadvertently clicked on an underage sex website. She quickly uploaded searches of many similar sites and fired hundreds of images and video clips off to the unfortunate athlete's personal computer. A brief denouncing email to his local police department, copied to a national newspaper, followed and she was done. As was the athlete. No gain, just pain, she mused. Now for Kelso. Where the hell was she?

******

Jake and Nisha pulled up at the house in Charente in the early evening. Alf had seen the car arrive, and not recognising it he was waiting in the shadows with his pistol drawn. He relaxed when he saw Jake stepping out into the light thrown by the security lamps.

"I've brought someone to help us, Alf," she said, sidestepping his kiss, "we can do that later. She's an internet expert. Her name's Nisha."

Nisha had been waiting in the car. Jake beckoned for her to get out.

"Nisha, Alf. Alf, Nisha," she said.

"Alf?" Nisha said. "No one's called Alf."

"He is," Jake said, "it's an affectionate nickname. I'll give you his real name when I remember it."

"Hello, Nisha," Alf said, "come in and I'll sort your luggage later. Jake, a word please."

Mel's door was closed. Steph was in the room with her, and Alf led Jake and Nisha to the kitchen.

"We'll be back in a moment," he said, leading Jake into the dining room.

"What's going on?" he asked once they were alone. "Who is she?"

"She's one of the Met's computer crime people. I've taken a gamble and entrusted her with some of the story - not all of it by any means. We need her, Alf, if we're going to beat Sykes at her own game. We can't do it on our own. Nisha's got the skills and knowledge we need, and I like her. We get on. It's a calculated risk, I get that, but we need her, Alf."

"How well do you know her?"

"Not that well. I didn't know you or Mel that well either once, remember? I'm following my instincts, and if I'm wrong, well…. Now, I'm parched and starving. Come here."

She held her arms open for him and he went to her. They kissed and held each other for a few moments.

"Later," she said, resisting his urgency. "Let's eat."

They went back into the kitchen.

"Well," Nisha said, "am I staying then? I've seen the gun on the sideboard and I'm not sure I want to know what the alternative might be." She gestured towards the spare pistol, Jake's, that was visible.

"Sorry about that," Alf said, putting the pistol in a drawer, "we're taking precautions. What's Jake told you?"

"She's told me Mel's here, and that Dido Sykes has tried to have her killed twice. I don't blame you for taking precautions, or for being spooked by the appearance of a total stranger. But I'm on Jake's side, yours too I hope. I'm here to help."

"OK. What are you going to need?"

"I need access to electricity, and a phone line for an internet connection. I'll be working at odd times, too."

"So you'd better be in the main house. The phone line is in the dining room; we're using it as a security control room but there's lots of space and no one else is in it most of the time. You can have my room upstairs. I'll move into one of the cottages."

"Where's Jake going to be?" asked Nisha.

"I'll be in the cottage too, Nisha," Jake said.

"Oh, I see. I thought it was you and Mel…."

"It's me and him too, Nisha. Like I said, it's complicated."

"None of my business," Nisha said. "Where's the bathroom? I'm bursting."

"I'll show you, bring your bag. Alf will get the rest of the stuff in and put it in the dining room," Jake said.

Upstairs Jake and Nisha quickly stripped Alf's bed and remade it with fresh linen. Jake showed Nisha where everything was.

"When you're ready come down and we'll have a drink and something to eat," Jake told her.

"OK," Nisha replied. "Jake, just tell me to shut up if I start to pry, won't you? It's just I want to understand how things stand with the three of you; it'll help if I do."

"Look, Nisha," Jake said, "the three of us, Alf, Mel and me, are close. Alf and I are close in quite a conventional sense, but we're both close to Mel as well. She just does things differently, in her own way. We've got used to that. Now she's been hurt our priority is making sure she gets better as quickly and as fully as she can; Alf and I will support each other through that. Afterwards we'll see where we are. This isn't making much sense, is it?"

"No, not really."

"I'll try to put it simply, then. We're all very close, the three of us, in just about every way. It sort of works."

"If you say so. I'm sorry I asked," Nisha said.

"You'll get used to it. It's not as mad as it looks. See you downstairs."

They relaxed over drinks at the kitchen table. Steph and Tracey joined them; Mel was still sleeping in her room.

"How's she doing?" Jake asked.

"She's doing really well," Tracey replied. "I think we can try the wheelchair tomorrow; her hip mobility seems OK, and as long as she's comfortable we can give it a go for a while. Steph and I are quite keen to get her moving, start to build her confidence up. She puts a brave face on it, but I think she's worried about how she's going to be in the future."

"And how is she going to be?" Jake asked.

"I don't think she'll go back to where she was. She was super-fit; we can hope she gets a lot of it back but I do expect some residual impairment. A bit of stiffness, a few aches and pains. There's been some nerve damage, which takes ages to recover from. We don't know what effect that'll have on her, sensation wise. She might have some numbness, maybe muscle coordination problems. Don't get me wrong, she'll still be in good shape, just not as good as she was.

"We've seen similar levels of injuries in the field, soldiers who've gone from being super fit and active to being more like ordinary people. The biggest issue once the physical signs of the injuries have gone is the damage to self-esteem. Some people feel it badly, get depressed about not being superb anymore. It's important that she has her friends around her, and that we all support her by pushing her to be as good as she can be. She'll shout a lot, but in the end she'll thank us."

"What are your plans, yours and Steph's?" Jake asked.

"We'll stay as long as we're needed. I reckon she'll benefit from us being here for another three or four weeks, then we'll start to back off. We've talked about it. Steph will stay on here, but I'll pull out when Mel starts to exercise her independence. Mel will let us know when she doesn't want Steph around anymore. If it looks like Mel needs us more or for longer, we'll change plans, but we're not expecting any major problems."

Steph hadn't said anything and was busy making a big bowl of salad niçoise.

"Are you alright with all that, Steph?" Alf asked her.

"Absolutely. Tracey and I discussed it at length. Mel's recovery depends more on her than on us; we won't outstay our usefulness. We won't leave you in the lurch either. We've both got lives to get back to, not that we're not liking being here with you lot. I think a nice fruity Loire white with this salad, don't you Trace?"

They chatted as they ate. Steph and Tracey never imparted anything about their private lives or asked about anyone else's. It was almost 11 by the time Nisha yawned and excused herself. Alf and Jake tidied up and loaded the dishwasher while Steph and Tracey checked on Mel. Tracey sat up with her for a while, even though she was still asleep, while Steph turned in.

Jake and Alf sat together on the small terrace of the guest cottage. He poured them both a whisky.

"Have you been thinking about what happens next?" he asked.

"In what way?"

"About Sykes. About us doing something to fix this."

"I have. That's why Nisha's here. I don't know what we're going to do or be able to do. Nisha's fairly confident she'll be able to find Dido, and when we know where she is we can think about going after her. We can talk about it in the morning. I'm looking forward to seeing Mel. I'm also looking forward to going to bed; I'm exhausted. Where's the shower?"

"I'll show you and leave you to it. Which room do you want?"

"I'm not that exhausted, Ferdinand. You've got one last thing to do before we go to sleep."

Chapter 23

In Montreal she was getting ready. She had two cases packed and had called a taxi. The ride to the airport took half an hour and she was dropped at the departure hall by the polite and helpful driver. A few moments later she emerged from the arrival level and stood in line for another cab, this time to take her to the Ritz Carlton back in Montreal. She checked in and waited while a porter delivered her cases to the suite, just for one night.

Once she had given the porter a decent tip and closed the door, she unpacked the smaller of her two cases. On the sofa she laid out her traveling outfit, a tailored trouser suit, silk blouse, a pair of heels and a pair of flat sneakers. She sorted her travel washbag, making sure that everything was in a small enough container to pass the recently reinforced security checks. Satisfied, she ran a bath. She removed all her clothing, the less costly items that she wore around Montreal. These she stuffed in the smaller suitcase. The last thing she removed was her hair, the light brown, shortish mop with a few golden highlights. The wig went in the case with the rest of her other self.

What was left of her own natural hair, long, lustrous and silky black when properly cared for, was very short, in fact shaved. In front of the full-length mirror in the bathroom she made sure all her other body hair was shaved too, and she finished off by running her razor over her head one more time. It was completely smooth now. She washed the bristles off in the shower before getting into the tub. She lay down in the warm water of the luxurious bath, letting the expensive lotions dissolve her bohemian traces, wash away the photographic artist with the loft studio near the river. It was time for her to move on, at least for a while. She liked Montreal; it was pleasantly anonymous and uncurious, and she would probably come back when her task was over. But she made a habit of never thinking about what would happen once a task had ended, she felt it made her careless. As the bath water began to cool, she dropped her hand beneath the surface and rubbed vigorously between her legs. It wasn't for pleasure - she felt little in that respect - or for satisfaction; it was merely to relieve a physical tension. For her it was an act as necessary as using a toilet, nothing more, something she had to do regularly to keep her body in balance.

When she was done, she got out of the bath, dried herself and put on a soft robe. She lay on the bed and let herself relax for an hour. Afterwards she would get up, get dressed, put on her new blonde hair and do her make up, then she would take the hotel's chauffeured limousine back to the airport for the non-stop Air Canada flight to Zurich.

Her first-class seat was at the front of the cabin on the right, as she preferred. She ate sparingly, and only sipped at her champagne. She managed to sleep for a few hours, but as always on a flight she was itching to get off the plane. It touched down in Zurich precisely on time and she walked through immigration and customs with hardly a pause.

"Welcome back to Switzerland, Madame Desbois," the immigration official said, stamping her Canadian passport.

She nodded and smiled politely. In the arrivals hall a young man waited with her name on a sign. She acknowledged him with a glance and followed him to a waiting Mercedes saloon.

"The terminal is only a few minutes' drive, Ms Desbois, and the aircraft is ready for you. Flying time to Geneva will be less than fifty minutes."

She didn't reply but nodded at him to let him know she'd heard. A little over an hour later she was in another Mercedes, this time speeding east away from Geneva airport towards the string of small exclusive towns and villages along the northern shore of the lake. Shortly after crossing the boundary between the Cantons of Geneva and Vaud the car pulled off the lake side road and stopped at a closed steel gate. She sat quietly in the back while the driver communicated on the entry-phone. The gates swung open and the Mercedes swept silently towards the porch of a substantial villa where a uniformed butler and a housekeeper were waiting attentively.

"Madame," the butler greeted her, "it is so good to have you back. Welcome home! Everything is ready for you."

"Thank you Hervé," she said in French, "hello Matilde. It's good to be back. Take my things upstairs. I'm going to swim, and then I'll take some green tea on the terrace."

"Very good, Madame," Hervé said.

They served her lunch, and afterwards she retreated to her office, or rather her suite of offices, on the upper floor of the villa with uninterrupted views of the lake. She'd bought the house a few years earlier on the proceeds of one of her first successful ventures. She liked the fact that the Swiss authorities were more interested in the colour and denomination of your money than where it came from or who you were, and they were more than happy to welcome Madame Marianne Desbois to their country. And also to sell her a very expensive house, of course. Apart from her sojourn in London, which had ended so badly thanks to bloody Kelso, she conducted all her 'business' in Europe from her house in Switzerland. Her Canadian bolthole was a good back-up, but the appeal of Montreal, pleasant as it was, was transitory. She had other places too, but Europe was where she felt she belonged - but not England, not again. It had been a mistake.

Her business now was largely maintenance and research. She had to ensure that her 'clients', those who reluctantly and regularly contributed to her upkeep because of her threats and demands, remained aware of their obligations. From time to time she needed to remind some of them, and very occasionally she had to make an example of one, just to encourage the others. The research side was a constant sweep to identify potential new 'clients' and gather sufficient material or leverage to be able to influence the way they interacted with her, not that they had any idea who or where she was. She also had to keep up to date. The internet and all its nuances were changing rapidly; she needed to get back into her old network of geeks and freaks, the same as she had in America, to keep her skills sharp. A 'conference' was coming up in France and she would need to go along.

But her most pressing occupation for now was Kelso. She wanted Kelso's downfall to be as prolonged, painful and humiliating as possible. Her plan was almost there, all she needed was the right lever to pull, the right hook, to make Kelso come to her. She downloaded her latest email trawl from Kelso's work account and started to read.

******

Nisha had set up her stall, as she called it, an array of laptops and electronic boxes, all neatly plugged in and glowing. She had cursed the French telecoms system, but with her advanced modems she'd been able to boost the internet speed sufficiently to do most of what she wanted. It was a good thing that they didn't want to use the phone to make any calls. Then she went to meet Mel Dunn.

Nisha knocked softly on the door of Mel's room. She'd seen Tracey come out a few seconds earlier. There was no response, so she pushed the door open.

"Hello?" she called.

"What now?"

"Mel?"

"Who are you? Where's Tracey?"

"I'm not a medic, Mel, I'm Nisha, I work for Jake."

Mel was eyeing her quizzically. Nisha had a moment to look at Mel, Jake's best friend. She saw a slim woman with close-cropped brown hair, barely concealing small scars and stitch marks on her scalp. Her face was drawn, her skin pale. There were rings under her eyes, and she looked exhausted. She looked back at Nisha, expressionless.

"How are you doing, Mel?" Nisha asked.

"Bloody brilliant," Mel said, sourly, "what is it you do for Jake? Are you another bodyguard or what?"

"I wouldn't know where to start guarding anyone's body. I'm in the computer crime unit. Jake's my ultimate boss."

"Does she know you call her Jake?"

"She said I should. We're friends now. She's asked me to help track down Dido Sykes."

"Dido? Why?"

"Hasn't she told you? Dido did this to you, she hired someone. She's taken a contract out on you and her, Jake."

"I know all that," said Mel, "I meant why has she asked *you* to help her find Sykes?"

"She thinks Sykes is behind an ongoing blackmail campaign. Jake got me to look investigate one case that was reported to her. I did and told Jake all about it when I'd looked into it. Things sort of moved on from there."

"Did they now," Mel said. "How are you going to go about tracking down Sykes?"

"I've got a few tricks up my sleeve, and a roomful of computers and things just across the hall. Dido Sykes is a hacker, so am I. If I'm better than her, I'll find her."

"You're a hacker?"

"Yes, but one of the good guys. I *am* a police officer, Mel."

"Oh, I thought you were some sort of analyst, like me."

"I'm one of those too. I think we're going to work well together, if you want to, that is."

"I want Sykes out of the game," Mel said, "I'll do what it takes. I'm sorry if I seem a bit snippy, but all this is a bit of a fucker. I want things to be how they were, or at least to be able to move on."

"Understandable," said Nisha. "That's what Jake says too."

"Have you met Alf?" Mel asked.

"Last night when we arrived. You were asleep so we didn't disturb you. I also met Steph and Tracey. Now I've met you all - the full set."

"So, what do you think?"

"About what?"

"The whole thing, this place, the set-up, us."

"I think it's mad. All of it. Jake tried to explain about the three of you, but to be frank I'm not sure what she was saying. It didn't make much sense to me. I'm just going to sit in my room and play with my computers and let you lot get on with it. Whatever 'it' is."

"Could you get Tracey back for me? I think I need the potty. Sorry I'm a bit grumpy, Nisha. I *am* glad you're here; we're going to need some help. I'll see you later."

Chapter 24

It was a warm day. By midday Nisha felt in need of a break, she stood and stretched her neck and back.

"I need a swim," she declared.

A few minutes later she had changed into her bikini and was powering up and down Alf's pool. They'd helped Mel into the wheelchair and pushed her onto the terrace and she was watching Nisha's sleek body in the water. Being sensitive to Mel's feelings, neither Jake nor Alf joined Nisha in the pool, but Steph did.

"Don't hold back on my account," Mel said, "it looks gorgeous in there. I'll be back in the water soon enough."

"I'm fine for now," Jake said, "and Alf's making the lunch. How are you doing today?"

"I'm glad to be out of that bed. I'm feeling OK, it's a bit painful now that I'm putting a bit of weight on my pelvis, but Steph says that's normal for the first few days. I'm going to try to wheel myself later; I've not used my right arm for weeks, but enough of that. Where did you find her?"

"Nisha? She's an Inspector in my department, but I'd never met her until a couple of weeks ago. She's a whizz on the internet. She told me she's a 'white hat hacker'."

"I've heard of them," Mel said, "not strictly legal, though, is it? Computer Misuse Act or something."

"That's right. She confessed all over a drink."

"Did you give her gin?"

"Now now," Jake said, but gently, "don't be like that. Nisha looked into an unusual blackmail, one without a demand for anything. You've heard of

Amelia Armstrong, the divorce lawyer? Well, someone broke into her computer system and copied lots of embarrassing stuff which they released to the press. The subject of the material was one of her clients, and it was all very salacious. Armstrong's as good as broke now, but she has told us that some other lawyers she knows received emails after her case went public, these ones did contain demands. Payments to named charities. We think one of the charities is controlled by the blackmailer."

"So why bring her here?"

"Because I think the blackmailer is Dido Sykes. I'm not sure why, it just has her smell about it. I told Nisha my thoughts, and about Sykes. In return Nisha admitted to me she hacks computers. If it is Sykes doing the blackmailing, we need to get into her communications system. With everything that's still flying around about Alf and the cases the three of us have worked on, I can't really do a regular investigation, especially as none of the blackmail victims have reported crimes to us. So, Mel, we're going to do it from here, just the four of us. You're going to help."

"I had a feeling that was coming."

Alf appeared from the house with a basket of fresh French bread and plates of charcuterie and cheeses. He set it on the table and went back for cold beers and water. At that moment Nisha and Steph emerged from the pool. Nisha was almost dwarfed by Steph, who was a lot taller and broader, but by no means fat. Steph had on a business-like black one-piece swimsuit, in contrast to Nisha's very small and racy orange and white bikini. They dried themselves; Steph went in to change but

Nisha took a seat on the terrace still wearing just her bikini. There was no disguising her curves, slender as she was. She seemed oblivious to the glances she was getting from the others. Nisha stretched her arms innocently above her head and lay back, eyes closed, facing the sun.

"This is a whole lot better than sitting on a bench in St James's Park with a scabby sandwich," she announced to no one in particular. "I think I like working for you, Jake."

"This is only day one, Nisha," Mel said, "you'll be eating your words by the time she's through."

"I'm great to work for," Jake said, "even Raj says so."

"Only because you keep threatening to send him to that police station at the opposite end of the District Line to where he lives," Mel retorted.

"There's something you need to know, Jake," Nisha said, "I was going to tell you earlier but you were busy with Mel."

"What's that?" Jake asked.

"Your work email - someone's reading it. I check mine out every day, and I did yours this morning too. Someone has found a way into the Met's email system - I can't say for certain whose accounts have been compromised, but yours definitely has. I went back a couple of weeks and checked for signs of dual log-ins. Until this morning your account was accessed every day around noon or in the early afternoon. Today it was accessed at 8am local time, that's 7am in London. I know it's not Raj because he's got official access to your email, and it's not one of the IT administrators. I'd go so far as to say it's no one internal at all. It's a hack."

"7am means it certainly isn't Raj," Jake said, "are you sure, Nisha?"

"Hundred percent. I'm going to go through the rest of your internal files later if it's OK with you. No one at the Yard will know; they don't know I can look at email access across the Met's system anyway. Not that I look at anyone else's."

"Can you see where the hacker is, Nisha?" Alf asked.

"Not yet. I started to do a trace but hit the usual dead ends, same as the blackmail emails. I mean the *same* dead ends, not similar ones. It's the blackmailer, Jake. She's reading your mail."

"Fucking Sykes!" said Mel.

"That's just what I said," Nisha agreed.

"Will she know I'm not in the office?" Jake asked.

"Possibly, probably. Have you used your Blackberry to access your email since we arrived here?"

"No."

"Good. Turn it off, just for now, and take the battery out."

"When we looked at her before," Mel said, "I tried to trace her email accounts, the ones she was using for the trafficking network. My Cheltenham mates and I got as far as north-east USA or lower Canada. That's a five- or six-hour time difference, isn't it? That fits with the midday / early afternoon access. It's when she'd be waking up."

"But if she's suddenly changed the timing," Jake said, "it could mean she's come here. To Europe."

"Fucking Sykes!" they said in unison.

"Let's think about this," Alf said, "if she *is* here, she's within our reach. And we have a way to talk to her."

"How?" Mel asked.

"Through Jake's email," he said. "We just need to work out what we want to say to her, and when."

"Then it's time for us to get sneaky too," Jake said.

"Goody," said Nisha, "can we have lunch first? I love French cheese."

Chapter 25

They started the following morning. Mel had joined them the evening before, the first time she'd been out of bed for a meal in weeks.

"Grown up food!" she said. "Booze too."

Despite her brave face and banter, Mel was feeling her injuries and found eating difficult. She barely touched her glass of wine. She asked Tracey to help her get ready for bed almost as soon as the sun went down.

At breakfast she seemed better, and the four of them (Steph and Tracey had gone out) started to discuss their options.

"First thing," Alf said, "is to find her. Mel traced her email trail back towards North America a few months ago, now we have a hint she might be in Europe."

"I had a look at the current crop of blackmail communications," Nisha said. "North America, rather Canada, does come into it, but it doesn't stop there. The dozen or so emails I've got aren't enough to be definitive - sure all of them are routed eventually through Canada, but I've got one or two which seem to go further. Back towards Europe, specifically Switzerland. It's a very complicated routing, and with such a small number of email trails to look at I'm doing a lot of guessing."

"But" said Mel, "sooner or later all the emails must get back to her, or to a server she can access at will. How hard is it to set up this sort of thing?"

"Bloody tricky," said Nisha, "she'd need to have a reliable chain of hacked servers and all sorts along the way. At any stage losing one link in the chain would stop everything dead."

"So, is she getting some help?" Jake asked.

"It's possible, but not essential. She could just be relying on unscrupulous service providers - and there are quite a few of those - who can give her the facilities she wants with no questions asked."

"And anywhere she's getting help, paid for or otherwise, we could have an opportunity," Alf commented.

"Got it in one," Jake said. "Now, while Nisha gets on with identifying the email chain, how can we find out where she is, even who she is at the moment?"

"She's a hacker, right?" Mel said. "Hackers need to keep up with each other or they get left behind. Things are changing and developing so quickly that the hackers need to tell each other about new defences and developments. They must talk to each other."

"They do," Nisha said, "we do. Online, on the dark web, and face to face. The really tight stuff is kept for face to face."

"How does that work?" Jake asked.

"Usually under the cover of a techie conference, you know, computer gamers and IT people, people like that who get together to push each other's buttons. They happen all the time. Most of us on the hacking side can't be bothered with the mainstream, but we have to use gatherings as cover. We know that a lot of people are after us."

"Even the white hats?" Mel asked.

"Especially them, us." Nisha said.

"So, how do you get to know about the meetings?" Alf asked.

"The conferences are advertised," Nisha said, "the sidebar meetings are arranged between us using our own communication channels. I've been having a look; some of the bad boys I keep tabs on are talking about a gig next weekend in Lyon - a low key games development conference at the university. It's not one of the flashy exhibitions, no sponsors or anything - just a bunch of grungy techie types."

"Sounds like fun," Jake said, "are you going?"

"I hadn't planned to, but I could. Do you want me to?"

"Let's talk it through," Alf suggested, "no point in doing anything unnecessary, there has to be a benefit. If Sykes is going Nisha should go, but we need to know. Do hackers have online identities, Nisha?"

"Of course," she said, "no one uses their own name. People know me as Tonto."

"Why?" Jake asked.

"Because I'm a bit nuts, and I always tell people I'm treated like the Indian sidekick where I work. I don't tell anyone where I do work, obviously."

"So, she might have heard of you, as Tonto?" Jake asked.

"Possibly. I'm quite famous, relatively speaking."

"How do you find out what other people are called?" Mel asked.

"They tell you; you don't ask. If you know someone's online handle, it's assumed they've told you."

"How could we find out what Sykes's hacker name is?" Alf asked.

"Don't know," Nisha said.

"Why don't we ask some of your mates?" Mel asked, "show them a picture and ask if they know her?"

"You mean do it the old-fashioned way? That's brilliant!" Nisha said. "Have we got a picture of her?"

"I have," Mel said, "on my laptop. You did bring it, didn't you, Jake?"

"Yes. It's in my bag in the room. I'll fetch it."

Ten minutes later Nisha had doctored Dido Sykes's image from one of the surveillance photographs Mel had kept on her machine. She made her a bit more downmarket, cropping out the designer clothes and messing the hair up a bit. She also made copies with different hair colours, one blonde-ish, another ginger."

"Hair and clothes like hers would stick out a mile at one of the hacking dos. Everyone looks like a sack of something, even if they're rolling in it. Some hackers make a lot of money, but they never let it show. I'll send this round and see if any of my closest group know her."

"OK," said Jake, "so now we wait while Nisha does her thing. I'll put the coffee on."

******

With nothing much to do while Nisha was doing whatever she was doing, and Mel being worked on by Steph and Tracey, Jake and Alf went for a leisurely swim. After ten minutes they both leant back against the side of the pool, close to each other.

"I could get used to this, Ferdinand," Jake said.

"I could get used to your company too," he replied.

"And everything else. Maybe we should just pack it all in and stay here, like this."

"You're not serious?" he asked.

"A bit. Since Mel got hurt I've been thinking."

"She didn't just get hurt, someone tried to kill her, twice. We can't stand aside and let that go, and we haven't done what we've done just to live comfortably off the money."

"Don't be angry with me, Alf. I know we need to see this through, not just for Mel but because it's the right thing to do. I'm just feeling a bit beaten up; I'm not used to playing catch up to someone like Dido Sykes."

"We'll get on the front foot soon, Jake. We just need to get a break, then we can do something. Let's go in."

Back in their shared space they showered and made love to each other. As they lay together afterwards their peace was shattered by pounding on the door.

"I've got something, Jake!" shouted Nisha, "put him down and meet me on the terrace!"

"You wouldn't think she was only an Inspector, would you?" Alf commented.

"She's certainly different from how they were when I was one. Come on."

Nisha and Mel were deep in conversation on the terrace when Alf and Jake arrived, Jake still a little pink from her exertions.

"Sorry to spoil your fun, but I've got her online name," Nisha said. "One of my geeky lot has seen her at a gig in the States. She's quite a big deal, apparently, but very stand-offish. She uses the name 'Leah'; and is always with a guy known as Sammy who follows her round like a poodle. I know Sammy. He lives in Vancouver."

Chapter 26

The plan started coming together. Now they had a name, Leah, Nisha was able to track back across dark web posts about hacker gatherings. She found that Leah had been to one about every three months, usually in the US or Canada. The man 'Sammy' had also been at every one she had attended. Sammy had been quite easy to identify. His name really *was* Sammy, and Nisha had been accessing archived flight manifests for flights between Vancouver and San Francisco for the dates of the most recent gathering that she could find where both Leah and Sammy had been present. She found Sammy, real name Samuel R Lubeck, US passport holder, travelling economy on an Air Canada flight both ways. Nisha compared the outbound and inbound manifests for Sammy's flights and found only one other name that appeared on both. Marianne Desbois, Canadian passport, who had booked separately from Sammy and had travelled from Montreal to Vancouver to connect with the San Francisco flight. She had returned the same way after the conference.

"I think she might be using the name Marianne Desbois," said Nisha, "but I could be wrong. Give me a few minutes and I'll check Desbois out."

"Marianne Desbois?" Jake said, "in the French version of Robin Hood his name is Robin Desbois, Robin of the forests, and she's calling herself Marianne. As in Maid Marian but using Robin's surname. She sees herself as a female Robin Hood."

"That explains the money in the blackmails," Nisha said, "she's given most of what she made to charity and only kept a few million for herself. Taking from the rich and giving some of it to the poor. Very noble. I've found her - I've got into the Canadian passport office records, here's her passport application. The photo is her, but with short brown hair. There's an address in Montreal."

"Look at Air Canada flights to Europe, out of Montreal first then out of Toronto," Jake suggested.

"Got her," Nisha said after a while. "First class open return Montreal to Zurich last week. There aren't that many direct flights to Europe from Montreal so I guessed she might be heading for Switzerland and checked those first. I'll do some digging to see if I can find her. The Swiss are totally secretive, apart from when they're not. They publish lists of who owns every vehicle and who lives in every property in the whole country, even if it's only a short-term rental. And they keep lists of every hotel guest which they collate in Bern. I love the Swiss!"

Nisha went off to her den and closed the door.

"Need to concentrate," she shouted over her shoulder, "I need coffee. And cake."

"She's good," said Mel, "it would have taken me much longer."

"I'll go get her fuel," said Jake.

An hour later they had it. Marianne Desbois, aka Dido Sykes, had taken a private jet from Zurich to Geneva. She'd paid by credit card. There were no vehicles registered in her name, but she was listed at a property in the Canton of Vaud, a substantial house near the shore of Lake Geneva near the village of Coppet. Alongside her name were those of Hervé and

Matilde Grossman, Swiss nationals. Nisha had written down the address.

"The address has three vehicles registered to it, owned by a limited company called Eris SA," Nisha said.

"Eris is another Greek goddess," Mel said, "the goddess of discord and strife. It's her alright."

"I'm looking for any bank accounts for Desbois and Eris," said Nisha, "but it's proving to be quite tricky. Money is a touchy subject in Switzerland and the bank systems are very good. The only way I'm going to get into her accounts is by her giving us the numbers and passwords."

"And she isn't going to tell us, is she?" Mel asked.

"Not knowingly," said Nisha, "but I'll bet she keeps a close eye on her money. I need to take a look at her house. Can we go tomorrow, Alf?"

"We can, but why?" he asked.

"I want to see what communications she has; if she's got a self-contained set up or if she uses the public phone system. I need to get into her communications, and I want someone to watch my back while I'm doing it. Does she know what you look like?"

"We've met, we've spoken, so probably. I did look a bit different then."

"We can give him a going over, can't we girls?" Nisha said. "Make it so even we won't recognise him."

"I'm not liking the sound of this at all," he said, as the women laughed.

Early next morning Alf and Nisha set off in his ancient Peugeot. Nisha was her usual morning self and didn't speak until they stopped for coffee near La

Souterraine. They sat opposite each other at a table in a roadside café.

"What do you think of your new look, Alf?" she asked.

"It'll grow back," he muttered.

"Why do they call you Alf?"

"It's just a name, nothing special."

"But your real name isn't Piet Kuyper, is it?"

"It is for now. Look, Nisha, I'm really not in the mood for the questions just now. Nothing personal, but let's just focus on what we're doing."

Nisha wasn't deterred.

"When I joined Specialist Crime I heard about Julia Kelso's big corruption case - the one where the Director General of the National Crime Squad and the head of CIB went to prison. All kinds of organised crime groups got wiped out. I was interested and read the case files, the ones I could get hold of, that is. Some are still locked away, and Jake has very wisely kept a lot of stuff off the computer system. I came across a name, a Detective Chief Inspector called Ferdinand who died. It's you, isn't it? You're Alan Ferdinand. You're dead."

"I don't look dead, do I? Alan Ferdinand is dead, he died at Beachy Head, like it says in the files. Now let's leave it."

"OK, Alf, if you say so. But I'm going to want the full story, from you or Jake or Mel, because you need me if you're going to get Dido Sykes, and I need to know I'm working with the good guys or I'm going home."

"Jake was right about you. You're really not a morning person, are you?"

"I'm serious, Alf. I'm sticking my neck out a long way already. You know I break the law for the right reasons, I need to know that you're doing it for the right reasons too."

"We'll talk to you about it when we get back, just not now. But believe me, we're doing it for the right reasons too. You haven't known us for long, but you must trust Jake to some extent, otherwise you wouldn't be here."

"True enough. I want to trust her, trust all of you. You need to trust me too. Can we do that?"

"Yes, we have to. Let's go, we've a long way ahead of us."

The next hundred kilometres passed in reflective silence. Nisha fiddled with the radio, trying to get some pop music or anything to ease the tension in the car. She was dying to ask about the relationship between Alf and Jake and Mel, but knew it wasn't the time.

"I'm sorry, Alf," she said eventually, "I didn't mean to be nosy, but it's in my nature. And I'm not that tactful sometimes. What's the plan, for later, I mean?"

"It's going to be late afternoon by the time we get there. If there's movement at the house the most likely times are late afternoon and early evening, and in the morning. We'll scout the area, see if we can keep a quiet eye on what's happening. You look for what you need, I'll look at the people and any defences or security."

"Are you planning to go in?"

"I'm not planning anything, just gathering information for when we need it."

"We'll need to stay the night, then," she stated, "so we'd best agree a story for the hotel or wherever. Am I your girlfriend or your niece or what?"

"We're a couple or we're work colleagues. If we're going up against Dido Sykes I don't want you to be in a room on your own, so maybe I should be your sugar daddy."

"What, in this old car? I can do better than that for myself, thank you."

"Don't worry, you'll be safe - from me anyway. But don't underestimate Sykes; she's vicious and nasty, and she may have vicious nasty friends too."

"I've only got my own passport with me. So, I'm Tanisha, and you're Piet, my Belgian boyfriend who's probably nearly twice my age. We're on our way back from Italy where we've been on holiday. I work in IT, you're an architect, hence the crappy car. There."

"That'll do, but don't volunteer anything. Don't speak French, just English. I doubt the hotel staff will be too curious. We'll just find a cheap motel near the autoroute."

"You old romantic. I'm going to close my eyes for a bit. Do you mind?"

"Not at all, carry on."

Nisha reclined her seat and closed her eyes. She was asleep in no time. Alf glanced down at her pretty, sleeping face. He liked the girl, but he really didn't know how far he trusted her.

******

They crossed the border into Switzerland near Geneva airport; there were only cursory checks. Alf showed his Belgian ID card and Nisha's British passport to a border guard who just looked at them and gave them back. After buying the *vignette* for the Swiss motorway system they drove on and pulled off the autoroute as soon as they were clear of Geneva. They followed the old road closer to the lake and were soon approaching the small town of Coppet. Nisha had printed off a map of the area and marked the house, which they found easily. Luckily, there were a few cars parked in the street outside, mostly of a similar style to Alf's - vehicles belonging to gardeners and tradesmen working in the grand lakeside houses. They pulled in at an empty parking bay and waited. They sat for ten minutes. No one approached them or showed any interest. The street was quiet, with very little passing traffic. They could see the tall steel gate of Marianne Desbois's house; it remained shut. Nisha got out of the car and strolled down the street, passing in front of the gate. Alf had noticed the security cameras but hadn't seen any sign of guards. Nisha kept walking, not showing any interest in the premises. She's good, Alf thought.

Nisha was gone for a good twenty minutes. She reappeared from behind the car.

"Nice house," she said, "got a pool in the front garden, we're at the back, I think. There's no vehicle access on the other side, and the garden goes right down to the lake. I've seen a satellite antenna as well as a landline going in, which is a bugger. I need to find out which one she's using most."

"How are you going to do that?" he asked.

"I've got a gadget in my bag, but we need to go somewhere private to set it up. It can pick up satellite traffic, but only at quite close range, like from where we are now. If she's using satellite, my gadget will show me. If there's no traffic, it means she uses the landline and public telephone network. Thing is, we don't even know if she's there."

"Let's give it a bit longer, see if there's movement. Then we'll find a hotel and you can set your stuff up."

"Make it within walking distance if possible. I'd like to set the kit running in the car and leave it here tonight. The battery on the gadget should last a good ten hours."

Just as they were about to leave a large Mercedes saloon came down the road. The gates to the Desbois property slowly swung open and the car drove in. It had blacked-out windows and they couldn't see if anyone was in the back.

"It's one of the cars registered to that Eris company. Let's go, at least we know there's someone there."

They found a motel just outside Coppet, no more than a fifteen-minute walk from the Desbois house. A room was available, and Alf carried two of their bags up. Nisha took her own computer bag. It took her around twenty minutes to sort her kit out and make sure the battery was fully charged. Then they both went back to the car. Nisha put a short, slim aerial on the rear parcel shelf. It was attached to a small box, which was in turn plugged into a laptop computer. Nisha set it up, turned off the laptop screen and put the laptop in the rear footwell. The box was on the back seat. She covered it with a travel rug. As an afterthought, she stuck a tiny camera with a wide-angle lens onto a side window. She plugged its lead into the laptop.

"It takes a shot every two minutes," she explained, "just make sure it's pointed at the gate. Bring back something to eat, please. Darling!" She kissed him playfully, just for show.

Alf drove back to the Desbois house. Their space was still empty, so he parked as before. He got out, and before locking the doors he placed a handwritten sign in the front window with the words *'En Panne'* - broken down.

He walked back to the motel, stopping at a convenience store on the way to buy sandwiches and beer.

"Good, I'm starving," Nisha said.

She was already in bed, sitting up wearing a tee shirt.

"I've had a shower, I really needed it. Your car's awful sticky in this heat."

"Sorry about that," he said.

"No you're not. I'll have the chicken salad sandwich and one of those cold beers."

He sat at a small table and ate, she stayed in the bed. There was only one.

After their frugal meal he took a shower. When he came out of the bathroom he was wearing his boxers and a tee shirt. There was a moment's tense silence.

"You don't mind if I'm on this side, do you?" Nisha asked. "I can move over if you want."

"I thought I'd be sleeping on the floor," he said.

"That would be silly, after all the driving and with more to do tomorrow you need proper sleep. And I'm not sleeping on a floor for anyone, not again. I did that enough at uni. We're both grown-ups, aren't we?"

"Fine with me. I'm bushed," he said, sliding in beside Nisha.

"Just going to clean my teeth," she said.

He watched her as she got out of the bed. She seemed completely unaware of her body and its effect on people; her tee shirt wasn't short but barely covered her bottom. She had no underwear on. He glimpsed her buttocks as she walked across the room. She was in the bathroom for just a few minutes and smelt freshly of toothpaste and face cream when she came out. As she walked back across the bedroom her dark pubes flashed in and out of view, again she seemed to neither know nor care. Her firm legs were dark brown, her thighs well-shaped. Her nipples were clearly visible through the fabric of her tee shirt. Alf turned on his side to face away from her as he felt himself becoming aroused. He felt her weight as she got into bed.

"Are we going to do the deep cover thing? You know, have sex? To make it look real."

"I wasn't planning on it," Alf said.

"We can if you want, I don't mind."

"No, you're alright, but thanks all the same. I'm shattered, and it wouldn't be a good idea anyway."

"Suit yourself. But if you change your mind in the night just be sure to wake me up first. And use a condom - there are some in my washbag."

"Just leave it, Nisha. Let's get some sleep."

"OK. Goodnight, Alf," she said, "just hit me if I snore."

"Goodnight, Nisha. Likewise."

He turned the light out.

Chapter 27

Nisha was asleep in moments, while Alf lay awake in the darkness thinking about the young woman lying next to him. He wondered what Jake had been thinking when she brought Nisha along, brought her into their private world and exposed their vulnerabilities. He wasn't just concerned for himself, he was also concerned for Jake and Mel, Jake especially. If Nisha were to voice her suspicions that the late Alan Ferdinand was far from dead, and that not only was he alive he was also deeply involved with Commander Julia Kelso, they could both be facing long prison sentences. He rolled onto his back and looked across at Nisha's sleeping face, innocent and relaxed. That she was half-naked in bed with him, a virtual stranger, was a puzzle in itself, even in the absence of any sexual activity. Was she that trusting, or was she so naïve that she didn't realise the implications of what she was doing or saying? Eventually his eyes closed, but his sleep was invaded by dreams of Jake in jail.

As daylight came, she shook him gently.

"I've made you some tea," she said, "we need to get going. You seemed to have had a rough night, tossing and turning and moaning a lot. Are you OK?"

He opened his eyes wearily.

"Just bad dreams. Did you sleep alright?"

Nisha was sitting on the bed with one leg tucked under her bottom. She was still in the tee shirt but seemed completely unaware that she was exposing herself to him.

"Weird dreams too, but not that bad. I can sleep anywhere, apparently. It's the mornings that are my problem. I'm surprised I'm so chirpy today."

"Can I ask you something?" Alf said.

"Sure," Nisha replied.

"Would it make a difference to you if I was Alan Ferdinand?"

"Don't follow," she said.

"You don't know what that would mean?"

"It could mean that you and Jake would be in a whole lot of trouble, obviously, unless it's all legit and just some super-secret double-bluffing. Look, Alf, I may be a bit gauche and geeky, but I'm not dim. And if you're going to ask me what I'm going to do about you being Alan Ferdinand, if that's who you are, the answer is nothing. I don't really know you, but I've spent quite a few hours alone with Jake Kelso - I know her better than she thinks I do. I trust her, but she's very vulnerable right now and she needs my help. I wouldn't do anything to hurt her. Now, I need a pee."

Nisha stood up, once again showing herself to Alf.

"Sorry," she said, noticing his look, "I've been told I'm an inveterate flasher. It's not deliberate, I just don't think about it."

He groaned and lay back on his pillow.

An hour later they walked cautiously towards his old Peugeot, still parked near the Desbois house. It had a parking ticket on it but was otherwise undisturbed. There were no signs of movement or interest in them or the car. Alf unlocked it and opened the bonnet. He quickly replaced the distributor cap lead, and after two attempts the car started. Nisha got in, and they drove off. Once clear of the house and neighbourhood they pulled over. She got into the back and checked her equipment.

"It seems OK, but I need to have a proper look. Let's go back to the hotel."

Back in the room she busied herself while Alf watched her. Her fingers flew across the laptop keyboard and her forehead was creased with concentration.

"Right," she announced eventually, "she's using satellite, and she's not using Tempest precautions, which is mad."

"What are Tempest precautions?" he asked.

"Tempest is a sort of codeword but also an acronym. I can't remember exactly what it stands for, but essentially it's about electronic and electromagnetic emissions. If communication channels aren't shielded a nosy person like me or the NSA or anyone with the right equipment can listen in by hoovering up the leaky emissions. I think I've collected enough data overnight with the kit in the car to get into her email, which I can do back at base. If not, we may have to come back and try to work out a longer-term collection strategy. We can't keep parking your beaten-up Peugeot outside her house."

Nisha started packing up her stuff. Alf packed his own small overnight bag. Shortly after 10 in the morning they'd checked out and were back on the road. They took one last pass in front of the Desbois house and were rewarded by another glimpse of the big Mercedes emerging from the gates. This time Alf was able to see the profile of the back-seat passenger through an open window. Although she was now peroxide blonde, he had no doubt that it was Dido

Sykes, aka Marianne Desbois. Alf allowed himself a smile.

"Nisha, I could kiss you!" he said.

"If you want to do that you should have done it last night when you had the chance. Too late now, but why?"

"That was Dido Sykes, in the back of the Mercedes, I'm positive. We're on to her."

"Game on then," Nisha said. "I've peaked. Wake me up when it's lunchtime."

Alf pointed the Peugeot towards France while Nisha reclined her seat and fell asleep.

******

It was early evening by the time they got to the house near Poitiers. Nisha locked herself away in her den of wizardry while Alf filled Jake and Mel in.

"Marianne Desbois is definitely Dido Sykes," he started. "The house near Coppet is where she's currently holed up; I saw her. Nisha, who is very strange by the way, deployed some of her gadgets and we left the car by the Desbois house last night. Nisha reckons she's collected enough leaked emissions, I know - it sounds awful - to break into her email traffic. That's what she's doing now. If she can't, we'll have to go back and have another go."

"Great stuff," said Jake, "but why is she strange?"

"It's just everything she says and does. I'll tell you later. But you do both need to know she's worked out who I am."

"What?" Mel said.

"Ferdinand, she knows I'm Alan Ferdinand."

"How did that happen?" Mel asked.

"She fronted me in the car. I blanked her, but she's guessed and convinced herself. This morning I asked her what she'd do if I was Ferdinand. I asked if she understood what it would mean. She does, and she says she won't tell anyone. She wouldn't want to hurt Jake. She also said that Jake is vulnerable and needs her help."

"Do you believe her?" Mel asked. Jake was sitting still, pale and silent.

"I don't know. I don't think we've got a choice for now. I think we have to take her at face value. At least here we've some control over her."

"While she's shut away with her computers and gadgets we've no control at all," Jake said, "but I agree with Alf. We don't have a choice. If she decides to blow the whistle, we'll have to deal with it when the time comes."

"You do know what that means, don't you Jake?" Mel said.

Jake nodded and reached out for Alf's hand, then with her other hand she took Mel's.

"Do you want me to talk to her when we're alone," Mel said, "fruitcake to fruitcake?"

"That would be helpful, I think," said Jake, "try to find out what she's really thinking about us."

At that moment Nisha appeared on the terrace grinning from ear to ear.

"I'm in!" she shouted. "We can read her traffic! I need beer."

Chapter 28

The next morning Jake spent an hour in the pool, swimming rhythmically up and down on her own. She was thinking. Alf and Mel sat together on the terrace talking quietly. Mel's wheelchair was under a parasol; they were both eating croissants brought by Steph from the village bakery and drinking far too much coffee.

"What do you reckon, Mel?" Alf asked. "What do you think she'll come up with?"

"Something quite sneaky, I suspect," Mel said, "but probably more subtle than anything you'd think of. You'd just want to shoot her."

"You have such a high opinion of me, Miss Dunn."

"Even if you didn't *want* to shoot her, you'd probably end up doing it anyway. That's what usually happens."

"It's always self-defence, well nearly always. What would you do?"

"I'd find out what she's been up to and work out a way to tell the Feds," Mel said, "wherever she'd get the toughest sentence. But that wouldn't work because I know coppers and they're all the same. They start off disbelieving everything, then they give their informants a hard time, then they start an investigation that goes on forever until everyone's gone gaga or died of old age. I would like Sykes to go to jail, and not just for what she's done to me - although I am *very* pissed off with her about that."

"We'll make her pay, Mel," Alf said, "but like you say it's got to be quick; we can't give her a chance to go to ground again. I doubt we'd find her so easily next time round, if there is a next time. Have you seen Nisha this morning?"

"No, but I know she was up nearly all night, I heard her. I don't sleep so well at the moment. Not enough stimulation - I can feel my brain turning to porridge."

With that, Jake emerged from the pool and took a seat on the terrace, not bothering to dry herself.

"Look at you, Kelso," Mel said, "all dripping wet and goose-bumpy."

"Good morning Dunn," Jake said, "I can't wait until you're well enough to get thrown in the pool."

"Have you thought of anything?" Alf asked.

"Yes, but we need Nisha to tell us if it'll work. Is she up yet?"

"I'll go and see," Alf said.

"Have you had your chat with her, Mel?" Jake asked.

"Not yet, I'll do it later while we're working on Dido's stuff. I'll choose my moment," Mel said.

Alf went upstairs to Nisha's room. He knocked, but there was no answer. The door wasn't locked, and he opened it quietly. She was lying on the bed, on top of the covers, wearing a creased cotton shirt with buttons down the front, mostly undone. The shirt was gathered in a ruck just below her chest, leaving her naked from the navel down.

"Nisha," he called softly.

She stirred and opened one bleary eye. She saw him but made no attempt to cover herself.

"What do you want? I'm asleep," she said.

"We need you," he said, "on the terrace. We need to talk something through with you."

Nisha grunted, then got up and went to the bathroom. He heard her using the toilet, then a tap running as she cleaned her teeth. She emerged, still with one eye closed and in the same shirt. She waved him towards the door and followed him downstairs.

"What?" she said to Jake, scratching a buttock unselfconsciously.

"We need to talk a plan through. We need you to tell us if it's doable."

"Give me a minute," Nisha said.

She stumbled towards the pool and threw herself in. After splashing around for a few moments, she climbed up the stairs and came back to the terrace, the wet shirt still largely unbuttoned and clinging to her shapely body.

"That's a bit better," Nisha said, squeezing water from her long black hair and reaching for the coffee pot. She took one of the cane chairs and slumped in it, holding one knee to her chest.

"That's one way she's strange," Alf said.

"Am I flashing again?" Nisha asked. "Sorry."

She lowered her leg but did nothing about the see-through wet cotton sticking to every curve.

"Is it possible, Nisha, to set up email accounts for Alf and me and make it look like they've been in use for quite a while? Also, make the email accounts seem like they've been sent from internet cafés in different places?" Jake asked.

"Should be, but it wouldn't stand up to too much scrutiny. I can mess around a bit with geography, but time is tricky."

"Could you also delete an email from my work account and remove it completely from the Met's systems?"

"That depends on how long it's been there. If it's more than a few hours old it's unlikely without getting access to the physical back-up tapes, which I don't have, at least not from here. The email system backs up at least once a day, sometimes more depending on the level of traffic. What do you have in mind?"

"I want Alf, as Paulo Silva, to send me an email on my work account, then I want it deleted as soon as Sykes has seen it."

"OK. But it'll have to be sent around 6am our time. She reads your email around 7; if I can see when she's done it then I can wipe it and get rid of any traces before the system backs up. It's not 100 per cent safe, but usually the back-up happens around 2am London time. Weekends are quite quiet, so if you do your email at 6am on a Monday Sykes can see it and I should be able to get rid of it well before the next day's back-up. I'll check to make sure the schedules haven't changed since last week."

"And can you set up the other email accounts before next Monday?"

"Course, but you'd have to give me the emails you want in them. I'm assuming you want Sykes to go after these other accounts?"

"I do," said Jake.

"I'm with you so far," said Mel, "what next?"

"We entice Sykes to confront me, then I can find out what it is she's after. If she just wanted me dead, it could have happened in Crete, I'm sure of it. She may still want me dead, but she wants something else as well. So, we set up a conversation between me and Silva, culminating in a meeting somewhere of our choosing. She won't be able to resist that."

"And in the meantime?" Mel asked.

"You and Nisha get into her communications, as much as you can find. Get material which the Americans or Europol will go mad for. Copy it all. Also, Nisha can find out if Sykes is going to that hackers' gathering in Lyon? If she is, I think you should go too, see if you can get to know Sykes or Leah or whatever she's calling herself. Alf can watch your back if you'd like. Then we take stock before we entice Sykes to our meeting."

"The hackers' gig is next week. The timing works," Nisha said. "I was up late last night looking at Dido's system. I can't get into everything as I know sod all about Greek mythology and all her passwords seem to have something to do with all that."

"I can probably help you there," said Mel.

"Good, thanks," Nisha said. "I've got into her emails, though and I've seen enough to hazard a guess about how she works. I followed my hunch and it's exactly as I thought. Everything eventually comes back to one place, in this case a rented server in a data centre in the Philippines. She can access it any time she wants, so can I now. She's definitely behind the blackmail campaign, just as you said, Jake. Not just the law firms, but also some celebrities and a handful of the oil majors. Reading the traffic, I'd say it's a fair bet she set off that disaster in Azerbaijan, you know - the oil well that's still on fire. I think she did it to encourage a few other oil companies to comply with her demands - there's evidence that they've paid up big time. I haven't got the smoking gun yet - the coded instruction she would have sent to a process control system to cause a catastrophic malfunction. It'll be hidden in her computer somewhere, probably on one in the Desbois house in Switzerland."

"The FBI would love to know all about that," said Alf, "what else have you found?"

"I've found old email accounts. I think they relate to the people-trafficking case Jake told me about, the timing seems right. There are hundreds of them. Older stuff too. She must feel really confident that no one would be able to crack her system - I'd have expected her to dump all that as soon as she didn't need it anymore."

"I think she does feel confident," Jake said, "and she also wants to keep it all so she can look at it in her old age - a record of past achievements, her life's work. It's sad, really, to think of what she's achieved as a criminal and what she could have achieved if she wasn't one."

"What have we got on the charity she's using to channel money to herself?" Alf asked.

"We know just about everything," Nisha said, "it's registered in the Caymans and it's supposed to support turtle conservation or some such rubbish. The charity's bank account she used for payments from the blackmail victims, also in the Caymans, has been emptied though. It's going to be a mammoth task to try to trace the transfers, all of which have been remote and electronic, with large sums going to various other accounts. There'll be a long chain to break. I'm trying to get into Sykes's personal computer - I'd bet she's got the final bank destinations in there somewhere."

"Good luck. We need to know where her money is so it can be taken away from her, if not officially then by us. So, what's the end game, Jake?" Alf asked.

"Ultimately," Jake said, "I'd like her to face justice for what she's done, but I think it's going to be too difficult and take too long. Mostly I want to stop her being able to do this again - ever."

"It's not helpful, I know," said Nisha, "but once a person with her abilities gets into doing this sort of stuff they only stop when one of two things happens: one of those is a road to Damascus moment, which does happen more often than you'd think, but I'm always sceptical about how sincere the converted actually are; the second is they get killed. That also happens more than you'd think, especially when organised crime is involved. Someone who's whizzy on the net is usually no match for an angry bloke with a machete."

"I don't think she's going to do a Saint Paul," Jake said, "and I don't want to kill her or get her killed. So, we'll have to find a third way."

"Good luck with that," said Mel.

"Nisha, how can we be sure she's going to Lyon?" Alf asked.

"She'll need to make arrangements. She could just rock up at the main conference, but the backroom stuff needs prior notice. I'm looking at her deep- and dark-web access to see if she's doing any planning. I should get to know."

"Good. Let's get going. Alf and I have got emails to write. You two can go off to the coven and do whatever it is you do in there." Jake said. "Nisha, is that a new shirt?"

"Yes, why?"

"It's too small for you."

Nisha looked down. The shirt was indeed too small, and after its immersion was now riding up above her thighs and straining over her chest.

"Hmmph! It's all cold and clammy anyway," Nisha said, undoing the remaining buttons and shrugging off the wet shirt. She dropped it on the flagstones, leaving herself sitting naked, damp and mad-haired in the cane chair, oblivious to the looks of the others.

"What?" she said when she noticed, "it wasn't covering anything up anyway!"

"Are you two related?" Jake asked, her eyes flicking between Nisha and Mel, who was grinning widely as she passed Nisha a towel.

"What do you mean, related?" Nisha asked, dropping the towel in her lap.

"Let's go in," Mel said, "you can get dressed and I'll explain what she meant. Then you can show me your magic tricks."

Chapter 29

The next few days were eaten up by preparations for Jake's email episode. Now that Mel was mobile and a bit more independent, Steph and Tracey were using their down-time to work out, run and swim. They still took turns to attend to Mel overnight.

"She's doing well," Steph confided in Jake, but we're not home and dry yet. Her head injury was worse than you'd think looking at her now, and there's still a possibility of seizures, especially when she's in bed and her blood pressure is fluctuating. Her hip, arm and shoulder are pretty much OK; the pelvis is mending but it'll take a while yet before it's really stable and strong enough to bear regular weight. The leg breaks look like they're knitting nicely, judging by her last x-ray. We'll only really know when the plaster comes off in the next week or two. Point is, Jake, we all know she's a fighter and once her leg is out of plaster she's going to want to go for it. We need to restrain her gently until she gets some of her strength back. Tracey's agreed to stay another month before we decide if she goes."

"I don't know what we'd have done without the two of you, Steph," Jake said.

In the dining room, now completely overrun with computers and electronic boxes and modems, Mel and Nisha were working well together. Mel's methodical mind and her ability to see patterns and make sense of vast swathes of data complemented Nisha's instinctive skill in penetrating systems and bypassing security measures. By the end of the week, they had amassed several files of copied data, now safely stored on one of

Nisha's machines. Mel summoned Jake and Alf. Nisha was working away in a corner and took no part in the conversation.

"What we've got," she announced, "is a good intelligence trail showing Dido's material involvement in the people-trafficking thing we all know about, plus multiple blackmails dating back at least five years. She has three campaigns currently underway, again they're the ones we know about. We have the warning emails, and the ones she used to make examples of her chosen victims - including Amelia Armstrong, a celebrity designer / architect who killed himself in jail, and that major oil company with the big fire in Azerbaijan. It seems she's also hit that one with a major Foreign Corrupt Practices Act case alleging huge payments to the president of an African country where they operate, all of it seemingly made up. There are emails showing that she shorted stock in the company before the FCPA allegations were made, and in other oil companies just before the Azerbaijan well blow-out. She's made a packet.

"What's more, we've found personal files on her computer relating to her little helpers. You know, Drew Strathdon, Jasmira Shah and the others. It all confirms our, or rather Jake's, supposition as to how, why, when and where they were recruited by Sykes. There's also a list of potential helpers, and files on potential enemies. The three of us figure quite prominently in that one," Mel told Jake and Alf.

"What's she got on us?" Alf asked,

"On Paulo Silva, next to nothing. She does question whether he is in fact Alan Ferdinand, but that's really quite recent."

"On what basis?" he asked.

"I can't really see anything - seems like a good guess, but how would she know about Ferdinand anyway? I don't see anything that suggests she follows the goings-on in the Met Police that closely, with one exception."

"That being me, I assume," said Jake.

"Correct," said Mel, "she's had a good rummage through the Met's systems looking for you, Jake. All your personal details, home address, family, career history, commendations and awards - you do have an awful lot of those - and your appraisals. I'll save your blushes. Obviously, she got a lot from Strathdon about your early life in the land of the blue-painted warlords. There's also a bit of social tittle-tattle about who you meet, and where. It mentions St Ermin's. It hasn't got much about any friends, but it does say I'm your closest one. You're a sad woman, Kelso."

"OK," Jake said, "it's a myth, by the way."

"What is?"

"The blue paint. The Scots never did that."

"Was it just the freezing rain then, that made them look blue?"

"Shut up. Now, what's she got on you?"

"Not so much, but enough. She's got my university record, and details of the time I spent in the civil service before NCIS. I don't think she's tried too hard to get into the NCIS systems, or maybe she did and she found out the truth, which is they don't really have any. She's got my old address in Raynes Park, details of the car I used to own, my old bank account, but it's all out of date. I'm the only one with comments about sexuality, and that's mostly from university days too. It says I was promiscuous and undiscerning, which is a bit bloody much!"

"But you were," Jake said.

"That's not the point! It was self-discovery, that's all."

"If you want," Jake quipped.

"Does it say anything about what she intends to do with any of this?" Alf interrupted.

"Not that we've found yet. I've asked Nisha to search for contacts with the guy in Colorado, the one who arranges, or used to arrange, assassinations. And to see if there's any mention of the people who accepted the contract on us. Spike's sources said it's a Dutch or Norwegian couple - it would be good to know more than that, if only to give Alf something to chew on.

"Some good news is that Sykes is going to the hackers' gig in Lyon, and Nisha's booked herself in too. That's right, isn't it Nisha?"

"Sorry, what? I wasn't listening," Nisha answered.

"I was saying about Lyon," Mel said.

"Oh, right. Yes, she's going, and so am I. Thing is, I have to go as Tonto."

"Which means what?" Jake asked.

"I go in cover. I travel as Tonto would, from London to Paris on a coach, then bus to Lyon. It takes forever, but it is what it is. And in Lyon I'd get a room in the students' residences, the gig is at the university. It means I leave here for London tomorrow and start travelling to Lyon the day after to get there late on Friday. Going back the same way I won't get back here until Tuesday or Wednesday. Is that OK?"

"I guess it has to be," Alf said. "I'll give you a French mobile before you go so you can contact me. While you're travelling turn it on at least once every two hours. If we need to contact you, you'll see a text message with the word 'cassoulet' in it. If you see it, call the number you'll find in the address book. Either me or Jake will answer it."

"That's all a bit Smiley's People, isn't it?" Nisha said.

"It's good undercover practice," Alf said, "If you need help or to speak to us just call the number, any time."

"So, you won't be riding shotgun after all then?" Nisha asked.

"It's up to you. If you want one of us nearby, say so. If you think you'll be more comfortable knowing we're nowhere near and won't get in your way, that's fine too."

"OK," she said, "I've been to these things before and I'll know a few people there, I'm sure I'll be fine. I'll text you when I get to Paris, and again when I'm on the bus leaving Lyon on Monday morning. OK?"

"That's fine," said Jake.

The next morning Alf drove a typically taciturn Nisha to Poitiers station for the fast train to Paris to connect with the Eurostar to London. Nisha had a backpack for overnight things and a laptop bag, complete with a computer. The emergency phone was in the pocket of her denim jacket.

"Take care, stay safe, Nisha," Alf said, "see you next week. Don't forget the drill if there's trouble, or if you need any help or information."

"Thanks, Alf," she said.

Nisha absent-mindedly stretched up to kiss Alf on the cheek before walking off towards the platform. Alf had offered her enough Euro notes to see her through with some to spare; she accepted a third of what he offered.

"Tonto doesn't really do money," she said, "but thanks anyway."

Alf watched her as she walked away.

******

That night, after a quiet dinner with the three of them and Tracey and Steph, Alf said he wanted an early night. Jake followed him fifteen minutes later and found him already in bed. Jake undressed, showered and joined him between the sheets.

"What's wrong, Alf?" she asked, gently touching his cheek. "You've been very quiet this evening; what is it?"

"Just a strange feeling, you know, uneasy," he said, "I think I'm going to go to Lyon anyway, regardless of what Nisha wants. She won't know I'm there unless she needs to."

"If you want to, but it's her turf, Alf. She knows these people."

"She doesn't know Dido Sykes."

"True. And Sykes doesn't know her, at least there's nothing in anything that Mel and Nisha have found to suggest it. Are you OK with the email thing?"

"Yes, I think it'll work," Alf said. "I'm thinking we set the meet for Montreux, say a week on Wednesday or Thursday. It'll give us time to debrief Nisha, and it gives Mel more time to dig deep into what they've found. I'd like us to have a package ready to go to the Americans or Europol by the time we have the meet. If Dido shows up, we'll play it by ear, if she doesn't, we'll need to make sure she's still in Coppet. If she is, we can spring the trap on her there."

"Except we can't," Jake said, "everything we've got has been obtained unlawfully - at best it's intelligence. If we give it to anyone they'll have to turn it into evidence before they can do anything with it. Even if anyone could do it, it would take forever."

"You're right," Alf said, "by the time they've tried to track down the material and obtain it evidentially she'll be long gone."

"So we need to do it ourselves, one way or another. Take her out of the game. Changing the subject, can I ask you something?"

"Given where we are I wouldn't have thought you'd need to ask for permission," he said, before kissing her softly.

"Why don't you ever talk about your family, your life before all this?" she asked, trying to ignore his lips on her neck, but not quite succeeding.

"It was all a long time ago, Jake, not a happy part of my life."

"Where were you, in Belfast?"

"In the Shankill, not Shankill Road itself, but one of the backstreets. It could have been the moon or Mars; it wasn't like anywhere on real earth. None of the working-class areas in Belfast were. I knew the few streets either side of ours, and the way to school or to the local shop, but until I was about thirteen that was it. You know, for years I thought the Ardoyne was a body part. You only ever heard of it when someone was 'shot in the Ardoyne', and it was just up the road from us. It was a mean time, nasty. My mother was a lost soul, or maybe she'd sold it. No siblings. I prefer to put it all behind me, that's all."

Jake kissed him.

"You say a lot without words, you know that?" she said, "you could never talk me into bed with the words that come out of your mouth. You did it with the words you never said."

"I don't remember us having much of a say in it. Dunn told us to."

"So she did. Are you sorry?"

"What do you think?"

"I think you're moderately content with the situation."

He kissed her lips, then started moving down her body.

"I am too," she said.

Chapter 30

Alf was in Lyon late on Friday afternoon. He'd taken the fast train to Paris, the Metro from Montparnasse to the Gare de Lyon and boarded the TGV. Arriving at the Gare Part Dieu, a few hundred metres from the university campus, he had time to get his bearings and check into the convenient Ibis hotel he'd booked. On a warm summer afternoon the university quarter was quiet, the regular students having long since departed for the summer break. He strolled through the campus looking for signs indicating where the computer gaming conference was being held. He found it with some difficulty, and got to see a handful of youngish people, all wearing grungy clothing and smoking roll-up cigarettes, busily erecting banners and posters and setting up screens in a medium-sized auditorium. As he passed a desk he saw a pile of papers, copies of the main conference attendance list which would be freely distributed to all attendees who wanted one. He picked one up as he passed and slipped it into a pocket.

He went back towards his hotel, finding a neighbourhood bistro on the way. He had an early supper with half a bottle of decent Burgundy, followed by a large whisky or two. In his room he turned the air-conditioning on full and took a long shower. Jake Kelso's well-meant and very enthusiastic attention the night before had left him tender in parts. What had got into her, he asked himself? Since that first time a year or so ago, in Mel's one-bed flat in Raynes Park, Julia Kelso had become ever more adventurous and voracious in bed, pushing him almost to the edge of his comfort zone. Of the three of them, he felt quite rightly that he was the least experienced sexually. Learning was good, though.

He lay in bed trying to get to the root of his unease. He couldn't quite get there, but it had started after Mel's account of the material she and Nisha had found. It didn't come, so he watched incomprehensible French TV until his eyelids drooped and he slept.

Around noon on Saturday he walked back towards the university campus. People were coming and going in dribs and drabs, so he found a pavement café with a view of the main entrance and spent a good while over a light lunch. At one time he glimpsed Nisha near the entrance, speaking intensely into a phone. She looked stressed. He surreptitiously checked the emergency phone in his pocket, but there were no messages or missed calls. When he looked up Nisha had gone. By 3pm he felt he couldn't linger any further. He paid his bill and took a casual stroll to his next previously identified vantage point, this one a shady bench inside the campus grounds - one of several he'd seen being used by local residents who were clearly neither students nor computer game developers. He had a paperback in his pocket, a French one, which he held loosely in his hand. He had to remember to turn a page every now and then as he pretended to read. He started to notice more of the techie types, people who tried to look like normal students but didn't quite manage it. Around 5pm he saw her.

Dido Sykes, alias Marianne Desbois and who knew what else, was wearing frayed cut down shorts showing off her tanned and toned legs, and a tee shirt. She had a backpack on, and a pullover tied around her waist. Her hair was no longer blonde, but an indeterminate light brown, cut around shoulder length. She's in good shape, Alf thought. Unlike many of the others he had seen, she had no obvious tattoos, torn tights or facial piercings. She seemed relaxed and at home. She paused, about 60 metres from him, to take a phone call. She hardly spoke; her expression remained the same, relaxed and neutral. She didn't look in his direction. It was only after she'd ended the call that a subtle smile flitted across her face, then she was gone.

So, they were both here. There was nothing more he could do but wait, and tomorrow he'd come back and watch and wait some more. Nisha had said the main conference would break up around four or five, but the hackers would stay on for another couple of hours.

******

The chair of the conference took charge of the proceedings as if it were a session of parliament. Nisha stifled a yawn. Her French was OK but not great. She'd chosen a seat mid-way down the auditorium but on the end of a row. The first speaker was introduced to demonstrate his latest iteration of a hugely popular and commercially successful game that featured zombies and racing cars. He spoke in American-accented English. Nisha was mildly interested, but after a while she stood up and leant against the wall for a stretch, as several others were doing. She looked around the hall. Dido Sykes was towards the back, also leaning on a side wall. She was alone, her eyes methodically scanning each row before turning her attention to people standing round the edges. Her eyes held

Nisha's for a second before moving on. Dido slowly moved from the back to the opposite side of the hall and started making her way towards the front. She was examining faces now, having already scanned backs and postures and hairstyles. Her eyes met Nisha's again and held them for a little longer. Nisha gave a brief involuntary smile and got one back from Dido.

The presentations went on and on. After the successful game developer there was a session on spotting and rectifying common glitches and coding errors, and on methodical product testing. This time Nisha couldn't suppress the yawn. A voiced to her left startled her.

"It is, isn't it?" the voice was soft, the accent sort of but not really American.

"Sorry?" Nisha said.

"Ball-breakingly boring. Do you want to get a drink?"

"Sure," Nisha said to Dido Sykes.

Outside the hall they paused.

"I'm Tonto," Nisha said, "I'm here for the after-party."

"Me too. I'm Poena."

"Pina?"

"P O E N A, but it's pronounced Pina. Have you come far?"

"London. You?"

"I'm from Canada, but I'm in Europe for the summer. I haven't seen you at one of these before. I mainly do the West Coast ones."

"I stick to Europe, and a few East Coast. What are your interests?"

"All sorts. I spent some time at Harvard when the net was growing up, now it's an unruly wayward teenager I'm interested in seeing what it gets up to. So, my interests are pretty general, but across all aspects of the after-party discussions."

"I'm a latecomer," Tonto said, "I started getting into it just for a living, writing code, programming, ironing out problems for people. Now it's a bit deeper than that, in more ways than one."

"Would I have heard of your work?" Poena asked.

"You've probably seen it, but I'm quite shy. For now."

"It's a good way to be. Here's a bar, what would you like?"

"Just a beer, thanks."

Poena ordered a draft beer and a green tea. Her accent puzzled the waiter momentarily, but her stern glance dissuaded him from the usual insults that proper French people like to throw at speakers of Canadian French.

"Are you staying in the student residence?" Tonto asked.

"Afraid so. It's a bit rough, but it's only a couple of nights. I'm glad I'm not here all year round."

"It's a bit better than my digs were at uni. My hall was worse than this, then after the first year we got kicked out by the college and had to get private rented accommodation. Brutal! What was Harvard like?"

"I wasn't a student; I was working there and I had an apartment in Boston. It was an interesting time, though."

"I'd like to hear all about it."

"Maybe one day."

Tonto had finished her beer.

"Fancy another?" she asked Poena.

"I'll have a rye whisky; the tea is foul. It must be the water."

The drinks arrived. Poena and Tonto were getting into deeper conversation and neither seemed to notice the nondescript man with very short hair stroll past the bar on the opposite side of the street. The women clinked glasses and toasted each other. An hour and two more drinks later Poena announced that they'd better go. They walked swiftly back to the campus and found the 'after-party', the hackers' gig. The nondescript man opposite the bar was no longer there.

******

Sunday followed pretty much the same pattern as Saturday. Poena and Tonto signed in for the main conference but left after opening speeches to go in search of lunch. They walked close together, talking earnestly to each other. The Saturday hackers' gig had revealed some interesting developments for both the hacking and the anti-hacking communities, not that the two were properly segregated. As always, smart hackers like Poena and Tonto quickly saw ways through new protective developments or had enough of an idea to know how and where to start building new attack vectors. Poena and Tonto were deeply engrossed, and had their conversation been overheard it is unlikely that anyone other than another hacker would know what on earth they were talking about.

Poena skipped the green tea and went straight to rye whisky, a Canadian one. Tonto joined her after one beer.

"Too fizzy and tasteless," Tonto gave her verdict on French draught beer.

"Canadian Club is neither of those things," Poena said. "*Santé*."

******

A little after 7am on Monday Tonto let herself quietly out of Poena's room, which was on the same corridor as hers in the students' residence. Despite the hour, she was neither sleepy nor grumpy. She hefted her backpack and set off at a determined pace for the bus depot near the Part Dieu station. Time to get back to the others. Alf followed her at a safe distance, having first checked that no one else was doing the same. He was surprised at Nisha's attitude having experienced her usual morning moods a few times. He wondered briefly and chauvinistically if she had maybe got lucky the night before. Maybe geeks are good at it, he thought.

In her room, Poena stretched in her dishevelled bed. Her clothes were rumpled on the floor, her hair lying on the desk like a small, eviscerated mammal. Tonto had gone. All was well, it had been a good weekend. Her train back to Geneva left at noon, so plenty of time for another nap. It had been quite a long night.

Chapter 31

Alf got back to the house near Poitiers late on Monday afternoon, just as Nisha was going through the Channel Tunnel on her long-distance coach. Jake and Mel were on the terrace enjoying the warmth of the summer air.

"How did it go?" Jake asked, passing him a glass of chilled water.

"Nisha found Dido. I saw them a few times; they seemed to be getting along just fine. I got a list of all the registered attendees. Nisha's on the list, she's spelt her name differently, but there's no Marianne Desbois. Somewhere in there is another alias for Sykes." He passed the list to Mel. "Now, what have you two been cooking up?"

"We've edited the emails we roughed out," Jake said, "Nisha showed Mel how to set up the accounts we're going to be using, and how to fake the sending date and time on an email. I think we should launch the next phase on Monday morning, in a week."

Jake handed Alf a slim sheaf of paper and he started reading through the fictional exchange between Paulo Silva and Commander Julia Kelso, which took place over a period of a couple of months following the operation to take down Dido Sykes' trafficking operation.

S to K: I've done what I promised. Your turn now.

K to S: All in good time. Wasn't Dartmouth enough for you? You had your fun with both of us.

S to K: That was just a pleasant appetiser. You owe me Julia. Please don't try my patience.

K to S: I'm working on it. What you're asking for isn't easy. There are other people involved.

S to K: That's your problem.

K to S: We need to talk. Just you and me this time.

S to K: We can meet when you've shown me some good faith. I want the intelligence files I specified.

K to S: That's more than we agreed. What do I get?

S to K: 70/30 in my favour.

K to S: Other way round. My risk is huge.

S to K: 50/50 then.

K to S: We'll talk. I'll bring the files.

"That should whet her appetite," Alf said, handing the papers back to Mel, "short and sweet, and nicely spaced out. It's how you'd do it. I like the Dartmouth reference; I'm assuming she'll have seen the photographs you told me about."

"I'd bet on it," Jake said, "who's hungry?"

Jake went inside to prepare supper.

"She's quite domesticated now, isn't she?" Mel said. "I think she enjoys living in your house."

"How are *you*, Mel?" he asked her.

"Frankly, Alf, I've felt better," Mel said. "I'm glad I've got something to focus on now; just lying around doing nothing was driving me nuts."

"Are you still in pain?" he reached out and took her hand.

"Aches more than pains, so better than before. It's what's going on in my head that bothers me. I've never been that introspective, but I'm worrying a lot about the future. What I'm going to be able to do, or rather what I'm not going to be able to do. They've told me I might experience some big changes."

"What sort of changes?"

"Physical ability, not being so fit anymore, knackered libido. That sort of thing. Can you imagine me not running or swimming or having sex? I can't!"

"You'll be fine, I'm sure of it. As soon as you get your leg back you can start your recovery. The pool's all yours, and there's enough space to walk around in the garden without going out. Once we've fixed Dido for good, life starts all over."

"I hope so, Alf."

She squeezed his hand; he lifted hers to his lips and kissed it gently.

Just then the emergency phoned beeped. Alf looked at the small screen.

"Nisha's home. She's going to take a day to sort herself out and be back here on Wednesday afternoon."

"Good," said Jake. "Did you and Nisha find anything about the couple, the hired killers? Dutch or Norwegian, weren't they?"

"I haven't seen anything," Mel replied, "and Nisha didn't mention it. I can have a trawl through the stuff we've downloaded tomorrow. Why?"

"Just an uncomfortable loose end," Jake said, "when we go to meet Sykes we'll be breaking cover. I'd feel happier if the killers were sorted out by then."

"I'll have a look tomorrow. Can we have the rest of the night off, do you think?" Mel said. "I was saying to Alf I've been a bit low. It'd be nice to have an evening like we used to, just the three of us."

"What," Jake said, "you want us to drink too much and shout at each other? We'd wake Steph and Tracey."

"Stuff Steph and Tracey," Mel said, "in the nicest possible way. But yes, let's drink too much and get noisy."

******

Nisha arrived back on Wednesday. Alf went to meet her at Poitiers station. She kissed his cheek again.

"How's Mel?" she asked him.

"She's got a hangover, out of practice. She was feeling a bit down in the dumps last night and she wanted a mini party. We obliged. I don't think Steph and Tracey approved."

"Why was she down in the dumps?"

"If you'd known Mel before the attack, you wouldn't need to ask. She's a very vital person, very passionate and energetic. She's also a control-freak. You put a person like that in a hospital bed for six weeks and then in plaster up to her waist, with 24-hour carers and you can only expect her to get fed up."

"Poor Mel, I wish I'd known her before. I really like her, she's smart, clever. She's much more clued-up on the internet than I was expecting. With a bit of training she could probably do my job nearly as well as I can."

Nisha stopped talking and watched the landscape roll past.

"You don't talk much, do you Alf?" she said, breaking the silence. "You don't give much away."

He didn't reply. She reached up and placed her hand on his on the steering wheel. He looked at her, her dark brown eyes holding his, almost challenging.

"We will be alright, won't we Alf?" she asked.

"I hope so," he said, turning his eyes back to the road.

"And we're doing the right thing? Shouldn't we get the rest of the police involved? Should we be doing this on our own?"

"Are you having a touch of the seconds, Nisha? Jake said she'd been through all this with you. If we left this to the mainstream she'd walk away laughing, Dido Sykes I mean."

"Not the seconds, not really. I'm not as brash as I make out, Alf, I just need a bit of reassurance from time to time."

Nisha took her hand off his on the wheel and dropped it to his thigh. He lifted it and gently pushed it away.

"And some warmth. Just sometimes, Alf," Nisha said, quietly.

"I'm not for you, Nisha, sorry. It's complicated."

"That's what all of you keep saying to me: it's complicated Nisha. Like I'm too stupid to understand," Nisha said, a little louder. "How complicated can it be?"

"It's also personal, private."

"So private that there are pictures of the three of you flying around?"

"What do you know about pictures?" he asked.

"They're on her computer, Dido's. Jake half-naked, with you wrapped around her, and Mel off to the side. I've seen them."

"Just leave it, Nisha," he said, gently. "Let's get this over with and we can all move on."

She lapsed into silence for the rest of the journey.

******

When they got to the house, Nisha was her usual bright and bouncy self again. Alf went to find Jake, who was resting in the room they shared.

"Nisha's back. I think you should have a quiet chat with her, she was saying strange things in the car and asking questions about us, the three of us. She's seen the Dartmouth pictures."

"Where did she see them?" Jake asked.

"She said she saw them on Dido's computer. Are they on there?"

"I wouldn't be surprised, but neither Nisha nor Mel mentioned finding them. I'll ask Mel later. Mel said she couldn't find anything about the hired killers either. We'll ask Nisha to dig some more."

"I'm going to spend the rest of the week in Switzerland. I'm going to check out Montreux and maybe have a few runs past the Desbois house. I'll go tomorrow on my own. Let's go and talk to Nisha"

"How was it, Nisha?" Jake asked when they were all on the terrace at the house.

"I met her, Poena she's calling herself. She approached me in the main hall at the start of the conference. There was some guy banging on about something or other; I was standing up to try to stay awake but couldn't help yawning. She saw it and said it's really boring, why don't we go for a drink."

"Just like that?"

"Just like that. We went to a bar near the university, then went back for the after-party, that's what we call the hackers' gig. It went on until around 2. She knows her stuff, Alf. We kind of hung out then, all day

Sunday. The whole thing wound up around midnight and I went to my room."

"What did you make of her?"

"She seemed nice, to be fair," Nisha said, "I mean, I know she's not, but she was friendly. Not open as such, but then no one is at these things. Like I said, she knows her stuff when it comes to the internet and hacking - she taught me a thing or two. I got the sense that she wasn't real, though. I think she has different personalities to suit whatever role she's playing. You know she wears a wig? She's shaved her head. New hair, new person. Poena's got shortish light brown hair and wears a lot of denim. You told me she's around mid- to late-thirties but as Poena she could pass for mid-twenties. All the time we were talking I was looking for signs of pretence, some indication that she was making it all up. There wasn't anything, she didn't miss a beat or say anything inconsistent; it was like she really was *being* Poena."

"Poena?" Alf said, "what does that mean?"

"It's Latin, and also Greek," Mel said, "I did classics, remember? The word 'poena' means pain or punishment, but it's also a version of the name of Poine. Poine was a servant of Nemesis, the Greek goddess of divine retribution. Poine was what they call a spirit, and her job was to hand out punishment for Nemesis. Kind of says it all, really. It's telling us her motivation. Retribution."

"Retribution for what?" Nisha asked.

"She had a bad time as a kid," Jake said," not that that should be any excuse for what she's done. She was the only daughter of a single mum who made a living selling herself round Hull docks. The mother would take her tricks home; Dido would have seen what was going on. I got this from Drew Strathdon when I interviewed him after he was arrested. Everyone knew, and they treated Dido like dirt, unless they were male and then they would assume she was just like her mum. She hates the world and what she thinks it's done to her, treated her with contempt and denied her what she felt she deserved - a little respect. If she hadn't gone so far, you'd almost have some sympathy."

"She gets none from me," Nisha said.

"Nor from any of us," Alf said, "she's ruined dozens of lives, if not hundreds, and killed quite a few people too. Not to mention what she's done to Mel."

"What name did she use to register?" Alf asked, "for the main conference."

"I don't know; I didn't ask, obviously. I introduced myself as Tonto, she said she was Poena, that's all. Hackers don't tend to ask for real names, or even made-up ones."

"So, now we've got her stage name what can we do with it?" Jake asked.

"Lots," said Nisha, "I'm already looking for her on the dark web. Also, her choice of name gives us an insight into how she's thinking, like her choice of the name Dido does. It's all wrapped up in Greek mythology and it's going to help us get at her."

"How so?" asked Alf.

"It's psychology," said Mel, "when Nisha gets round to having a go at her, knowing the way she thinks will be a big help."

"I don't follow you," said Alf.

"Nisha and I have been talking," said Mel, "we're going to attack her, get into what she's doing online. When you're being hacked by someone like Sykes, your best defence is to hack her back."

Chapter 32

"Spike?" Alf said, "it's Piet Kuyper. Can you talk?"

"Sure, Piet. How's everything going?" Spike answered.

"It's going well. Steph and Tracey are terrific with Mel. Look, we're moving into another phase of this thing. Can you meet me in Switzerland on Saturday? Business arrangement, obviously."

"I could, I suppose. What's happening?"

"I'd rather explain face to face. Can you be in Montreux around noon on Saturday?"

"OK. I'll call you on this number when I'm there."

"Thanks, Spike. I appreciate this. We all do."

Alf ended the call; Julia watched him and nodded her agreement.

"I think it's sensible to have Spike's people as back up when we have our 'meeting'. I'm surprised Nisha hasn't found anything at all about the hired killers. Sykes must be in touch with them somehow. I've asked Mel to have a good look as well, in case Nisha missed something. When are you going?"

"I'll head out this morning. I'll take your hire car; even I've had enough of the old Peugeot. It predates aircon."

"By about thirty years," Jake said. "Coffee?"

Alf left the house near Poitiers later that morning and headed east towards Switzerland, along a road that was fast becoming too familiar. Jake's rental car was faster and infinitely more comfortable than the old Peugeot and for a while Alf actually relaxed as he drove. He'd booked a room at the same motel near Coppet, and he arrived after dark. He'd passed the

Desbois house and had seen lights on inside, but no sign of movement. He wondered for a moment how Sykes was entertaining herself inside the opulent house, and what she was thinking. In his room he poured himself a scotch from the bottle he had with him, and after a soothing shower he fell asleep. His dreams featured both Jake and Mel, and strangely also the shapely and worrying Nisha. When he awoke, he found he was both aroused and perplexed.

The next morning, after another drive-by of the Desbois house, he headed east again for the lakeside town of Montreux. It was pretty, elegant and decidedly affluent. Riggers were taking down the stages used for the jazz festival a few weeks before; the squares and open spaces were teeming with tourists. He parked in a multi-storey and took a couple of hours to wander the streets, stopping for coffee and again for lunch. He was sizing up places for a meeting with Kelso, looking for one which was open enough and public, but with good vantage points for covert surveillance. He came up with a short list of two: the open space near the Freddie Mercury statue and the area close to the pier where the Lake Geneva steamers loaded and discharged their passengers. Both were busy public places, not attractive for assassins. He returned to Coppet to rest. After a modest supper he fell into bed, but this time sleep evaded him. He lay awake for hours, plagued by images of death and destruction, of Jake dying, of Mel dead.

He was up early on Saturday morning. The now usual drive past the Desbois house, again no sign of movement, and on to Montreux again. Spike called him around 11. Alf said they should meet at the pier.

Alf was there first, or so he thought. Spike, the short and stocky ex-SAS man, suddenly appeared at his shoulder.

"Hiya Piet," he said, "nice place. You seemed to be deep in thought. I've been watching you for at least ten minutes."

"Sorry, Spike. A lot on my mind. Thanks for coming."

"You're paying. What's up?"

"We've found a way into Dido Sykes. We've got into her communications, and we know she can read Jake's email. Sykes knows me as someone called Paulo Silva. The plan is that I email Jake as Silva, redirect Sykes to another email address and let her read about a planned, possibly acrimonious, meeting between Silva and Julia Kelso. We think Sykes won't be able to resist coming along. She's got a contract out on both of us, but we think she wants to do more than just kill Jake, which is why we think she'll show up. Jake wants to talk to her. We thought we'd do it here."

"But it's a gamble," said Spike.

"Right. We haven't got a handle on the killers who had a go at Mel in Crete, and we don't know if there are any others out there working for Sykes."

"So, you're wanting me to put a team on to cover the meeting, looking out for the Crete couple and anyone else who seems likely?"

"Can you do it?"

"Sure. It'll be the same team. I'm assuming once you and Jake have had your 'meeting' you'll part company. Sykes may not show while you and Jake are together. With four guys we won't be able to cover both of you fully after you split up."

"I'd guessed that. Play it by ear; ideally one of you can get me back to my car and the rest stick with Jake."

"Good choice of location, by the way," Spike said, "we've ready access to weapons here; everyone in Switzerland has at least one gun, and we've plenty of old friends hereabouts. When are you going to do this?"

"A week today, next Saturday."

"Time enough. I'll get the guys together and we'll get here mid-week. For this Op the fee will be fifty grand, Euros, all in. No hidden extras. Is that OK?"

"Fine. I'll meet you here on Friday with the cash. Now, where do you suggest? I thought either here, or by the Mercury statue."

"Let's go have a look," Spike said.

******

Alf arrived home around breakfast time on Sunday morning. After he'd left Spike in Montreux, he drove almost non-stop through the night back to France, pausing only for toilet stops, coffee and fuel. He arrived at the house near Poitiers stiff and aching. He peeled off his sticky shirt and jeans and plunged into the pool, luxuriating in the cool cleanness of it. Jake appeared in a dressing gown.

"I thought we'd been invaded by seals or something," she said.

"Why don't you come on in?" he said.

"OK."

She dropped her dressing gown and plunged in as well, wearing nothing at all.

"Bliss," she said, "I will always thank Mel Dunn for introducing me to the joys of skinny-dipping. No sane person's ever even thought about trying it in Scotland."

She swam up to him and stood facing him, her arms on his shoulders.

"How did it go with Spike?"

"Fine, it's all set. He'll be there mid-week onwards with the guys, the same team as we had in Crete. I'll see him on Friday, you turn up on Saturday and we'll see what happens."

"Doesn't feel right somehow," she said, "like going into a lion's den."

"She's no lion, Jake, she's just a criminal. We've dealt with criminals before - tougher ones than Dido Sykes."

"True, but this one is so personal. Vicious."

"We'll take her down, one way or another."

"I hope you're right, Ferdinand," she said, pushing herself away from him and swimming a couple of lengths.

He followed her.

"Have you still got your boxers on? That's disgusting!" she said.

She pulled them off him and threw them onto the pool apron.

They swam together, pausing to talk quietly every few minutes. They looked up and saw Mel and Nisha on the terrace, watching them. Mel had a mug of coffee and she looked at them with a degree of sadness. Nisha was wide-eyed, despite the relatively early hour.

"Is this a private party, or can anyone join in?" Nisha called.

She didn't wait for an answer but pulled off her shirt and ran naked to the pool.

Jake laughed, but as she looked up she saw Mel's retreating back as she wheeled herself away and into the house.

Chapter 33

They prepared the email exchange on Sunday evening. Nisha had shown Mel how to monitor Dido's response, just in case she was having 'one of her mornings' on Monday. Mel, Jake and Alf were up before 6 and had gathered in the dining room. Nisha was nowhere to be seen. Alf read through his draft email one last time.

'This is taking too long. I've told you before not to test my patience. You have one more week.'

He was logged into his new fake email account as Paulo Silva. The draft was addressed to Julia Kelso's official Met Police email address. He pressed send.

Julia held her Blackberry and waited. A few seconds later the device bleeped and Silva's message appeared.

'I don't know who you are or what you want. Don't contact this email address again.'

Her message appeared on Alf's screen. He smiled. Julia logged into her own fake email account and sent another email.

'I know you're impatient, but don't use my work email. I've got what you need. Meet me in London this week and I'll give it to you.'

Silva responded: *'I'm not stupid. I'm not coming to UK until everything is fixed. I want to meet somewhere neutral. Switzerland?'*

Julia's response: *'OK, but soon - this week.'*

'Montreux, next Saturday morning, 11am. By the Mercury statue,' was his answer.

"I'll go get Nisha," Jake said.

Nisha appeared ten minutes later, half asleep. She waved coffee aside and took her place in front of her screens. As soon as she touched the keys she became alive and alert.

"She's read the Met Police account. I've deleted the message exchange and it won't be on the back up tape. I'm just checking to see if she's taken the Paulo Silva bait and got into his account. It may take her a while, but we've made the password easy enough."

Nisha went to the kitchen and came back with an apple and a mug of tea. She checked her screens again.

"Bingo," she said, "Dido's bitten. She's checking out Silva's account."

Mel was wheeling herself towards Nisha to see her screen, but before she got there Nisha had turned it off.

"I'll check her stuff later to see if she's saying anything or speaking to the killers. I'm going back to bed now!"

Nisha stood and walked out of the room. Mel went to her screens and turned them on again, but she couldn't recover the site Nisha had been looking at, the one which showed Dido getting into Silva's account. Mel frowned but said nothing.

Later that morning Alf made the trip to Bordeaux again to withdraw more cash, another €80,000 to cover Spike's fee and other mounting expenses. Jake and Mel relaxed by the pool; Nisha stayed in her room until lunchtime.

"What's going to happen, Jake?" Mel asked.

"If we're on track, Dido will show up in Montreux on Saturday, watch me and Paulo Silva have a shouting match and then make her move on me. Alf's arranged some back up, just in case she's got other ideas and wants to set her dogs on me or him. Once I've had my little chat with Dido we can work out the next steps."

"I've got a strange feeling about all this, Jake. Something doesn't add up, but I don't know what. Maybe it's just that we aren't in full control of this, and I haven't got the whole picture."

"None of us has, Mel," Jake said, "Dido's got the upper hand for now, but I think we can change that after Saturday. Having Nisha with access to Dido's systems is a godsend, but it still doesn't put us inside her head. That's why I need to talk to her."

"Changing the subject," Mel said, "Steph said they're going to take me to the orthopaedic guy again this week. They think he'll give the OK to remove the cast from my leg. Steph says I'll still need the chair for the first week or two, but I can start trying to stand and walk with crutches. I never thought I'd get this excited about the prospect of simply standing up."

"That's excellent news, Mel," Jake said, smiling, "we'll arrange a special standing up party, with lots of cake and gin."

"I'll keep my diary clear," Mel said. "You and Alf seem to be getting along well, not that I'm jealous or anything just because you're having lots of sex and frolicking about in the pool like randy teenagers. You're practically shacked up together."

"I suppose we are," Jake said, "not that it was planned to be like this. He's opening up about himself more these days. If you weren't all crocked up this could be heaven for the three of us."

"I think I'd end up being a gooseberry," Mel said, "could you get me some more coffee?"

******

On Wednesday Jake took the train and ferry back to London, travelling on the Belgian identity card Alf had given her. From the borrowed SIS flat she booked a BA flight to Geneva for the following Friday, and a room at an airport hotel, all in the name of Julia Kelso. For good measure she booked a first-class seat on the 9am train from Geneva airport to Montreux. She called her boss, Will Connaught, just to check in. His tone was cool to say the least, the subtext being that Metropolitan Police Commanders who disappear without trace and without contacting base for weeks on end are doing themselves no favours. She tried to keep the conversation light but failed. She hung up after a few closing pleasantries. She took herself off to a small restaurant she knew vaguely and ate a solitary dinner, glaring menacingly at anyone who looked like they might be thinking about starting a conversation with her. She walked home and enjoyed the feeling of being completely alone in her own space for the first time in what seemed like ages.

On Friday she took a taxi to Heathrow and then a plane to Geneva. She turned on the secret phone she and Alf used and called him. He was in Montreux and had met with Spike. Everything was set.

At 9 on Saturday morning Julia Kelso boarded the train for Montreux. It sped along the lakeside, stopping only at Geneva Central and Lausanne. It was a beautiful morning, warm in the summer sunshine, but still she shivered. It was less than 500 metres from the station to the Freddie Mercury statue and she had almost an hour. She stopped for a coffee and afterwards strolled along the lakeside path, cool in her dark blue linen suit. She rehearsed the script in her head.

Just before 11am she walked into the open space near the Freddie Mercury statue, it's bizarre pose completely at odds with the staid grandeur of the lakeside resort. She looked at it while also scanning the area. She didn't see Alf or Dido. She checked her watch. It was 11. He appeared from behind her.

"Hello, Julia," Paulo Silva said, loudly enough to be heard by anyone nearby, "you came."

"Obviously. I have the papers you want." She handed him a thick envelope from her bag. She imagined she could hear a camera shutter clicking rapidly as he accepted the envelope.

"Now, what do you have for me?" she asked.

"As we agreed, access to an account with the sum we arrived at. It's at your disposal."

"So, we're done?"

Silva laughed.

"Nowhere near done, Julia. This is just the start. I hope it's the start of something beautiful, like Dartmouth all over again."

Julia's face clouded with anger. She slapped Silva hard across the face with her right hand.

"If I ever see you again, Silva, you are a dead man!" she hissed. She turned on her heel and walked towards the lake.

He stood there, almost stunned. A few onlookers were staring at him, attracted by the volume of Julia's outburst and the sound of her slap. He turned and walked in the opposite direction, his face still stinging from her blow.

From the shade of a nearby terrace the tall Dutchman watched the scene unfold. The instructions she had sent had been specific. Let the meeting take place, then take the man, and when he was down, search him. Bring her anything he had on him. No excuses, no mistakes. He set off to fall in behind Silva, the thin blade concealed within the sleeve of his shirt. His wife was waiting at the hotel with their daughter. He planned to take them to the children's play park for a picnic when he was done. He was gaining on Silva, just a few metres behind now, but not crowding him. There were still too many people around. He had surveyed the area well; he knew that Silva would have to pass through a narrow quiet alleyway to get to the nearest car park. She had said he would be in a car, not on the train. She was right.

Silva turned to his right into the narrow alleyway. It wasn't very long, but long enough. He was only three metres or so behind Silva. He lost sight of him for a split second, and when he followed his quarry round the corner into the alleyway he was surprised to find himself looking down the barrel of a silenced pistol in the hand of a stocky black man wearing a ski mask. He let the knife blade slip from his sleeve and caught the hilt in his hand. He brandished the long blade at the stranger, lunging at him. There was no sign of Silva. The masked black man was unperturbed. Without a word he pulled the trigger twice. The tall Dutchman looked down at his chest in disbelief, seeing the deep red stains blossom across the lemon-yellow fabric of his shirt. He looked up as he fell. The black man had gone. He was on his own. He died face down in the deserted alleyway, alone. Back in their hotel, his widow sang to their daughter as they waited for daddy to come back.

Spike caught up with Alf in the car park, as arranged.

"It was him; he had a knife and was about to do you. He's sorted," Spike said simply. "Ewan was behind him just in case, the others stayed with Jake. She's shown up, Sykes."

"Thanks, Spike, I appreciate what you've done. See you around."

They parted without a handshake or a backward glance.

Chapter 34

Julia turned and walked quickly past the covered market heading for the pier and the train station. She'd caught a brief glimpse of Ricky, one of the SAS team, so she knew she had some protection but she hadn't yet set eyes on Dido. There was a patch of dark shadow near the entrance to the covered market.

"That was quite a slap, Julia," a voice said from the shadows, "it looked like you meant it."

Dido Sykes stepped forward. Her hair was blonde, almost as blonde as Julia's own. She was wearing stylish but casual clothing, pale creams and yellows, cool for the summer heat.

"What are you doing here?" Julia said.

"What's the saying? Everybody has to be somewhere," Dido said. "Actually, I'd heard you'd be here, so I thought I'd say hello."

"You've got a nerve! After everything you've done - you do know there's a warrant for your arrest, don't you?"

"So, why don't you do it then, Julia? Arrest me. Oh, but you can't, can you? Not just because we're in Switzerland, but also because I've got photographs of you handing a package to Paulo Silva - a man you said doesn't exist. How would you explain that? What was in it, Julia, and what do you get in return?"

"You took a contract out on me," Julia stated, ignoring Dido's question.

"Did I?"

"Yes, and on Mel Dunn and Silva too. Did you have Mel Dunn attacked in Crete?"

At that moment the wail of a police car sounded a couple of streets away. It was quickly followed by the sound of an ambulance siren.

"I did, Julia, and unless I'm mistaken those sirens are for your friend Silva too. Two out of three; is that a good ratio?"

"Why? Why did you want Dunn and Silva dead? Or me?"

"The young kids call it being 'dissed', disrespected. I don't like being disrespected, taken for a fool. You hurt my business, Julia, you destroyed something that had taken me a considerable effort to build up. Someone has to pay for that, in this case it's you and your 'friends'. Are they just friends, Julia? I don't think so. The pictures tell a different story. Who would have thought the holy Julia Kelso, saintliness personified, is nothing more than a grubby little corrupt perverted whore, just like the rest of us? That's the truth, isn't it Julia? Dunn and Silva - only that's not his name - are your lovers. I should say were. I don't think Mel Dunn will be doing much more of that sort of thing, and Silva or Ferdinand, or whatever his name is, died a few minutes ago."

"So why am I still here?" Julia asked.

"I was going to have you killed, Kelso," Dido said, "but I had second thoughts. Do you know what humiliation is, Julia? Real humiliation - not just knowing that I gave your boyfriend sexual thrills in a punt when you were no more than five feet away, not just knowing that I put him up to screwing Jasmira Shah and filmed it all while you two were planning your wedding. No, that's just mild embarrassment. I know what humiliation is, what it feels like, and I want you to feel it too. Once you've experienced it, you won't need me to kill you - you would do anything to do it yourself. I want to hurt you, Julia, badly. I hate you more than anyone else alive. But before that, you have work to do for me. Now that I've got pictures of you giving a package to someone who Drew Strathdon will identify as Paulo Silva and who others will identify as Alan Ferdinand, and no doubt I can find or manufacture payments to a secret account you hold, you are all mine. I can take you anytime I want. All you can do about it is do exactly what I say, when I say it, and hope that I'll keep your secret safe. I might, I might not, you'll never know until it's too late. I wonder what it's like to be a bent copper in a British jail, Julia? It can't be very relaxing. I'm going now, but we'll talk again."

"But why, Dido? Why do you hate me?"

"Because you're perfect. Your entitlement, background, your contacts, your privilege, everything. Everything fell into your lap; you never had to fight for anything in your entire life, ever."

"And you did? Is that it?"

"You'll understand, when I'm done with you."

With that, Dido Sykes melted back into the shadows. Julia lunged after her, but she had gone. Julia scanned the aisles of the covered market looking for Dido's hair and clothing. She realised in a moment that the hair would have come off or been concealed, and the clothing would also be covered with something different. Julia ran as fast as she could, dodging the crowds through the thronged market. She emerged in the adjacent parking lot just in time to see the back end of a large Mercedes saloon pulling onto the main street and powering away.

She made her way towards the area where the sirens had come from. She saw a police cordon at the end of a small alley. An ambulance waited, its back doors open. A small crowd was gathering.

"What's happened?" Julia asked a young man, speaking French.

"I heard there's been a murder - a mugging gone wrong. They think it's a foreigner who's been killed - Dutch or Belgian. That's what the police officer was saying.

Julia's heart was pounding, panic rising. She pressed forward, trying to catch a glimpse of the fallen victim, but she couldn't get near enough to see. She felt a presence next to her and turned to face Ewan, another of Spike's team. He said nothing but smiled at her and winked. Then he too melted away, his message delivered. Julia exhaled and felt herself starting to shake.

She forced herself to move away and walk towards the station to get a train back to Geneva. Once seated in the first-class carriage she took the secret phone from her bag and turned it on. She pressed Alf's number and waited.

"Where are you?" Alf's voice was tinny in her ear.

"Thank God!" she said, "I thought you'd been killed."

"Again?" he said. "Where are you?" he repeated.

"On a train back to Geneva."

"Does it stop anywhere?"

"Just Lausanne."

"OK, get off there and wait in the station café. You'll probably be there before me." He ended the call.

In the end, Julia waited in the station buffet with an untouched coffee for nearly 20 minutes before Alf came into view. He didn't approach her but bought a sandwich and a cold drink to take out. Julia rose and followed him. He went into a tunnel under one of the platforms and emerged onto a side street just below the station. He was waiting by the old Peugeot.

"You hit me like you meant it," he said.

"It's called method acting," she said. "What happened?"

"After you socked me in the face, I went back towards the car park as I'd arranged with Spike. Ewan was behind me, Spike was ahead. The two of them must have been in touch by phone or radio. Ewan clocked the Dutch guy - the one from the dive school in Crete - and saw that he was after me. He must have been lined up by Sykes. I went into the alleyway and Spike was there. He told me to get out fast, so I did. I didn't see what happened next, but Spike caught up with me as we'd planned. He just said he'd sorted the Dutch guy, who'd had a knife and was going to do me."

"Dido was behind it, she as good as told me. She came out of the shadows by the covered market. She'd been watching us." Julia recounted what Dido had said, word for word.

"I tried to follow her in the market, but she'd done a quick-change act and vanished. I think I caught a glimpse of the tail end of her Mercedes. She's convinced I'm corrupt and said we'd talk again, Alf."

"What do you think she meant?"

"Just that. She wants to hurt me by humiliating me, but she says she has enough on me to make me 'hers' for as long as she wants. She'll try to make me do something for her, I'm sure of it. But she knows more about our set up than we thought, she knows you're Ferdinand and she knows all about you and me and Mel."

"How could she?" he asked, only the three of us know all of it."

"She might have guessed; she might have got into the investigation files and put two and two and two together. Once she finds out that it wasn't you but her tame assassin who got killed, she's going to go crazy. We need to get back to Mel."

"OK," Alf said, pulling away.

"But I want to see her place first, Alf. Can we go that way?"

"Sure," he said.

******

Mrs Greet Visser closed the hotel room door as the solemn young police officer withdrew. She'd asked him to give her a moment while she dried her eyes and made herself more presentable. A female police officer would come to the hotel room to stay with the child while Greet went to the mortuary to identify the body of Wim Visser, her dead husband. The police officer had said he appeared to have been the victim of a robbery or mistaken identity.

She was alone with the child for a few minutes. The child was puzzled by her mother's change of mood and started to grizzle. Greet Visser rapidly opened her laptop and sent a single-word email, the code word which meant that the operation had failed and that one of them was dead or taken. The word was *Thanatos*, the name of the mythological Greek god of death. Had the mission been successful, the codeword would have been *Nemesis*, the goddess of retribution. When she was done, she attended to her daughter.

An hour later the email was read in the lakeside villa near Coppet. She read it and howled with rage, although she already suspected something had gone wrong when the killer hadn't shown up as planned to hand over the package Kelso had given Silva. She threw open the balcony window and stepped out. The sun was fading on the lake. Dido, her eyes filled with tears of frustration, let out a furious blood curdling scream.

The two people in the old and slightly battered Peugeot parked in the lane outside heard the sound and shuddered at the horror of it. The driver started the motor and drove off steadily to the west.

Chapter 35

They drove through the night again, tense and almost silent. Close proximity to death and malice had disturbed them both. It was still dark when they pulled up at the house near Poitiers. Tracey stood on the terrace, partly shielded by a large terra cotta pot, a pistol in her hand. She relaxed when she recognised Jake and Alf.

"Hi Tracey," Alf said, "everything OK?"

"Yes, all good. It's just I heard the car and I wasn't expecting anyone. Can't be too careful."

"Right enough. How's Mel?" Jake asked.

"Good. The cast came off yesterday. She tried to stand too quickly and took a bit of a tumble, but it's only her pride that's dented. She shouted at everyone quite a bit, so we've given her something to help her have a good night's sleep."

"And Nisha?" Jake asked.

"She's OK. She's been working most of the day. She went to bed a while ago, but had a bit of a skinful before she turned in. She seems tense."

"We're going to get some sleep now, Tracey," Jake said, "could you ask Steph to give us a shake at 9 if we're not up and about by then?"

"Sure. It's nearly 4 now, Steph takes over at 6.30. Goodnight, what's left of it."

They took turns in the shower. Jake insisted Alf went first. She was sitting in an armchair with a tumbler of scotch when he came out.

"Penny for them," he said, pouring a glass for himself.

"I'm trying to figure out how Dido knows what's going on. So far, the most logical thing I can come up with is she's broken into the Met's IT systems and the HOLMES accounts for all the cases we've worked, and she's come up with the right answer."

"If she's made sense of HOLMES she deserves to win," Alf said. The Home Office Large Major Enquiry System, or HOLMES, was a massive, automated information catastrophe that tormented senior investigating officers with endless pointless questions.

"True enough," Jake said, "but I can't see it being anything else. I mean, no one except the three of us knows the story, do they? Nisha's guessed bits of it, but why would she tell anyone? Could the Americans have worked it all out? Why would they? Has Dido got someone inside Hugh Cavendish's lot at Vauxhall Cross? I just don't know, Alf."

"Get showered," he said, "you're beat; you need some sleep." He poured himself another whisky.

"OK," she said, "see you in a while."

Alf lay on the bed listening to Julia Kelso in the shower. By the time she came out he was asleep, his glass still half full on the bedside table. She pulled a sheet over his sleeping body and climbed in beside him. She was asleep in seconds too.

******

Both were wide awake at 8. Alf went to swim in the pool while Julia sat on the terrace, a bathrobe over her two-piece swimsuit, sipping fresh coffee. She heard a shuffling sound and looked round to see Mel, upright and moving carefully on crutches. Julia smiled at her and waved.

"She moves! That's wonderful, Mel!"

"I fell over yesterday and went into a massive strop. Did Tracey tell you? I expect they'll make me do the washing up all day to say sorry. Is that coffee hot?"

Mel eased herself into a chair next to Julia and took her hand.

"I'm glad you're both back, Jake," she said, "I was worried."

"I saw Sykes. She tried to have Alf killed in Montreux, but luckily he'd seen that coming and enlisted Spike and the boys to watch our backs. The guy who tried to kill you - he's Dutch, by the way, was foolish enough to threaten Spike with a knife. He's not around anymore. Spike sent me the guy's name, he was called Wim Visser, and his address. It seems Spike helped himself to his wallet to make it look like a robbery. Can you do anything with it?"

"I might if I could get near the internet. Nisha's using all our connection time, and I'm still concerned about Dido locating us if she knows my IP address. I'll see if I can jump on to one of Nisha's machines when she's not looking."

"How are you getting on with her?"

"OK, but she's a strange one, like Alf said. We've had our little chat, by the way, while you were both away. I convinced her that you aren't on the wrong side, and that everything to do with you and me and Alf is just private chemistry. I said you're the most honest person I know, and that I wouldn't have anything to do with you if you weren't."

"And what did she say?"

"Nothing, for a while. She listened very carefully, watching me. Then she sat for a few minutes, and in the end she said she believed me, believed I was telling her the truth. Then she said an odd thing. She said she wouldn't be talking to anyone else about us. Not anyone, full stop, but anyone else."

"You think she's already told someone?"

"It did cross my mind."

"Who?"

"No idea. Can you get her out of here for a few hours? I'd like to have a rummage around now I'm a bit more mobile. Just her computers and any phones I can find."

"So you really don't trust her?"

"I just don't know, Jake. I want to, and in many ways I do. We do need to be sure though, don't we?"

"I'll ask her to come food shopping with me; I'll take her into Poitiers and drag it out to include lunch. Will that do?"

"Yes, it should be fine. Do you trust her, Jake?"

"I do, I did. She's not given me any reason not to. But it's as well to be cautious, Mel. Do what you can. Here's Alf."

He arrived, drying himself with a large towel. He hugged Mel warmly.

"Welcome back to the land of the vertical," he said, "we've missed you. How are you?"

"I'd forgotten all about gravity. It's coming back to me now, but it'll be a while before I'm racing Kelso round the park again. Jake said you had an interesting time in Montreux."

"We did. We need to talk it all through, just the three of us, but not right now. I've something I need to do this morning, something which will please Commander Kelso."

"You're not, are you?" Jake asked. "You're going to change that bloody awful car! Please get a decent one this time!"

"You've beaten me into submission. I do admit that having been back and forth to Switzerland in it a few times I'm starting to see the benefits of air conditioning and functional seats. I'll go to my man in Bordeaux to see what he's got."

"I'm going for a swim," Jake announced.

Mel and Alf watched her as she took off her robe. The small scar on her abdomen looked pinker than usual against her pale skin. Jake walked to the pool and lowered herself in, starting to swim rhythmically with long, powerful strokes.

"She is gorgeous, Alf," Mel said, "we're very lucky. I'll be glad when I'm back in full working order, I can tell you."

"We'll be glad too."

"She's going to try to get Nisha out of the house for a while today. I want to have a look at what she's been doing while I've not been looking over her shoulder," Mel said.

"Why? Do you think she's not being straight with us?"

"I'm not sure. Just being cautious. I hope I don't find anything."

"I reckon Dido knows that her efforts to get me out of the way have failed. We've taken out one of her killers, but if Spike's intelligence is correct the husband and wife work together as a team. We'll need to be careful for a while longer. I'd like to know if you or

Nisha pick up anything at all about Sykes's intentions now. Did Jake tell you that Dido said they'd be talking again, whenever Dido wanted to?"

"She didn't tell me that, no. I don't like the sound of it, though. It suggests she can contact Jake whenever she wants. Which could mean she knows where we are."

"That's what I was thinking. While I'm out looking for a better vehicle, I'm also going to firm up the rental on that place Jake and I looked at near La Rochelle, just in case we need it as a back-up. We've done all the paperwork in Jake's name, so there's no tie up to me or here; I just have to give the agent some money. I don't want to give up this place now, but I don't want Sykes and her killers finding us here either. I'll let Jake know, but I suggest you don't tell anyone that we might be moving out just yet."

"OK," Mel said, "I'm just going to have something to eat before Steph comes after me. She's threatening to start my physio today, and she's a brute. In the nicest possible way, of course."

"*Bon appétit*," he said, "I'm going to get dressed."

"I wouldn't be in too much of a hurry. Jake's just getting out of the pool and she's got one of her hungry looks on. Not for food, either."

"What have you done to her, Mel? She can't get enough these days."

"Are you complaining?"

Chapter 36

Far away to the north, the widow Greet Visser sat with her mother. Despite losing her husband to a violent mugger just a few days earlier, Greet seemed remarkably calm. She was giving her mother instructions about the child. What and when she ate, when she had to go to bed, what her favourite stories were, what she needed to cuddle in the night. The mother knew all this of course, but she indulged her daughter. She felt Greet must be going through some kind of internalised hell.

When she was done Greet finished her tea, held her daughter for a few seconds and kissed her head. The child wriggled to get free of her tight clutches.

"I'll be a few days. I have some of Wim's affairs to settle, then I'll be back. Take care of her." Then Greet was gone.

She had been curt with Greet when she had called the emergency number. She used foul language and told her to use the email - only the email.

"I need you to help me find him - find them. Wim is dead. I need to finish it. Not for you, for me!"

"If I knew where they were I would have already told you and your incompetent husband!"

Greet had to pause to calm down when she read this.

"Find out! Give me something to go on at least."

"Contact me tomorrow."

******

In her house by the lake she considered the Dutch woman's messages. When you are looking for something or someone, the starting point is always the place where the person or thing was last seen. She spent the morning hacking into mobile phone providers' billing systems looking for calls made to or from Montreux around the time she met Kelso. It was a long process, and boring. But in the end she found something.

A French mobile had called an Italian pay as you go phone twice. Once an hour or so before the meeting, again the day before. A different French mobile had called the first French mobile moments after her meeting with Kelso, a call which went unanswered. The first French mobile called back half an hour later and this time there was a brief conversation. The original French mobile was located in Lausanne, near the station, and the service provider's data indicated that the second phone was located with the first one shortly afterwards. The two phones travelled together going westward through Switzerland towards France but taking a detour through the village of Coppet.

She went back to the Italian phone, which had been busily in contact with three others - all Italian pay as you go phones as well. There were a lot of short calls, many unanswered, which looked to her very much like some sort of surveillance operation. A picture was starting to form.

She now hacked into the Italian mobile service and looked back at the call records for the phone she was interested in. Her research gave her two new numbers, both British, which had made calls to one of the Italian phones and it didn't take long for her to find out that both had been located in Western France for the last couple of months. Unfortunately for her, there was no fixed or regular location other than the general area of Poitou-Charente. Both British phones seemed to be turned off for long periods. Closer, but not close enough.

The French mobiles she had identified were both switched off before they left Switzerland. One was activated briefly near Lyon, but otherwise both remained silent.

By late afternoon she hadn't got much further. Then an idea came to her.

She sent an email.

"Turn on your phone," was all it said.

"It's too risky," came a reply.

"Too late to worry about that," she wrote.

"No. Give me one hour, I'll call you," came back, after a pause.

An hour later her phone rang. She picked up immediately.

"You've been holding out on me," she said, without preamble, "I need to know exactly where you are."

"I can't tell you!"

"You can, and you will. If you don't they will all know your secret, know what you've done. I'll find out where you are anyway, but it will be better for you if you save me some time."

"I don't want to be a party to any murders!"

"You already are! People are dead. Send me the address. You have one more hour."

She cut the connection.

Thirty minutes later an email arrived, and she had it. She copied the address - it was in Charente, near Poitiers - and sent it to Greet Visser.

Chapter 37

Julia didn't pay much attention to the VW camper van parked in the village square as she drove through in the hire car. Such vehicles were a common enough sight. Had she looked closely, she would have seen that it had Danish number plates but an oval 'NL' badge on the back, signifying the Netherlands. Greet had stolen the plates from another van she came across in Belgium on the way down. The van itself was not stolen, not as such. The van's owners were inside, crammed into the small space beneath the rear bench seat. They would have been very uncomfortable if they could feel anything at all.

Greet had flagged down the van near a campsite in the dunes between Amsterdam and The Hague. She had been wearing her hitchhiking costume - frayed denim shorts, tee shirt, a sweatshirt tied around her waist, hiking boots and a rucksack. The rucksack contained two handguns with ammunition, a two-kilogram demolition pack of C4 military explosive, two detonators, a fresh sealed pack of batteries, her favourite stabbing knife and some apples. It also held spare shirts and underwear, a few toiletries and a bottle of water. The camper van, decorated with the usual paraphernalia of the hippy trail, was the third vehicle that passed her and it stopped, as she knew it would.

The occupants were a pleasant middle-aged professional couple from Amsterdam trying to recapture their misspent youth. They had been to a mini-festival and were now heading south for some sun and, hopefully, some adventurous sex. They were happy to take her along with them.

They had stopped for the night at a campsite near Charleroi in the south of Belgium. The woman had prepared some food while the man opened some wine and rolled three large spliffs. They ate and drank and smoked, and as the couple made their intoxicated move on her she killed them. They had already removed most of their clothes, and as Greet encouraged the man to embrace her she slid her long, thin blade into the gap at the base of his skull and upwards into his brain. She twisted the blade savagely. The woman started, alarmed by the spasms of her man. Greet leaned forward, stroked her face kindly and slid the same thin blade between her ribs and into her racing heart. There was hardly any blood.

At 3am Greet unscrewed the number plates from a Danish vehicle parked nearby and as an afterthought helped herself to a bicycle propped alongside it. It fitted in the back of the van easily. She drove 'her' VW camper van back to the autoroute. By daybreak she was well past Paris heading for Poitiers.

******

Greet sat in front of the small café in the village square and got a sense of the rhythm of the place. It was a sleepy town. Lunch started around 12.30 and everything closed until almost 4pm. The occasional dog wandered up to lounge in the shade of parked cars or drink water from the little fountain by the *Mairie.* There wasn't much traffic. She saw one marked police car from the Municipal Police, occupied by a grey-haired officer on his own. He looked a kindly sort.

She loitered as long as she reasonably could before going back to the van. As she opened the door she noticed that it was starting to smell quite bad, but she didn't want to waste time disposing of the bodies just yet and it did hide the faint smell of the explosives. Also a few additional body parts in the debris of what she was planning would confuse things nicely. She wound the window down and drove away from the square towards a small, wooded area she had noticed. She found a shady clearing and manhandled the bicycle out of the van. Being Dutch, she was as comfortable on a bike as she was walking, and the terrain was gentle. It took her less than 30 minutes to find the address, a spacious plot with a sizeable farmhouse and a few outbuildings. She saw the unoccupied gatehouse, and she noticed the discreet cameras in the gateposts and under the eaves of the main building.

She dismounted and pushed the bike along the track, looking for vantage points and different ways to access the property. Whoever had chosen the place had done well. It wasn't overlooked and there were no tracks or footpaths along the boundaries. She saw a corner of the swimming pool and the side of one of the barns. She didn't see or hear any people. It was eerily still and silent.

Greet continued to circle around the area, trying to appear to be an aimless tourist. She noted that the track past the end of the driveway to the property led only to the village in one direction, and to a few other even more remote properties in the other. It meant that anyone going to or from it from the village and anywhere beyond would need to pass down the track leading south. This track had several tight bends and a couple of passing places, as well as plenty of wooded areas for cover. Her plan was starting to take shape.

She had no idea how many people were in the farmhouse compound, whether they were armed or not, or if they had any emergency communications or back-up. She needed to level the score - she owed it to Wim - but she didn't want to be killed or taken; she needed an escape route. That meant she couldn't risk a frontal assault - she was on her own after all - and if she were to drive the van primed with explosives into the compound there was no guarantee that those she needed to kill would indeed be killed, although she probably would be. Greet wasn't that familiar or experienced with explosives; they were more Wim's sort of thing. She preferred the surgical precision of the stiletto or a silenced pistol, or poison or a well-placed fire. Wim had liked the violence and noise of rapid gunfire and explosions.

But she'd only have one chance, and she knew it. She remembered some of the training camps she had been to years ago, the camps where seasoned warriors from Abu Nidhal and the Baader Meinhof Red Army Faction and ETA and the IRA all came to instruct and guide young violent revolutionaries. She recalled the pillow talk with an IRA man from Tyrone who had waxed lyrical about the culvert or roadside bomb detonated by a command wire. Effective, he had said, flexible and almost guaranteed not to blow up a bus load of school kids, which would generally be bad for the cause.

She pedalled steadily back to the van. She had searched the bodies of her unwilling benefactors and found that they had several hundred Euro in cash as well as a couple of credit cards. She had seen that he was a senior official with Amsterdam city council and she was a teacher at the university. She had taken their cash, and now she was going to use it to buy what she needed.

Opening the van windows wide, she drove towards Poitiers, stopping at every filling station to buy a 5-litre plastic fuel container and fill it to the brim, some with petrol, some with diesel. By the time she got to the Auchan hypermarket near Poitiers she had 35 litres of inflammable liquid in the back of the van. At Auchan she bought two reels of thin single-strand electrical wire, the longest she could find, a roll of heavy-duty adhesive tape, and three bargain two-kilo packs of assorted nuts, bolts and screws. She also bought herself a small dark green tent, a hooded top, some long trousers, some bread and cheese and three bottles of screw-top red wine. At the hypermarket filling station she topped up the van's fuel tank and bought two more 5-litre containers of petrol. Satisfied, she drove back towards the farmhouse complex as the light started to fade.

She had found a place where she could drive the van a good way into the trees, out of sight of the track. The van was well hidden by the time it was properly dark. Closing the van doors and windows tightly to contain the noxious smell, she pitched her small tent upwind and settled down for the night. She allowed herself a few moments of self-pity as she lamented her dead husband, then she drank a bottle of wine and went to sleep. She woke at dawn, peed in the bushes and set herself up to watch the track.

She saw the postman and two tractors before she saw anyone from the farmhouse. She recognised Kelso driving an ordinary looking saloon car. There was another woman in the passenger seat with short dark hair. They both came back less than 30 minutes later - clearly a quick trip to the village for something. She saw the man a little later. He was driving an old noisy Peugeot. The windows were open, so it had no air conditioning, and he was carefully avoiding potholes. He came back about two hours later, but this time he also had a female passenger. His one looked similar to the one with Kelso but with lighter hair, also cut quite short.

So there were at least four of them, five including the Dunn woman who was unbelievably still not dead. That would be rectified. The man was the main target, though, and now she knew what car he drove.

Greet spent the rest of the day setting up the van. She placed the rucksack packed with the slabs of C4 primed with a detonator. The detonator wires were twisted to join the electrical cable she had bought, still on the reels. The batteries were safely in her pocket. She piled up the petrol and diesel containers around three sides of the rucksack, but not too close. She didn't want them to absorb any of the blast, just fuel the fire. In front of and close to the rucksack, between it and the sliding door, she piled the bags of nuts and bolts. She ran the cables under them so that the weight of the shrapnel would hold the electrical wires firmly in place. She had no idea if 50 metres was far enough from the bomb for her to be safe, but that was the length of the cables, so she had decided to spend some time making herself a foxhole shelter in the woods.

When she was done, the only thing she still needed was transport to make her getaway. In the morning she would ride the bicycle into the village to look for a car or motorbike she could use, just to get her as far as Poitiers after the bomb went off.

Chapter 38

The peace of the breakfast table was shattered by a shout.

"Jake, Alf, I need you! Now!" Nisha called. "It's not good!"

They appeared almost simultaneously.

"What is it?" Jake asked.

"We've got a leak. Sykes knows where we are."

"What?"

"It's in her emails. She sent our address, this address, to some Hotmail account I haven't seen before. I've no idea whose or where it is."

"When was this?"

"I've just seen it. The email was sent the day before yesterday, in the afternoon."

"How does she know?" Alf asked.

Nisha gave him a sideways look.

"I'm guessing someone told her, or she's done something super clever with what little phone communicating we've been doing. It's not from my machines."

"But no one uses a phone in the house," Jake said, "we go to the village or into town to make calls. My Blackberry's off unless I'm away from here. We never use the landline. Could it be through the internet?"

"Extremely unlikely," said Nisha, "I haven't seen anything to suggest it, and my activity is well camouflaged."

"So, someone has let something slip," Alf stated, "accidentally or deliberately. And I'm really hoping it's not deliberate!"

"Let's look at everyone's movements first of all," Jake said, "whose been off site in the last few days?"

"Everyone, except Nisha and Mel," Alf said.

"That's right," Jake said, "I've been into the village a couple of times. I took Tracey with me this morning but I went on my own yesterday."

"I went into Poitiers to pick Steph up," Alf said. "She'd been to Paris for some medical things she couldn't get around here."

"When I went to the village yesterday I found Tracey in the square by the café. I didn't know she'd gone, and when I asked her she said she'd needed a walk. When did Steph go to Paris?"

"She went the day before yesterday, around lunchtime. I took her to the station," Alf said.

"Where's Mel?" Nisha asked.

"Mel's here," Mel said. She had propped herself up on her crutches by the open door and had been listening.

"I want to look at everyone's phones. Can you collect them, Jake? Here's mine for starters."

Jake had all of their phones laid out on the table. They were all turned off. One by one Mel turned them on and examined the call records and text messages."

"No harm in turning them on now, is there?" Mel had said when Tracey started to protest.

As she completed her examination she handed each phone back to its owner. Nisha's, Jake's and Alf's were clear of any calls or messages for several days. Her own phone was clean too. That left Steph's and Tracey's. Before she turned them on Mel turned to them both.

"Am I going to find anything you need to tell us about?" she asked quietly.

"I made a few calls on the train to Paris and back," said Steph. "Just domestic catch-up stuff. All to UK numbers - family. I can tell you who they all are."

"Tracey?"

Tracey sat quietly; she looked uncomfortable.

"Well?" asked Jake.

"I did use my phone quite a lot from the village yesterday, and I might have made a couple of calls from here too. It's personal, but I've got a bit of a situation, domestic like. I haven't told anyone where we are, no one at all!"

"Mel?" Jake prompted.

Mel looked at Tracey's phone. The call record was full of numbers, mostly but not exclusively UK ones. There were text messages too, incoming and outgoing, all of an increasingly frantic nature.

"I don't like to ask, Tracey," Mel said, "but what does all this mean?"

"It's my ex," Tracey said, "it's a long story. In a nutshell, he's a junkie. He got hooked while he was in the army and got kicked out. We've got a kid - he's supposed to be looking after her while I'm here. Frankly, we need the money. Anyway, he's gone off the rails and he's wanting money and drugs off me. I left the military because I'd been pinching stuff for him from the pharmacy and it was about to go public. If I hadn't left I would have been dishonourably discharged after a couple of years in military prison. So, now he's been threatening to dob me in unless I get him cash and dope, not pharmaceuticals anymore but Class A. I'm about to finish my final exams to be an ICU nurse and…." Tracey tailed off, her eyes reddening as she tried not to cry.

"Sorry," she said, pulling herself together.

"Has he told anyone yet, about the drugs or where you are?" Alf asked.

"He says he hasn't told anyone about the gear, and I'm pretty sure he doesn't know this address, just that I'm working in France. When he's off his face he gets hellish busy with emails and texting and stuff though, so who knows. Thing is, we had a huge barney over the phone and by text that lasted a couple of days."

"Show me his number, Tracey," Mel asked gently.

"It's that one," Tracey pointed. There should only be that one, and two others - one for my mum and the other for my counsellor - I'm trying to get help for us."

"What about this one here?" Mel asked, "the foreign one?"

"What foreign one?" Tracey said,

"This one," Mel pointed.

"I don't know, I've never seen it before. Honest!" Tracey looked at each of them in turn, horrified. "I haven't blown our location! I wouldn't do that! We're a team! Steph! Tell them!"

There was a long moment of silence. Tracey's startled eyes jumped from one face to another, seeing nothing but blank stares.

"No! No! I didn't! I wouldn't!" She rushed from the room as her floodgates opened.

"Phew!" Jake broke the silence.

"I believe her," Steph said, "we've been through a lot together, me and Tracey, I trust her with my life."

"The point is," said Alf, "there's a number on her phone she can't or won't account for, and we know that Dido Sykes knows where we are. Tracey needs to stay in her room, with no phone or internet or anything. I want someone with or near her all the time. If it wasn't her we'll find out. And if it was, well we've more pressing things to worry about just now."

"I'll go and tell her," Steph said, "and I'll sit with her for a while. She's a good person and a brilliant medic. We still need her."

"Anyone got anything to say?" Jake asked, directing her question at Mel and Nisha.

"We'll start looking for confirmation, one way or another," Mel said. Nisha nodded.

Outside Alf spoke quietly to Kelso.

"We need to move, quickly. Do you remember how to get to the place we looked at, the one we've rented as a back-up down near La Rochelle?"

She nodded. He gave her a set of keys.

"Get everyone together, tell them to get an overnight bag each and pack up whatever kit Nisha needs. I want you all to be ready to leave together in one hour, or when I give you the word. Keep your phone on."

"And what will you be doing?" she asked.

"I'm just going to scout around the area to see if we've already got company. If I find we have I'll try to call you; if I can't you'll hear shooting. Either way, pile everyone in the hire car and get the hell out of here. If you don't hear anything, move out in one hour, tops. I'll come to meet you at the new place."

A silence followed. She didn't need to say anything.

Chapter 39

Alf had come to know the land around his house very well. When he'd been there on his own he walked each day and had explored every corner of the surrounding woodland and open country for three kilometres in any direction. He knew that any attack would need to come from the track into the village, so he circled out away from his house towards the south, moving parallel to the track but staying inside the tree line. The camper van was less than a kilometre from the house. It had been driven off the track into the trees and it was now almost hidden in a small clearing. It couldn't have been seen from the track, but from his vantage point in the woods he could look down on it and survey the site.

Some 50 metres or so from the van was a one-man tent, covered in twigs and foliage to disguise its outline. In another direction, also about 50 metres from the van but going back towards the track was a newly excavated depression with soil banked up on the far edge. In his brief time in the British army he had seen such excavations while doing the training for deployment to the bandit country of South Armagh. It was a foxhole, a shelter from which a hiding terrorist could initiate an explosion, a culvert or vehicle bomb.

He lay prone and silent, listening for any sound and examining every inch of the site for signs of life or movement. Everything was perfectly still. On the gentle morning breeze he caught the rank smell of decomposing flesh which seemed to be coming from the van. After 20 minutes he knew he would have to go and look more closely.

******

Greet Visser had ridden the bicycle into the village. She hadn't ridden it into the square but had propped it against a shelter in the car park of the small village supermarket, alongside a few others. She walked to the square and decided to have coffee and something to eat at the café. It was a pleasantly warm morning and for a few moments she was able to forget why she was there.

She thought briefly about the child, her daughter. Before the child had come along she and Wim Visser were already working together as a team. He hadn't long been out of the army; he had resigned after a tour in the Balkans and had been having flashbacks of some of the atrocities he had witnessed. They'd met at the psychotherapist's office where they were both receiving treatment. She had been referred by her own mother who was concerned at Greet's increasing fascination with extreme cruelty and violence, having found her watching all sorts of gruesome material on the internet. Greet had nowhere else to live and had to go along with her mother's wishes or become homeless.

She had immediately bonded with the tall, quiet ex-soldier and they soon became lovers. He had also been getting treatment, not so much for the harm caused to him by his flashbacks, but for the intense pleasure he got from remembering the pain he had seen inflicted on others.

It was Greet who introduced him to the sick pleasures of the dark side of the internet, but it was Wim's idea to make use of their shared enjoyment of other people's misery by offering to cause it, in return for payment. And so it had started. Slowly at first, just bodily harm for a few Euro, but it soon progressed as the strange couple gained a reputation for good planning and execution. It transpired that Greet had the aptitude for planning and carrying out the more controlled acts of cruelty, while Wim provided muscle and the extreme explosive violence needed to subdue a victim until she could inflict whatever pain or punishment had been commissioned.

The more bizarre and extreme the pain they inflicted, the more aroused they both became, and it was after a particularly satisfying and prolonged session involving successive amputations of the extremities of a debt-ridden, but still conscious, Amsterdam pimp and drug dealer that their passion resulted in her pregnancy. They married soon after they knew about the baby, and now he was dead.

Greet finished her breakfast and went to find some transport. She found a house that looked closed up for the summer. In an outbuilding she found a Renault Twingo with Paris number plates. It was covered in dust, had the battery disconnected, and the fuel tank half full. She had it started in a few minutes and having closed the outbuilding doors securely she set off back to her camp.

******

Alf approached the camper van cautiously. He looked for signs of booby-traps or tell-tales but found none. The smell got stronger as he neared the van. He covered his nose with a handkerchief. He slid the side door open and the eyewatering stench hit him. He noticed that crows were starting to gather in the branches nearby. With the door wide open he tried to hold his breath as he scanned the interior. He saw the clear plastic bags of nuts, bolts and screws and he saw the plastic fuel containers, nine of them. He also saw the rucksack and the reels of thin electrical cable next to it.

He cautiously opened the rucksack and instantly recognised the demolition charge, a detonator already in place. The two wires from the detonator were twisted around wires from the reels of cable but weren't covered by insulating tape. Alf untwisted one wire from a reel to the detonator, moving the charge slightly to cover the loose end. He traced the cable back and found a place where the wires were covered by one of the bags of steel nuts and bolts. He had a small torch in his coat pocket and he removed the battery. He found the wire cutters and tape that the bomb maker must have used, and he cut both strands of the electrical cable near the bag of shrapnel.

He quickly stripped the wires to expose the bare copper. He twisted the bare ends of each strand together, leaving a centimetre of exposed wire on each one. Taking two one-cent coins from his pocket he placed the battery from his torch between the exposed copper wires. He wiped the coins and battery carefully to remove any residual fingerprints, then firmly taped the coins over the ends of the battery to hold the wires secure. He hardly dared breathe as he did this, half expecting his life to end in a massive explosion. But it didn't come. He concealed the battery and the re-joined wires beneath the shrapnel bag Now the bomb was booby trapped and as soon as the bomb maker reattached the loose wire to the detonator it would explode. He carefully gathered the small pieces of insulation and fragments of wire to leave no trace of what he had done.

His work done, he closed the van door and retreated carefully back to his vantage point in the woods. No sooner had he settled down to watch, he saw a small Renault come up the lane. The driver parked it some way from the van, but then approached on foot. He recognised her from the photograph at the dive centre in Crete - it was the Dutch woman.

He watched her scan the site and, satisfied that all was in order, she opened the driver's door of the van. She started it and manoeuvred carefully back towards the track. He saw her pull the van into a passing place on the track just up from the clearing. He watched her descend, open the sliding door and emerge a second later with the reels of cable. She closed the door, rolled the cables under the van to the concealed side and retreated to her foxhole. She settled in.

Alf retreated slowly and silently. When he was well clear of the site he took out his phone and called Jake.

"Get in the car now, all of you. As soon as you get out of the gate, turn towards the village and drive slowly to the first bend. Once you get to the bend, floor it and drive as fast as you can. You'll see a VW camper van a few hundred metres up on your right - it's a bomb. I think I've disabled it. If you get past as fast as you can she won't have time to try to detonate it. Tell everyone to try to keep their heads down so she can't see who's in the car."

"Who is 'she'?" Jake asked.

"No time. Just do it, now!" He cut the call.

It was less than two minutes but it felt like forever. He saw the hire car come tearing down the lane and in seconds it was well clear of the van. Nothing happened.

******

In her foxhole Greet swore as the saloon sped past her bomb. She hadn't had time to touch the loose wire to the battery terminal. She had seen the blonde head of the driver, presumably Kelso, but she hadn't seen the man. She would have to wait until Kelso came back or the man drove past.

She heard the rattle of the old Peugeot before she saw it. She got ready. She saw the Peugeot round the bend slowly and move towards her trap. As it drew level with the back of the van she touched the wire to the battery terminal. She closed her eyes in anticipation of the blast, but nothing came. The old Peugeot kept going at the same speed and disappeared towards the village.

She cursed again. She emerged from her foxhole and followed the wires back towards the van. The battery was safely in her pocket. She was looking for breaks but found none. She opened the side door and choked back an urge to vomit. The cable went under the shrapnel as it should. She tugged the cables gently and they seemed firm so she didn't disturb the heavy bags. She had placed them like that to avoid the risk of the wire or the detonator being pulled out of the charge accidentally while she was moving the van. She opened the rucksack and saw in an instant that the one of the detonator wires had parted. She thought she had fastened it firmly, but now it was clearly loose. She looked for any sign of disturbance. Not seeing any, she bent forward over the rucksack to reattach the loose wire.

******

Julia and the women had nearly reached the village when they heard the explosion. Julia pulled over and tried to call Alf. There was no answer. She got out and looked back in the direction of the house and saw the plume of black smoke over the forest. People were starting to come out to look. The siren on the village fire station started to wail.

Julia almost fainted with relief when she saw the old Peugeot coming towards her. He didn't stop or acknowledge her; he just kept going.

Chapter 40

The new house fell silent. They had arrived the day before; Alf had still not appeared. The house was comfortable, but nowhere near as homely as the one near Poitiers. There were four big bedrooms upstairs and one downstairs, a large terrace with distant sea views, and a decent sized pool. Nisha, Tracey and Steph had adjacent rooms upstairs, alongside Jake's one, which would presumably be shared by Alf as and when he arrived. Mel had chosen the downstairs one with its own bathroom. Nisha's equipment had been set up in a spare downstairs room.

Her morning physio had been painful but mercifully brief and now Mel was alone in front of Nisha's computers. Nisha and Jake had gone out to buy provisions. Jake said they would have lunch in La Rochelle.

She knew Nisha's log-in by now and she started scrolling through files that Nisha hadn't looked at while Mel was with her. None of it made much sense, so she gave up. Turning to a pair of phones she'd found in Nisha's computer bag - neither was the one Nisha had presented when Mel checked all their phones back at the house near Poitiers - she was on more familiar ground. One phone was obviously Nisha's personal one. There were lots of contacts in the address book and loads of innocuous text messages, some to do with work but mostly personal stuff. The second phone was different.

It took a while for Mel to work out the PIN code to get into the phone. Eventually she remembered that Nisha had a tendency to use patterns rather than words or numbers for her passwords; she'd watched her fingers fly over the keys as she logged in. She tried a few patterns that seemed familiar, eventually hitting on the shape of an N: *1#3 on the keypad. The phone unlocked. It was a UK mobile on a pay as you go number. Mel looked first at the text messages. There were a few, only a few, all between T and L. T was obviously Nisha, and whoever L was he or she was using a mobile number beginning with +352. Mel checked; it was a Luxembourg number. The messages went back over several weeks, and the last exchange was only a few days ago. All were brief, suggesting that the correspondents knew each other well enough not to waste words. One message, less than two weeks old, from T to L caught her attention. It read:

"He will probably be around. Make like we've never met."

There was no reply. Mel checked the call records. Very few voice calls had been made, but there was one to a French number, also about two weeks ago - when Nisha had been in Lyon. The call lasted less than a minute. Mel checked back in the text messages and found an earlier message from L to T consisting of a long number, the same French phone number that Nisha must have called as T. The French number had called Nisha's T phone once only, two days after the Lyon trip. It hadn't been answered, but Nisha's phone had dialled the French number again just two days ago, the day Jake and Alf had returned from Montreux. There was no call duration recorded, so no conversation had taken place. Mel's training as an intelligence analyst told her that you don't always need words to communicate.

Mel turned the phone off and put it back where she had found it. She returned to the computer screens and examined the browsing history of each machine. On two of them the history was complete, on the third there was nothing at all. Looking at the programme settings Mel found that a TOR browser had been uploaded - this was the machine that Nisha used for her dark web access.

Mel was puzzled and worried. She couldn't go any further, not yet anyway, so she closed everything down and slowly walked out to the terrace on her crutches. She tried not to think too much but failed miserably. Where was Alf?

******

Jake and Nisha got back first.

"She said she had a stomach bug," Jake explained to Mel, "and didn't want lunch. She's gone for a lie down."

"How did she seem?" Mel asked.

"What do you mean?"

"Was she nervous at all, tense?"

"Not really; she was quiet, but if she isn't feeling well, it's understandable."

"Have you spent much time with her since Montreux?"

"A bit, she does tend to follow me into the pool. She seems normal, for Nisha that is. Chatty and a bit daft. Why?"

"I found a phone. It's hers, and I think she's communicating with someone in secret. I want to be sure before I say anything else."

"What are you saying, Mel?" Jake asked.

"I don't know. It could be nothing at all; it could be nothing to do with us. She is a hacker, after all, and she'll be in contact with all sorts of strange people all the time. Did she know Alf would be in Lyon?"

"We discussed it with her. In the end we said he'd be there if she wanted him to be. She said she didn't. We didn't talk about it any further, so no, she wouldn't have *known* he'd be there."

"Do you think she could have seen him, or worked out that he'd go?"

"Both are possible. Why?"

"She sent a text message to someone. She said *'He might be around. Make like we've never met'*. She sent it to someone she knows as L - Leah, maybe? Dido's old hacker name"

"And this was when exactly?"

"Two weeks ago. Before the Lyon trip. When she was in Lyon she called a French mobile number that L had sent her. She spoke for less than a minute."

"You think she's talking to Dido Sykes?" Jake asked.

"It's one explanation. There could be a lot of others."

At that moment Nisha appeared on the terrace, dressed for the pool.

"Feeling better?" Jake asked.

"A bit. I think I was dehydrated," Nisha smiled and sat down at the table with them. "I don't feel like doing any work today. Is that OK? There's nothing pressing, is there? Sykes is keeping her head down - she hasn't even checked your emails for a couple of days, Jake."

"Have the day off, Nisha. You've been at it non-stop," Jake said.

"I'm going for a swim. Coming?" Nisha asked.

"In a while. There's stuff to put away first."

Jake and Mel watched as Nisha walked to the pool. She kept her robe on until she got to the water's edge before removing it. Her lustrous body set off the colourful bikini she wore. She tied her hair back and dived in, swimming smoothly and powerfully in the cool clear water.

"Seems she only does the flasher stuff when Alf's about," Mel said. "Do you think she puts it on?"

"She didn't seem to care when I went to her house that time, but it was early. Maybe she's making an effort for us," Jake said, "or maybe you're right. She might just want to have a go with Alf. He said she'd tried it on with him in the car, not full-on or anything, but he politely declined."

Jake watched Nisha swim, trying to figure her out.

******

Their peace was disturbed by the rattling sound of the old Peugeot as Alf coaxed it up the steep drive when he arrived shortly after Nisha entered the pool.

"I thought you were getting rid of that old thing," Mel called as he walked across the terrace towards them.

"I have. I've been down to Bordeaux - we're picking up two new ones in a couple of days. We can get rid of the hire car then as well."

"I hope you've got something decent for a change," Jake said.

"I think you'll be content, Ms Kelso, I've found you something suitable."

"Mel wants a word," Jake said, "about Nisha."

Alf listened intently as Mel quickly repeated what she'd told Jake, keeping her voice low and her eyes on Nisha in the pool.

"What time did she make the call in Lyon?" he asked.

"Early afternoon on the Saturday. It was brief."

"I saw her using a phone. I'm pretty sure she didn't see me - she gave no indication. Which means she really didn't see me or she's very good at counter surveillance. Is she trained, Jake?"

"I don't think so. There's nothing in her personal file and she's never mentioned it."

"So, what do we do?" Jake asked.

"What do you need to get into her dark web machine, Mel?" he asked.

"Her passwords for a start, and then the sites she's visiting."

"How can you get that?" he asked.

"By sitting next to her and watching, or by using something called a key logger, which I don't have. It's a gadget to record secretly the key-strokes a user makes."

"And she's not going to do anything interesting while you're watching her?"

"Not a chance."

"OK. I'm going into town. I'm going to get you something so you can watch what she's doing without her knowing."

"What if we just front her with it?" Jake asked. "If she is up to something it would stop her."

"True, but we wouldn't know what she *has* been up to," Mel said, "if it's legit, in a loose sense, she'd probably get the hump and walk out. We still need her if she is on our side. And if she isn't, we need to know for sure."

Chapter 41

The memory cards in the two tiny cameras that Alf had bought after their discussion were large enough to capture what Mel needed. He retrieved them when Nisha had gone to bed and Mel downloaded the footage on her own computer.

"I think I've got her log-in, which is great," Mel said. "The shots of the screen aren't too good, but I can have a stab at the sites she may have visited, and any secure email she's got. I'll need to get on her machine, though. I'll try when she's having her swim tomorrow."

"I've replaced the memory cards," Alf said, "so if she does any more before then you'll be able to see that too. Now sleep!"

The next morning Alf and Jake left early for Bordeaux in the two cars. They said they should be back within four or five hours. Nisha was still asleep. Alf had looked in on her before they'd left and said she was completely gone.

Mel took her chance. A notebook beside her, she entered the log-in name and password the cameras had captured and the TOR browser opened and allowed her into the darkest depths of the web. Two hours later she heard footsteps on the floor above; she quickly wiped the browsing history and closed down the machine. By the time Nisha appeared on the terrace Mel was sipping coffee and reading a paperback.

"Morning Nisha," she called, "how are you today?"

Nisha grunted a reply and sat down heavily in a chair. Mel poured her a coffee. Nisha drank it quickly and held out her cup for a refill.

"That's better," she said after ten minutes. "Morning Mel. What's new?"

"Alf and Jake have gone for the new cars. Steph and Tracey are plotting my next torture session."

"Poor you. Is the physio really horrible?" Nisha asked.

"Yes," Mel replied, "but better than the alternative."

"I suppose it is," Nisha said, "I'm going for a swim."

When Nisha was in the water Mel hobbled back indoors. She knew Nisha would probably spend around an hour in the pool, as she always did. She took her seat at the computer table and logged in to Nisha's dark web account again. She was completely absorbed and didn't hear her.

"What are you doing, Mel?" Nisha asked.

She was standing in front of Mel, a bathrobe over her wet bikini, her bare feet leaving damp marks on the floor. In her right hand she held a pistol. It was pointing straight at Mel's head, unwavering.

******

Jake dropped the hire car off near Bordeaux railway station and climbed back into the old Peugeot, hopefully for the last time. They stopped for a quick coffee in town before heading for the car dealer on the *Rocade*, Bordeaux's manic ring road.

"I'm worried about leaving Mel alone with Nisha," Jake said.

"I'm sure she'll be careful," Alf said, "we'll just pick up the cars and be back in a couple of hours."

Jake was appreciative of Alf's choice of vehicles for a change. He had selected an enormous Citroën station wagon for general use and for long journeys, and for Jake he had chosen a relatively new automatic BMW 5 series saloon.

"Very good, Ferdinand," she commented, "a proper BMW and a bungalow."

"It's a very comfortable bungalow, as it happens. It's quite fast too."

They started back towards La Rochelle in convoy, her in the lead. They'd been away from the house for nearly three hours.

******

"What are you doing, Mel?" Nisha asked again.

"I know what you're up to, Nisha," Mel said, "it's got to stop."

"And you're going to make me, are you?"

"If I can. If I can't, Kelso will. You've got to stop it, Nisha. It's going to stop."

"Have you any idea what I've put into this? How many hours of work - how many hundreds, thousands, of hours? You think I'm going to stop, just because you say so?"

"You're working for Sykes, aren't you?"

Nisha's eyes widened; she laughed out loud.

"You have no idea, do you?" Nisha was raising her voice.

"So tell me," Mel said.

"What then, Mel? What if I do?"

"If it makes sense, maybe I can help you. If I'm wrong about what you're doing and you're not working for Sykes, then it could be you're doing something worthwhile."

"And if it's not worthwhile, in your opinion?"

"I'll have to stop it, Nisha."

The gun had not wavered in Nisha's hand once. It remained deadly still, aimed directly at Mel's forehead. Nisha saw Mel looking at the weapon.

"I do know how to use it, Mel. I've done the course, got top marks too."

"Talk to me, Nisha. Did you tell Sykes where we were?"

"I had to; it bought me some time. I just picked up Tracey's phone and made a call; after I'd spoken to Sykes I sent her an email. I didn't know she was going to send the Dutch woman but it doesn't really matter, does it? I can get on with things now."

"What exactly is it you're doing, Nisha?"

"I'm taking control - she's had it her own way long enough. She thought she was invincible, hiding behind her different names and aliases, invisible. I've been on to her for ages, long before all this. I've worked my way in. She thinks I'm a low life, but she knows I've got skills. I'm as good as she is, better in fact. She thinks she'll dispose of me when it suits her, but by then it'll be too late. She'll be finished."

"It's about defeating Dido Sykes?"

"Or whatever she's calling herself when it all ends, yes. It's about defeating her, and it's about me winning. She's done OK, but I can do better."

"You're taking over? You're replacing her?"

"Improving on her performance."

"You're taking over her criminal business? The trafficking, the blackmail, extortion, everything?"

"Like I said, improving on her performance."

"You can't! I won't let you!"

"But you're not in any position to stop me, are you? You're broken, Mel; she nearly killed you. She was sloppy, again. I'm fit; I have a gun pointed at you." Nisha was completely calm. The house was silent, still.

"I've written down what I know, Nisha, and sent it to Kelso. She'll know what you've done if you kill me."

"Kelso! Julia 'Jake' Kelso! I've got enough on her and Ferdinand to see them both behind bars for a very long time. She's on my list. He is too. It's a pity he's so stuck on the two of you, you and Kelso. I did quite fancy him - he's quite cute in a grumpy old man sort of way. I offered it to him on a plate, did you know that? Even though I was actually in bed with him with no pants on and inviting him to have sex with me that first time we went to Switzerland, he wouldn't do it. All I wanted was a condom full of DNA to seal his fate and Kelso's. If we'd actually done it maybe I'd have kept him to myself for a while for entertainment. But no matter, I've got what I need now."

"I can still stop you, Nisha!"

"No, you can't Mel. I like you, I really do, but you can't stop me. I won't let you."

Nisha levelled the pistol at Mel's head. She took up the pressure on the trigger.

"Goodbye, Mel. I'm sorry, I really did like you," she said, starting to squeeze the trigger.

A single shot rang out.

Chapter 42

Alf had stopped for fresh bread so Julia arrived back at the new house first. At first she was puzzled by the complete lack of movement, then by the silence. She parked and went towards the house, turning a corner to see Steph sitting on the edge of the terrace, her head in her hands.

"What is it, Steph?" Julia asked. "Where's Mel?"

Steph gestured towards the house. She was silent, her hands shaking. Julia went swiftly to the downstairs room where she saw the body. She rushed over and bent to check for a pulse. Nothing. A pool of blood was still spreading across the floor. Julia stood and went quickly to Mel's room, where she found Tracey.

"What's happened?" Julia asked.

Tracey looked up. Mel was on the bed, her face peaceful, eyes closed.

"She's in shock, I've given her a tranquiliser. Steph heard voices, like arguing. Mel sounded like she was getting upset, so Steph went to see what was happening. Nisha was pointing a gun at Mel, looked like she was about to fire, so Steph drew her own weapon and shot Nisha. One clean head shot. She had no choice. I've checked the gun Nisha had - it was cocked, and the safety was off. She could have fired any second. Steph's a bit shaken up; we're trained to do this sort of thing, but it's been a while since either of us had to shoot anyone for real. If you stay with Mel, I'll go see how Steph's doing."

"Do you know what they were saying?"

"No idea, I was in my room, I'm still confined to barracks, remember? I didn't hear anything - just the shot. I came running and found Steph in the doorway with Nisha on the floor. Mel was at the desk, but she was just freaked out of it. Like I said, I've given her something to calm her down for a while, just while we sort this out."

"OK," Julia said, "go to Steph. I'll need to speak with both of you in a while."

Tracey did as she'd been asked, coming back a few moments later with the tear-stained Steph. Julia went to the kitchen and came back with water for them all.

"You did great, Steph. Without you Mel would be dead," Julia started, "I need you to talk me through what happened, as much as you can remember. Alf will be here soon, and he'll want to hear it too, so maybe take a few minutes to get your thoughts together."

Julia went to the terrace to wait. Alf pulled up a few minutes later.

"What's wrong?" he started.

"There's been an incident. It looks like Nisha and Mel had a set-to, and Nisha pulled a gun."

"A gun? Nisha?"

"Yes, one of the spare ones that we've been using - I put them in a drawer in the kitchen. Steph heard arguing and went to see what was wrong. She's waiting to speak to us, but it looks like she saw Nisha ready to shoot Mel and she got in first. One shot to the head. Nisha's dead."

Alf was silent, but he gestured that they should go inside to see Steph. He left Julia to do the talking.

"How are you doing, Steph?" she asked gently.

"I'm OK, just a bit shaken, it's not what I was expecting."

"What happened?" Julia asked.

"I heard voices, they sounded tense, so I went to the downstairs room door. I saw Nisha with a gun pointing right at Mel's head. It looked ready to fire, I could see the hammer was in the cocked position. I didn't say anything or make a sound as I thought Nisha would shoot as soon as she heard me, and probably shoot both Mel and me. I drew my weapon - Tracey and I always carry around the house - it was already racked and the safety was on. I released the safety and aimed at Nisha. I saw her move her gun as if she was going to fire, so I let loose one round, aimed at Nisha's head. I didn't shout a warning or anything. It was all I could do. My shot was good, and she went down without a sound. Mel went white and started screaming - that's when Tracey arrived to take care of her. I checked Nisha for signs of life, but she was dead. Then I went outside to sit and try to calm down. You arrived about ten minutes afterwards."

"Nisha had the gun in her hand? Which hand?" Alf asked.

"Her right, but she steadied it with her left, under the butt - you know, the standard police shooting stance as they're about to fire."

"Where's her gun now?"

"Tracey's got it I think."

"And you fired one round only. Where's the casing?"

"I didn't pick it up, so it must be on the floor in the other room."

Alf went away for a second and came back with the brass cartridge case in his hand.

"I want you to give me your weapon, Steph, then go and scrub your hands. Also get showered, wash thoroughly and change your clothing - all of it."

Steph nodded.

"Tracey," he continued, "I want you to scrub Nisha's hands to get rid of any gun oil or powder traces. When you've done it get some water from the pool and wash her hands with it. I've seen her and she's wearing swimming stuff, so I'm guessing she was in the pool."

Tracey nodded too.

"I want your weapon too, Tracey, then you make sure your hands are clean. I'll collect the other pistol from the drawer and dispose of all four of them. When that's all done, Julia will call the police. The story is that Nisha was on her own in the downstairs room when an intruder came in. The intruder must have been after the computers, and she spooked him into shooting her. Everyone OK with that?"

They nodded in unison. Alf took a moment to gather up the concealed cameras hidden around the downstairs room.

"Just so we're all clear," Julia said, "I rented this place for Mel to convalesce in after a road accident in Greece. Mel is like a sister to me; Nisha was a mutual friend who came to join us and was doing some research - she said she was thinking about a PhD. Tracey and Steph are trained nurses hired to look after Mel."

"And I'm not here at all," Alf said, "is that clear with everyone?"

"What about Mel?" Tracey asked.

"Keep her sedated until the police have been and gone," Julia said, "as far as we're concerned, she didn't see or hear anything. None of us saw the intruder."

Fifteen minutes later, after all Alf's instructions had been followed, he left the house and Julia picked up the phone to dial 112 and tell the police about an apparent burglary and the shooting of her friend. She sounded appropriately upset.

The first police car arrived in less than ten minutes, the CID about twenty minutes after that. Julia's French was good and she did all the talking. The CID officers took details, sent for scenes of crime, an examining magistrate and an undertaker, took photographs of Nisha's body and the downstairs room, and the wide-open doors on the terrace at the side of the house. Easy access for any burglar. They searched high and low for the bullet casing but couldn't find it. The killer must have taken it with him, they said. They had found the spent bullet embedded in the wall, misshapen and of little evidential value in terms of identifying the weapon it was fired from.

They took statements from Tracey and Steph, with Julia acting as interpreter. They looked in on Mel and saw her lying in her bed, sedated and asleep. They went to ask at neighbouring properties, all of which were some way off, if anyone had seen or heard anything. No one had, but everyone was blaming the seasonal migrant workers who traversed southern France in their beaten-up unregistered white vans every summer.

By the time everything was completed, Nisha's body had been removed and Julia had called the British consulate in Bordeaux to notify them of the sudden death of a British national they were all exhausted. The last thing Julia did was put in a call to the Metropolitan Police to let them know that Inspector Tanisha Chakrabarti, studying in France with Commander Kelso and others, had been killed by a burglar. She asked them to notify Nisha's family and gave the name of the consular official in Bordeaux who would coordinate all the formalities concerning liaison with the French police and repatriation of the body.

As the sun set after Alf had returned, the four of them sat round a table on the terrace with strong drinks and a sombre ambience. Tracey went to check on Mel, who was starting to come round. Alf decided to go and sit with her.

When she opened her eyes, she saw him and the ghost of a smile flitted across her face, to be quickly erased by the memory of what had been about to happen.

"It's OK, Mel," he said, "you're safe now. Nisha's gone."

"What happened? She was going to shoot me."

"Steph got her first, but don't worry about that now. Do you want to tell me what happened?"

"It's all a bit fuzzy. Nisha's not what she seems - she's not good, Alf. I said I had to stop her, she said she couldn't let me. Too much to lose. Then the gun - it seemed so huge. I heard the noise and I must have passed out. Is she dead?"

"Yes, Mel, Nisha is dead."

"Oh," Mel said quietly. Tears began to roll down her face.

Alf held her hand, then raised himself to lie on the bed beside her. He held her close while she cried in silence.

Chapter 43

None of them slept much that night. Jake and Alf sat on the terrace in the near darkness for many hours. She was stressed and fretting, blaming herself for having brought Nisha into their midst.

"You can't blame yourself, Jake," Alf was saying, "she targeted you. For all we know she engineered the whole thing. We might know more when Mel's awake and with it in the morning."

"I suppose, but this has to end, Alf! I've got to finish it, and soon."

"And so you will, just as soon as we know what needs to be done. Now, have another drink or go to bed."

"You go, I'm going to stay here a while longer."

He left her and walked slowly upstairs to their room. He didn't hear her come in, but when he awoke at first light, she was there beside him, a frown engraved on her usually calm and flawless face. He got up quietly, pulled on his swimming trunks and went to the pool. After thirty minutes he felt better and went to the terrace. Mel was there already, dressed in a plain tee shirt and shorts, a livid scar on her right thigh. He couldn't help noticing how much her muscles had wasted - her legs were now thin and pale.

"Sexy, isn't it?" she said, noticing that he was looking at her legs.

"They'll be back to normal in no time," he said.

"Want to put money on it?"

"If you want. How are you?"

"Not so good, to be honest. I've spent my entire life not getting murdered, now someone tries to do it four times in just one summer! I'm not keen, Alf. But why am I telling you this? You're already dead, at least twice."

"It's not so bad," he said, "once you're used to it. But it's nearly over, Mel, we just need a bit more to work out what we have to do. Will you help us?"

"You know I will, I've already decided. First, I need coffee, then I need to be left alone with Nisha's laptop, the one she used to do all her dark web skulking. I'm pretty sure that it's got the most interesting stuff hidden away in it somewhere. Can you search her room, maybe the one at the other house too? I think she might have something written down; her codes and passwords are complicated - she must have them recorded somewhere. In good old-fashioned writing, I would imagine."

He went to dress, then started methodically searching through Nisha's things. Mel was right: in the lining of her backpack, concealed in a carefully made hidden pocket, was a standard issue office memo book, as supplied to the Metropolitan Police. Most of it was empty, but on various random pages there were lines of closely written script, the handwriting small and precise.

"Is this the sort of thing you meant?" Alf handed Mel the notebook.

"Looks like it," Mel said as she skimmed through the pages, "thanks. See you later."

She went inside and closed the downstairs room door behind her, trying to ignore the strong smell of disinfectant and cleaning fluid, and the wet floor that still bore a dark stain despite the best efforts of Steph, Tracey and Jake.

They sat and waited. And waited. Steph and Tracey tried to relax by the pool, Alf and Jake sat under a shady parasol on the terrace. At lunchtime Mel called for food. It was late afternoon before she emerged, a sheaf of paper covered in handwritten notes in her hand.

"Is it too early for strong drink?" Mel asked, "I need one of Jake's gins."

When it arrived, she started.

"As far as I can make out, Nisha was on to Dido Sykes a long time ago, at least a few years. She was busy hacking long before she joined the computer crime unit and she's kept files of some interesting things in a password-protected hidden directory in her laptop. It doesn't look like she's entrusted it to anyone else - no back-up files, so the laptop must have been very precious to her. Nisha started targeting Dido through hacker networks, making sure she went along to some of the gigs Dido went to, even sending covert emails to her. I've found a lot of those. Nisha was playing the innocent aspiring apprentice; she flattered Dido and wanted to learn from her. It worked. They got to know each other, quite well by the look of things.

"Nisha hacked into Dido's systems, and she's kept copies of some of the things Dido said about her. It seems Dido keeps notes too. Nisha found it amusing, judging by her comments. Dido reckoned she was recruiting Nisha, seducing her physically as well as technically. Nisha wasn't very complimentary about Dido's style in bed by the way, but I digress.

"Nisha has a comprehensive dossier on everything that Dido Sykes, alias Marianne Desbois, alias a lot of other things, has been up to over the past few years. It's all there - blackmail, which we know about, people trafficking, which we know about, targeted assassinations of potential rivals, which we know a little bit about, peddling secret information, which we haven't come across. There's also stuff that's just malicious - remember that old actor, everyone's favourite grandpa? Dido destroyed his life and reputation with entirely false evidence, and showbusiness being what it is it wasn't long before all sorts of deranged wannabees joined in the attacks on him. Poor old guy's gone crazy and he's locked up in a comfortable and expensive asylum in California. Dido did that to him just because she could and she wanted to. She told Nisha he didn't mean anything to her, she just didn't like him.

"The list goes on. Dido's made millions, a lot of millions. Nisha knew where it all is. It's all in there, banks, account numbers, access codes and passwords, everything. She also found all of Dido's files. They're on the servers in the Philippines, the ones I found earlier, or rather which Nisha let me find. Nisha got access to all of those too, but I don't know how she did it.

"Nisha was also after you, Jake. I'm certain that she wasn't the person she seemed. Her dottiness, all the exhibitionism, the allergy to early mornings, it was all an act. She was as sharp as a razor, and totally in control of herself. She found the connection between you and Dido going back to your time at Oxford. It looks like she thought you and Dido might be in cahoots at first, but she changed her mind when she saw how you went after the trafficking operation. Nisha deliberately got herself posted to the computer crime unit. She found out what Dido was up to with the blackmail primer involving Amelia Armstrong, and she actually contacted Armstrong first, through Llewellyn, her business partner. She planted the idea that only Julia Kelso could be trusted to handle such a delicate matter, which is why she got in touch with you in person. Then Nisha made sure she got the enquiry from you. She set it all up."

"Christ almighty," Julia said, "do you think she knew about the attack on you in Crete?"

"I was wondering, but I don't think so. It played into her hands, though. Nisha was thrilled to bits when you got friendly and asked her to come down here to help."

"But why, Mel?" Alf asked. "Why did she want Jake?"

"It's not clear, but I think she saw Jake as a threat. She knew that Jake was after Dido, and Nisha's plan was to usurp her. She wanted Jake out of the way so she wouldn't intervene or disrupt anything. If Dido had been taken out, it would have made it very difficult for Nisha to do what she wanted, which was to take over *all* of Sykes's activities, including her wealth, properties, everything. She told me she thought she could do better, improve the performance of Dido's criminal enterprises. I think she was planning to take over Sykes's identities and actually become her, which she couldn't do if Dido was locked up somewhere."

"So," Alf said, "just to make sure I've got this right, you now have access to all of Dido's information and her money?"

"Not quite," Mel said. "I know about it, but I can't get at it; I certainly can't hack into the servers in

Manila, or into her bank accounts. The codes Nisha left don't let me do that, there are other stages that are needed, stages which Nisha kept to herself. So, unless we can find them all we have is enough to disrupt, if that's what you're thinking."

"It is what I'm thinking," said Jake. "How can we do it?"

"With the Manila servers, it's easy, relatively speaking. We pretend to be Dido and close the account with the server operator, instructing them to delete everything on her servers, including all back-up copies over the normal monthly cycle. It's standard practice to run daily back-ups, and Dido's stuff will be there. It will take about four weeks for all her back-up copies to be overwritten and permanently disappear, but once her account is closed she won't be able to get at those files anyway. I've got her user identity, her passwords, and her security check words - it should be enough. It'll be the same as wiping Dido's memory. Nisha worked out that all of Dido's eggs are in this one basket. So, we can stop her dead, but…."

"If she still has her money," Jake said, "she can start again."

"Correct," said Mel, "Nisha worked out that it took Dido a long time to get to where she is. She had an early advantage with the knowledge she picked up at Harvard way back when, but now everyone in the hacking business has that knowledge and the internet has moved on. She wouldn't find it so easy to recover her position; without her financial cushion she'd be just another jobbing hacker scraping a living with small-time scams, not her style at all."

"And you can't hack into her accounts?" Alf said.

"No, I can't. It's beyond my skill set, and I don't think like a hacker. But I can mess her about a bit, probably enough to make sure she can't get at her own money either."

"How?" he asked.

"When we delete everything on the servers, we'll be wiping out most of Dido's financial stuff too - her references to access her accounts. She might have them in other places too, but if we time it right we can imitate her in communications with her financial institutions, Nisha identified five numbered accounts, not named ones. Two are with institutions in the Caribbean or Central America, the rest here in Europe, and she didn't think there are any others. We just tell them to change the access codes, passwords and security questions, say there's been a security breach. We can do the same to the accounts for Eris, Sykes's company in Switzerland - it has no employees and doesn't do any business, but it is her source of 'legitimate' funds to pay her bills. Eris owns her house in Coppet, so we can deny her that too.

"Once we've done that, the accounts are effectively changed; she won't be able to access them with her old codes. The money stays where it is, she just won't be able to get her hands on it and the banks will have no way to contact her - they don't know who she is. She'll be completely broke, to all intents and purposes. It's all about the timing."

"What are your thoughts on that?" Jake asked.

"It takes a couple of days to action an account closure with the server operators. They work twenty-four seven, but with limited customer service at weekends and public holidays - I've checked. They take advantage of quieter periods to do maintenance and things like that. So, if we close her account on a Friday before a public holiday, she won't be able to stop it happening. Manila is six or seven hours ahead, so we issue the cancellation around 4am our time. It won't affect anything Dido does on that Friday, but it will start to show on Saturday. National Heroes' Day is a public holiday in the Philippines, always on a Monday and it's coming up next week. That means she won't be able to do anything about her account with the service provider until Tuesday, which will be too late. Her access and all her files will be gone and within a few weeks will have disappeared completely and forever. If we change her bank codes at the close of business on the same Friday it should have all been actioned before she can attempt to recover her codes on Tuesday. Job done."

"Great stuff, Mel," Jake said. "Get it all set up for Friday. I'll leave for Switzerland on Sunday to have a chat with her on Monday."

"To say what?" Alf asked her.

"Just to tell her it's all over, that she's finished."

Chapter 44

They all had things to do. Julia had calls to make concerning Nisha, first to the Met's welfare people, then to ask one of her senior officers to go to see Nisha's family in Surrey, and finally to the British Consulate in Bordeaux to agree to cover their costs in repatriating the body once it had been released by the examining magistrate. It wasn't considered a complicated case, although it would probably never be solved given the numerous bands of itinerant criminals who roamed Europe these days and were virtually untraceable. Luckily there had been very little media coverage of the murder of Inspector Chakrabarti, thanks mostly to the influence of the lucrative tourist industry in that part of France. The consular official had been advised by the police in La Rochelle that Nisha's body would be released after the post-mortem and could be returned to the UK in a week or so.

Mel was worked on by Steph and Tracey when she wasn't busy with Nisha's laptop. She was making steady progress physically, thanks to her well-established fitness over the years. It didn't stop her complaining, though. In Nisha's files she found more emails between her and Dido, not adding anything new but confirming beyond doubt that Nisha had been playing her like a fish.

Alf spent a day carefully dismantling four handguns and two assault rifles which he had gone to recover from their hiding place in the big barn near Poitiers. He burnt any wooden parts and reduced the metal components to a pile of unidentifiable scrap. These he bundled into separate hessian sacks to be dumped in various bodies of water, ideally the Atlantic or the tidal Gironde estuary, over the next few days.

They called a halt to everything on Thursday and decided to have a day off at the beach on the Île de Ré. It was a welcome respite from the growing intensity of the atmosphere around the house. They lunched on fresh fish and seafood; Steph and Tracey swam and played in the Atlantic waves while Alf and Jake kept the somewhat wistful Mel company on a shady terrace. Mel found it hard to believe there was actually a village on the island called 'Ars' and kept asking excitedly to go there.

Back at the house near La Rochelle later they drank a bit too much and went to bed quite early. Mel was awake at three in the downstairs room with Jake sitting alongside her. Together they had a final review of the messages Mel would send as Dido Sykes / Marianne Desbois to the server operator and the five banks. Satisfied with their work, they logged in to Dido's covert email account and sent them one after the other in quick succession. Acknowledgments were immediate from Manila; Mel promptly deleted all of them, as she did with the sent messages. Mel knew that Sykes did not check her covert email on a daily basis, but she still needed a bit of luck to be on her side, and her luck held. By the time the banks opened later on Friday morning Mel was able to see the acknowledgements from each, together with confirmation that her urgent instructions had been actioned, and she deleted all of them too. Dido would never know, unless she delved deep into the email servers, which belonged to someone else who was not especially interested in keeping copies of anything at all. The destruction of Dido Sykes's criminal business empire had been irrevocably set in motion.

On Saturday Jake and Alf stayed in bed for a long time, tensions eased and enjoying each other as they had before it all started. Mel had studiously avoided talking about having any kind of sex, but privately Jake and Alf wondered if and how they should ever raise it with her again. Jake in particular missed Mel's special skills, energy and touches, despite Alf's diligence and enthusiasm. It's all very lovely with him, but just not the same, she thought.

On Sunday morning she left. She rose early, before the rest of the household stirred, threw a small bag in the boot of the BMW and set off on the long, familiar drive to Geneva and beyond. She spent Sunday night in a plush hotel on the outskirts of Geneva, and at 10 on Monday morning she was parked outside the lakeside villa near Coppet.

******

"Tell Madame Desbois that Tonto needs to see her, it's urgent," Jake spoke in French into the speaker by the gate.

"Just a moment," said a disembodied voice, then a pause. The gate clicked as the locks were undone. She walked up the drive to the front door. An elderly maid stood in the porch, gesturing for the stranger to enter. Guests were not frequent at the villa; Madame had blanched when the name Tonto was spoken.

"Madame is in the drawing room on the first floor," the maid said in heavily accented French.

Julia climbed the stairs slowly, wary and alert. Dido Sykes stood with her back to the door, staring out over the lake. She was elegantly dressed, her hair once again long and very blonde.

"What do you want?" she said, without turning round. "Why have you come here?"

"Hello Dido," Julia said.

Sykes spun on her heel.

"You!" she hissed, hurling herself across the room at Julia, her fingers outstretched like talons. Julia sidestepped, sweeping Dido's legs from under her as she lost her balance. She fell heavily, winded and gasping for breath despite the thick carpet which had cushioned her fall.

Dido reared up and lunged once more for Julia. In a second she was prone again.

"I can keep this up all day, Dido, but I'm sure you'll be more comfortable if we just sit down and talk," Julia said calmly.

After one last attempt Dido gave in. Julia didn't help her up but stood at a safe distance while the breathless and clearly angry Sykes raised herself.

"OK," she said, "what do you want?"

"I want to talk to you about Tonto. Nisha as I call her. She's dead, Dido."

"What do you mean?"

"Tonto. She was Tanisha Chakrabarti, a police officer, an Inspector. Didn't you know that?"

"Of course I know that. I put her up to it, Kelso. I told her to infiltrate your department to get to you. She was mine all along."

"I thought she was mine too, but she wasn't. She wasn't yours, either. She played us both, Dido, your Tonto, my Nisha, she wasn't ours at all."

"How did she die?"

"She was shot. She was about to kill Mel Dunn. Mel's not dead, despite all your efforts. By the way, the merry widow from Holland, your hired assassin, *is* dead. She and her husband both failed you."

"There will be others. Dunn's tenacious, I'll give her that, I was wondering. When Tonto sent me messages from your little hideaway in France she never mentioned Dunn, just you and Ferdinand. I know about him too. The undead detective."

"I'm not interested in what you know, not anymore. It's over, Dido. Your reign as a criminal mastermind, a blackmailer, pornographer, pimp, trafficker, exploiter of people, murderer, it's all finished."

"Is it now?" Sykes said, scornfully.

"Your Tonto was going to take you down. She'd been working on you for years; she's got everything there is to know about you and she was going to take you. Now I've done it instead; like I said, it's over."

"You wouldn't know where to begin, Kelso."

"We'll see about that, won't we? Tell me one thing, Dido: how did little Carol Jones from Hull turn into you?"

Dido's eyes flared with anger.

"You have no idea about Carol Jones. She's dead, along with her waste of space of a mother. They're both long gone, and good riddance. Dido Sykes came out of the ashes of Carol Jones, after some reinvention and some levelling of scores. I know you've killed, Kelso, I read it in your file - that Ukrainian killer. Sloppy and incompetent, he deserved to die. But you know what it feels like. The first time is the best and the worst: the worst because you never know how it's going to feel or if you'll ever have that thrill again, the best because it's intense, better than any other feeling. I killed Carol Jones's mother because she deserved it for what she'd done to Carol. There have been lots of others, some up close, some not so. I like killing at a distance too. It's precise - clean and satisfying. It's a pity about Dunn, I've enjoyed killing her, even if she's not dead yet. I enjoyed it because I knew it would really hurt you."

"And Ferdinand? Did you think you'd killed him in Montreux?"

"I would have done if it hadn't been for *your* hired killers. If he'd been on his own he'd be dead, and yes, I would have enjoyed it. He's still going to die, one way or another, so are you; I've got enough on both of you to tell your bosses that you're corrupt, a liar and a perjurer; that you've perverted the course of justice. That's what they call it, isn't it? I've got proof. Tonto was going to get me physical proof - DNA from Ferdinand."

"Where is your proof, Dido? Is it in Manila?"

Dido's head shot up.

"What do you know about Manila?"

"Probably all I need to. I told you, it's all over. It's all gone, everything you had in Manila, every single file and picture and email, all gone for good. You're finished."

"You're lying, Kelso!"

"Why would I lie, Dido? Check for yourself, log in - or try to. Your account's closed; everything's been wiped clean. Even the back-ups will be gone soon, not that you could get your hands on them anyway."

Sykes tried to remain calm as she walked over to a computer on a desk. She keyed in her access code, frowned and tried again. She glared at Julia.

"So what? You've landed one blow! It's inconsequential!"

"Far from inconsequential, as you well know. It's your life's work. Nisha found out all about it. She was going to take it; I've deleted it so it can't do any more damage."

"You fucking bitch!" Sykes screamed.

"That's not all," Julia said calmly, "if you thought you'd still have a comfortable retirement, think again."

Sykes laughed. "I'll end up in prison, you mean?"

"If you do, it'll be nothing to do with me. I'm not interested in prosecuting you or putting you in jail, not anymore."

"So what? You'll kill me?"

"Not that, either. I keep telling you, it's all over! I mean it, you're finished, Dido. You have no hateful information, and you have no way of getting any more. You also have no money, none at all."

"You've stolen it?"

"Nothing so crass. I don't want your money, money you've extorted and stolen from others. I've just put it somewhere you can't get at it, that's all."

Sykes flew across the room again, clawing for Julia's face. She ended up on the carpet once more.

"Don't just take my word for it. Try to check the balances in your five accounts - there are five, aren't there? Of course there are!" Julia watched as Dido's face went white.

She rushed for the computer, searching for the files with her access codes for her accounts. They'd all gone.

"Why don't you call them if you can't find the access codes?" Julia suggested. "You must have fall-back verbal security systems. Only they've been changed too. I have no idea what the new routines are, no one does. And these aren't the sort of banks where you can just rock up with a passport and a utility bill, are they, Dido? These are dodgy banks that take dodgy money. I've told them there's been a security breach and they need to change the access procedures, on your behalf, of course; they're very efficient at things like that. What goes around comes around. How long have you got here before you can't pay the bills anymore? A few days, a few weeks? Enjoy it, Dido. I'm going now. I just wanted to make sure you knew - that you're done, I mean, once and for all."

"You won't get out of Switzerland alive, Kelso! I'll see to that. I'm not done yet!"

"Yes, you are, Dido," Julia said, walking slowly down the stairs.

Dido flew down the stairs after her, a long metal poker in her hand. She swung it hard at Julia's retreating head.

Chapter 45

She had spent all day on Tuesday trying to salvage her business and recover her money, without any success. Her blow had connected with Kelso's head, making her tumble down the stairs but not doing any real damage. Kelso was on her feet again in a moment and launched a savage counterattack at her, leaving her battered, bloodied and bruised, cowering at the foot of the stairs. The maid had come to see what the commotion was all about but had run away screaming. By the early evening she knew Kelso was right; it was all over. Everything had gone, everything had been taken from her, and she knew she could never rebuild it. Her fury turned to denial, then to disappointment, which turned to self-pity and finally bitter resignation.

She walked slowly down the garden to the small jetty and untied the rowing boat she kept there. A modest and simple craft, but one she had become fond of. She sat in the boat and rowed out onto the lake. She undid the small shackle which secured the anchor to the boat. Unwinding a length of anchor chain, she wrapped it around her leg and refastened the shackle so that the anchor was now attached to her. She rowed slowly further out into the lake.

It was the off-white shape the kayakers noticed first, floating and ghost-like, just below the surface of the water. At first they thought it might be a dead animal, a dog or cat drowned in the lake - it happened. The members of the kayak club formed a circle for stability and pulled at the floating mass. One of the kayakers uttered a curse as the hair wrapped itself around his hand - it was a long, blonde wig. A short time later they found an oar floating loose. One of the kayakers, an off-duty traffic policeman, gathered the oar and took the wig from his friends. He would need to report this to his sergeant.

******

Julia had sat for a while in the car and dabbed at the cut on the back of her head. She'd been careless; she should have anticipated one final attack. Dido had come close, but not close enough. Julia had left her barely conscious on the floor of the villa. As she drove back towards Geneva, she was half expecting the flashing lights of a police car to force her to stop. They didn't come. She crossed the border back into France, breathing a sigh of relief.

Overwhelmed with fatigue, Julia stopped at a roadside motel and booked in for the night. After a long shower she collapsed into a deep, dreamless sleep. The next day, Tuesday, she resumed her journey. She was back at the house near La Rochelle by mid-afternoon.

"Whatever you said to her, Jake," Mel started, "it drove her crazy. I've been following her all day on Nisha's machine - she's been sending hysterical emails to the banks and the server operator, but because she doesn't know the new access routines the banks won't talk to her. The server operator is talking to her but says there's nothing they can do. They complied with her instructions and irrevocably deleted everything as she'd demanded. They won't give her access to the back-ups either. She's furious, but she's signed off now. What do you think she'll do?"

"There's not much she can do," Jake said, "she's got no proof of anything against us, and even if she did go to the authorities, she'd end up inside in an instant."

"Your head's got dried blood on it, Jake," Mel said.

"It's just a bump."

"You should let Steph or Tracey have a look at it. I think it might need a stitch."

"I'll leave it. Where's Alf?" Jake asked her.

"He went off to chuck stuff in the sea, from the ferry at Royan. He said he'd be back by five."

"I'm going to take a bath - it was a long drive," Jake said.

"Shall I do your back?" Mel asked, a smile crossing her face.

"Are you in the mood?"

"I think I am. It's been ages."

"OK, let's go."

Mel was using a single crutch to support herself. Jake waited and they walked slowly up to her room.

******

Two weeks later they moved back to the house near Poitiers. On the way they passed the burned-out patch of trees and saw the crater caused when the VW camper van exploded. Trees and foliage had been shredded by the storm of shrapnel from the bomb.

"The papers said they found remains of three people in the wreckage," Jake said, "they've identified two as a couple from Amsterdam, but they don't know who the third one is - there's not much left apparently. The police are speculating that it was all something to do with the Basques."

They bid an emotional farewell to Steph and Tracey. Mel hugged them both, tears in her eyes.

"I don't know why I'm crying," she said, "you two put me through hell!"

"No pain, no gain," Steph said, also a bit tearful. "You've been brilliant, Mel, you'll be fine. We've got to go, things to do, places to be."

"See ya, Mel," Tracey said. "Don't forget to exercise that leg every day."

They got in the waiting taxi and rumbled off down the drive.

"Just us again," Mel said, "are we back to normal?"

"I think so," Alf said.

"So, what now?" Mel asked.

"Pool, drink, dinner, bed," Jake said decisively.

"I meant later, the future," Mel said.

Alf sat silently, watching Jake's face.

"Shall we take it a day at a time, at least for another couple of weeks or so?" she said. "I've got to get back to work sooner or later, and you need to see your mum - she must be going out of her mind by now."

"She's fine, I phoned her the other day and told her I'm OK and I'll see her soon. They're used to not seeing me for months on end. What about you, Alf?"

"I've no idea. I suppose I'll just stay here for a bit. I need to see Eugene in Dublin, or rather I want to. I miss the old guy. Plus, I need to finish painting the barn. The fast lane, right?"

In the days and weeks that followed the old barn kind of changed colour and Julia Kelso spent many hours on her own in the dining room, either on the phone or sending messages on her Blackberry. Mel

Dunn swam and walked and exercised, trying to rebuild her strength and vitality.

The leaves were changing colour as autumn approached; there was a pleasant chill in the air. Jeans and fleeces had replaced shorts and tee shirts, but still they delayed moving indoors for meals.

On what was to be her last day at the house for a while Julia sat with Mel on the terrace. They were watching Alf scooping dead leaves and insects from the pool. They watched him lower the pool cleaning thing into the water and set it about its underwater business. Then he went for the paint and rollers and brushes to carry on his battle with the stubborn green paint on the side of the barn.

"Why would you paint a barn anyway?" Mel asked. "Who does that? If it was up to me I'd just set fire to it and build a new one."

"That's because you're a pragmatic analyst, albeit an arsonistic one. I'd do the same though. He must have put five coats on now and you can still see that lime green coming through." Jake paused.

"What is it, Jake?" Mel asked.

"I'm leaving tomorrow," she stated. "I'm going back to London. I've booked a taxi to take me to Poitiers for the train. Are you coming with me, Mel?"

"It's a bit sudden, isn't it?" Mel said.

"It's coming to a head, work wise. I need to go to see them and make my decision."

"What decision?" Mel asked.

"Whether I stay with the Met or move on. There are people who want me out, I know that, and I need to make my mind up about whether I want to fight them or not."

"What'll you do if you don't stay with the Met?" Mel asked.

"I don't know; I've got options."

"Why did you ask if I was coming with you?" Mel said.

"I just thought you might want to."

"What about Alf?"

"I don't think he wants to come to London," Jake said.

"True. I thought I might stay here for a bit longer - if it's alright with him, that is. I'm not sure I'm ready to get back to the grindstone just yet."

"Have you mentioned it to him?"

"No."

"When I go, are you going to have sex with him?" Jake asked.

"Just be blunt, Kelso, why don't you? I haven't really given it any thought," Mel replied.

"Will you, though?"

"I don't know, Jake. Does it matter?"

"I suppose not," Jake said, "I'm just a bit unsettled by everything. What we've been through, what we've done, us."

"Us?" Mel said.

"The way we are, the three of us."

"You mean you think it's strange?" Mel said.

"Obviously it's strange," Jake replied, "but that's not it. Look, I'm used to being in control of my life, and with us I'm not. I'm just not."

"Are you unhappy about that?" Mel asked.

"No, far from it; that's part of the problem. I need to go and sort my head out, that's all."

An hour later Alf came back to the terrace. Jake told him she was leaving the next day; he was quiet but looked crestfallen.

"It had to happen, I suppose," he said, "will it be long before you come home?"

"Home?" Jake asked.

"It's what it feels like, isn't it?"

******

Jake was woken before 6 the following morning by the alarm clock ringing insistently on the far bedside table. For a moment she was confused by Mel's presence in their bed, then she remembered her appearing at their bedroom door in the early hours, ghost-like in one of her long pale tee-shirts.

"Can't sleep," Mel had mumbled.

Jake had stretched over Alf's body and lifted the duvet on his side; he had grumbled in his sleep as the cool air touched his skin. Mel had slipped into the bed and reached across his sleeping body to hold Jake's outstretched hand. She was asleep in moments, but Jake had lain awake for ages listening to her two lovers breathing in unison.

Jake rose quietly and went to pack her things. She was sitting alone on the terrace with hot coffee when Alf appeared wearing a bathrobe.

"I didn't want to wake you," she said, "I wasn't going to slip off without saying goodbye. You do know that, don't you?"

"Yes. Is Mel going with you?"

"She wants to stay for a while, she says. Is that OK with you?"

"You know it is," Alf said.

"Good. Be gentle with her - and take good care of yourself too."

"You'll be back soon though, won't you?" he asked.

Before she could answer the village taxi appeared in the drive. Jake picked up her bag, kissed Alf quickly and was gone.

******

As the TGV whisked her through the French countryside Julia scrolled through the emails on her Blackberry. The messages from her boss, Will Connaught, were becoming terse. She sighed. Her work mobile rang.

"Kelso," she said.

"Ah, little Jake! Hugh Cavendish here. Sorry to bother you at this early hour. Are you well? I gather you've been away."

"Hugh? This is a surprise! Is everything alright?"

"Don't worry, it's not your family or mine, everyone's OK as far as I know. I was just wondering if you'll be in London anytime soon, actually very soon, or if I can come and see you? In the words of that American astronaut fellow, the one who was a master of understatement, we have a problem. I may need your help, and that of your 'unorthodox resource' if you get my drift."

"It just so happens I'll be back in London later today; I'm on the Eurostar from Paris this afternoon." She gave him the train number.

"Good, I'll be at Waterloo to meet you. We can talk over dinner."

"It must be serious, Hugh," she said, trying for levity.

"I'm afraid it is," he said, "but I can't say more on the phone. I'll see you later."

Julia ended the call and slumped back in her seat. The house near Poitiers (was it home?) already seemed a long way away.

Other books by Jo Calman

The Kelso series:

Book 1: A Transfer of Power

Book 2: A Price for Mercy

Book 3: An Inner Circle

By Jo Calman and Casey J Smith:

Viktor

All available on Amazon, in some larger bookstores to order, and as eBooks with the Kindle app

or through

www.jo-calman.com

Printed in Great Britain
by Amazon